KYPease .

BROWN JADE

Yong Pease

Pen Press Publishers Ltd

First published in the UK by
Pen Press Publishers Ltd
39-41, North Road
Islington
London N7 9DP

ISBN 1-905203-95-0

Printed and bound in the UK

A catalogue record of this book is available from the
British Library

Cover design Jacqueline Abromeit

Dedication

I wish to dedicate this book to my children
Dawn and Peter.

I would also like to thank all my friends for their love,
friendship and continual support.

PART ONE

Chapter One

Malaya 1958

It was six o'clock in the morning. The air was cloaked in a mixture of sleep and body scent. Jen crept out of bed and fumbled her way down the rickety stairs and into the kitchen. Standing on tiptoe she ran her fingers along the top of the larder for a box of matches to light a candle, but she wasn't alone.

There were spiders weaving intricate patterns across the larder to the windowsill. Cockroaches scurried across the mud floor and disappeared into cracks in the wall and holes in the floor. Rats the size of cats drank from the puddles dotted around the water urn. They looked at Jen with disdain and carried on drinking. A dog howled and barked in the distance. A cacophony of cock'-a-doodle-doo followed in rapid succession.

Jen, quite unperturbed, picked up the blackened kettle and sat it down by the urn. She removed the heavy wooden lid with both hands. Plunging the jug into the cold water sent a shiver down her skinny body. Jug by jug she filled the kettle. Squatting by the clay stove she gathered a handful of wood shavings and placed them on the slatted grid. Finely splintered firewood was carefully arranged over the shavings before several large chunks of charcoal were positioned around them. Jen struck another match and fed it to the kindling. She gently blew on it as smoke started to rise. As the firewood caught alight and the smoke gave way to sparks she stood up and stifled another yawn.

While the kettle was boiling she headed for the back door. The rusty bolt and the heavy wooden hinges creaked, squeaked and squealed like cornered pigs before springing open like a jack-in-the-box. Jen stepped out into the cool clean air and walked towards the bottom of the garden. In one corner sat a raised wooden shed that served as a latrine. In the other corner, enclosed in a three feet high concrete wall was a well.

Jen climbed the couple of steps and stood on tiptoe to reach the catch. As she threw the door open the whiff of human waste smacked her in the face. Instinctively she pinched her nose and held her breath. Squatting awkwardly over the bucket she distracted herself by pulling a couple of newspaper squares from a hook and crushed them in her hands. It was the best way to soften them before cleaning herself with them.

She leapt out of the latrine and let the door slam behind her, took a deep breath and walked over to the well. She found a bucket with a sturdy rope tied to its handle. With one hand she held on to the end of the rope, and with the other she threw the bucket into the well. Jen looked down into the dark, shimmering surface of the water and was pleased to see the bucket cut the surface like a knife. The pull on the rope informed her that the bucket was filling up. She hauled it to the surface, and with a grunt and a tug she landed it on the ground beside her. As she half carried and half dragged it indoors the cold water splashed over her feet making her flinch.

Her morning wash consisted of more splashing of cold water on her face and arms and rubbing down with a small towel that the whole family shared. There was no toothpaste in the tin, so she took a few grains of salt from the larder and rubbed them on her teeth and gums. She then peered at her face in a small cracked mirror hanging on the wall by the window. Screwing her eyes up and pulling faces was also part of her morning ritual. It helped to put her face back together again after the wash in cold water. Jen didn't like her face too much but she was pleased that she had no spots unlike some of her classmates. In a few months time she would be a teenager, Jen wondered about her future.

The rising steam from the boiling kettle interrupted her contemplation. She turned the fire down by shutting off the air vent on the stove. Jen made the coffee and replenished the two thermos flasks with boiling water. Next she threw another large lump of charcoal into the stove to keep the embers going till lunchtime when her mother would cook their main meal. She refilled the kettle and set it back on the stove to catch the rising heat of the smouldering coals.

The dawning of a new day threw shafts of hazy light onto the dappled and uneven mud floor. Jen looked down at her feet; the wooden clogs were worn down to a thin plinth. The pink plastic strips that held them to her feet had loosened allowing her toes to poke through the edges. She must remember to ask her mother for a new pair for her birthday she thought. On second thought she hoped to receive a new pair for her thirteenth birthday.

It wasn't the done thing to ask for a present, not in her family anyway.

It was time to get her brothers Tam and Lee out of bed and ready for school. Jen sighed heavily. She left her clogs on the bottom step and climbed the stairs barefooted; mindful of the wobbly treads and loose nails waiting to trap her callused feet.

* * *

Jen pushed her brothers' bedroom door ajar. The sound of them snoring quietly comforted her sense of isolation but it also fanned her frustration.

'Tam, Lee, time to get up,' Jen called quietly and waited. No answer came from the sleeping boys. They were curled up on the mats spread out on the floor with only a cotton blanket between them. Jen edged towards the slumbering bodies and tugged at the blanket.

'Tam, Lee,' Jen shook Tam by his shoulder. Tam lifted his head from his pillow, opened his eyes, looked at Jen and went straight back to sleep again.

'Get up!' Jen shouted losing her patience.

'What!' Tam lifted his head off his pillow again. He blinked at his sister. 'What d'you want? Go away, let me sleep.'

'It's time for school,' Jen snapped back.

'Stop shouting at me,' Tam answered indignantly and at the same time he wrapped the blanket even tighter round his shoulders and went back to sleep.

'Lee, time to go to school,' Jen shook Lee's shoulder vigorously. Lee made a grunting noise but didn't stir.

'This is my last call,' Jen threatened her brothers. 'You're both going to be late for school if you don't hurry, and get up *now!*' Jen felt the heat on her cheeks as she left the room.

Jen shared a room with her mother and her five-year-old sister Min. They all slept on the floor too with a curtain separating her mother's space from hers.' Jen got dressed in the dark and nearly trod on Min's head when she stretched over her to reach her uniform. The makeshift clothes hanger, a piece of bamboo attached to a piece of string, kept her uniform neat and tidy with all the pleats in the right places. She felt transformed as soon she put it on; a quivery feeling ran down her spine. Jen loved going to school.

She heard scuffling noise from the boys' room, and then the soft thuds of footsteps as they jostled each other to get down the narrow stairs first. They had a competition each morning to see who got to the latrine first. The loser had to put up with the stink of the winner's flatulence. Jen secretly smiled at their childish game but outwardly she adopted a mocked contempt.

'Mum,' Jen stood over her mother's sleeping form. 'Mum,' Jen called quietly again. Lian woke with a start.

'Yes...Oh! Jen you gave me a fright. What is it?'

'Can I have some money for the bus fares please?' Lian slipped a hand under her pillow and brought out her purse. She rolled over on to her tummy and emptied all the coins on to her pillow. She picked up a few square ones and gave them to Jen.

'Are your brothers ready for school yet?'

'Yes mum, they are having their breakfast.' She stood looking at her mother deep in thoughts. 'Mum...' Jen hesitated, 'can I...' but she didn't finish what she was saying. She had already seen the contents of her mother's purse.

'Close the door quietly, or you'll wake your sister up.'

As she walked down the stairs she felt the heat burning on her face and the tightness in her neck squeezing her voice. It was her school sports day and she would have liked to have had some money to buy an ice cream. But she couldn't bear to hear another apology from her mother. Poverty was part of Jen's life and she had long stopped asking why. She knew why.

Her father died when Min was born. Ever since then her mother had worked from home; taking in washing, sewing and mending to feed and clothe all five of them. Now that Tam and Lee were also in school, their mother found it increasingly difficult to juggle the finances. She had spoken to Jen about her leaving school at the end of the year when she turned thirteen. Jen was expected to get a job to help pay for her brothers to remain in school. The thought turned into a knot in her stomach. She visibly shook her head to stop herself thinking.

When Jen walked into the kitchen she saw that her

brothers were half-dressed and still eating their breakfast. 'Have you two finished? Please hurry up or we'll miss the bus again.' Jen sounded dejected and defeated but her brothers were oblivious to her distress.

As if on cue they started arguing about whose fault it was that they missed the bus the day before. Lee was flicking a rubber band at Tam, and Tam was dodging it by ducking under the table. Tam at eleven was two years older than Lee, but Lee was usually the instigator of most disputes in the home.

'Come on you two, stop it! You'll wake Min up and then *there'll be trouble,*' she snapped impatiently.

'What's the matter with you?' Tam asked, surprised at Jen's tone of voice.

'Nothing…just put your shoes on! *Lee*, watch what you're doing with that mug, and you've got your shoes on the wrong feet.'

'He likes it that way,' Tam piped in.

'It's comfortable like this. Anyway- nobody will notice,' Lee answered innocently.

'I noticed,' Jen spoke quietly. She had realised for sometime that Lee had problem distinguishing his left from his right.

'Let me help you.' Jen untied the laces and changed the shoes over. 'You must try to get them on the right feet,' she said to Lee.

'There're just shoes,' Lee replied, pointing to them, 'this one looks like this one.'

Tam started to giggle. Jen gave him a dark look. She straightened herself up and gathered all her books together and picked up her brothers' school bags. As each of them went through the front door she handed them their bags, and straightened their clothes. After a moment's pause she caught Lee by his arm and ran a comb through his hair much to Tam's amusement.

Chapter Two

The air was warm and humid. The rising sun cast a golden glow in the horizon. A clock struck seven as Jen walked past an imposing house fronted by a large, well-tended garden. A five feet high wire fence gave the air of protected privacy. Bougainvillias in full bloom threw out rosy bracts in gay abundance. Orchids in various hues of pink and red gracefully intertwined with weathered bamboo canes. Evergreen shrubs dotted along the gravelled path reflecting their glorious beauty in the ceramic pots that held them in regimental order.

Jen turned around to check on Tam and Lee. 'Lee, do you have to do that? Your shoes are filthy.'

Lee was kicking stones at Tam and whipping up clouds of dust and dirt. Most of them were on his white canvas shoes.

They turned down a narrow path between two rows of houses and after a further hundred yards they took a sharp right along a dried-up ditch. The ditch was used as a local rubbish tip and all manner of household waste, bits of machinery, and broken furniture ended up in it.

'Look at that bike,' Tam said pointing into the muddy depths at a half-buried bicycle. 'Bet I could fix it and sell it to a shop.'

'Bet you can't.' Lee dared him. 'It's all rusty and broken up, and it's only got one wheel.'

'There's more than one bike in there, I can use them as spares,' Tam sounded confident.

'Could you two please keep to the path,' Jen shouted over her shoulder.

'There're no snakes in the grass. You're just like mum, nag, nag, nag,' Lee said pulling a face behind Jen's back.

Jen stopped, looked round and saw Lee standing in the long grass on the edge of the ditch looking in.

'Okay,' she said, 'If you get bitten by a snake don't come crying to me.' Jen stormed off.

Tam got Lee by his sleeve and pulled him back on to the path. 'Quick, I can hear the bus.'

Tam propelled Lee towards a makeshift bridge. A plank about thirty feet long and no more than a foot wide was balanced precariously over the narrowest part of the ditch. As Jen walked across the plank it bounced with her weight and the two ends resting in the hard-baked mud lifted with each step she took. Tam stood waiting on the path till Jen got to the other side before he stepped on it. Lee however, followed closely behind Tam. Their combined weight made the plank bounce even more vigorously. Lee caught Tam by the shoulders, half pushing and jostling to get past. Jen heard them laughing and struggling together but she refused to turn round; instead she quickened her pace and headed for the bus-stop.

When Tam and Lee finally arrived at the bus-stop Jen was already on board the bus. She was standing near the door as the bus was already packed with school children.

'Come on, come on, you're holding up the bus,' the driver called out.

Tam stood aside for Lee to get in first and squeezed in after. There was barely a hand's space between him and the open door of the moving bus. The morning breeze was whipped into a mini tornado by the speed and juddering, and the vibration pinched and shook his cheeks into a comical grimace. He gripped the metal rung on either side of the narrow steps with the tenacity of an octopus. He enjoyed the ride. It was an adventure, the danger of falling off added to his excitement.

He arrived in school most mornings as he did that morning; dishevelled, dusty, exhilarated, and with only minutes to spare before the school bell sounded.

Jen's heart was beating furiously as she arrived at her school gate late as usual. As she ran across the school field clutching her bag to her chest she mentally ticked off her homework and scanned her timetable for the morning. The noise of lively discussions drifted through the open doorways as she neared her classroom. There were no windows in most of the rooms, only doors, which were permanently left open to let the air and light filter through.

She slipped into the back of the class quietly and sat down next to Patricia.

'Good morning Jen.' Miss Chan greeted Jen with a smile.

'Good morning Miss Chan. I'm sorry I'm late again,' Jen blushed bright red and lowered her gaze.

Some of her classmates turned and looked at her knowingly, but nothing was said. The teasing and taunting came later, in the playground and in the toilets.

'We're discussing the merits of good preparation for your forthcoming exams. It's only four months away and I hope all of you are taking your revision seriously.' Miss Chan looked around the class and saw forty pairs of anxious eyes following her.

Jen liked Miss Chan, her form teacher. She was strict but fair. Standing barely five feet tall, her long dark hair coiled into a bun and pinned into the nape of her neck gave her an air of reserved dignity. Jen admired her authority and knowledge. She imagined herself standing before the class moving gracefully back and forth imparting wisdom like Miss Chan.

'Did you finish your maths homework?' Patricia whispered with a hand over her mouth.

'Yes, did you?' Jen kept her eyes on the blackboard.

'No, can't work out the question,' Patricia answered leaning closer to Jen.

'Pay attention girls, can you see the board, those at the back?' Miss Chan raised a quizzical brow pointedly at Patricia. 'Please reserve your chit-chat till break time, thank you'

The class fell into silence as forty heads bent over forty wooden desks. Their collective brains hunched into a frenzy of solemn activity in a language that was foreign to most of them. Jen, like most of her classmates only ever spoke in Chinese at home, but Patricia was different, she spoke English at home.

Patricia's father was a British soldier on peacekeeping duties when he married her mother, a local Chinese girl. When Patricia was still a baby he returned to England alone. Her mother had refused to leave her family to join him. In keeping with her father's wishes her mother had always spoken to her in English. Jen found it all very puzzling and sometimes she felt very frustrated that she could not speak to her best friend in her mother tongue. But their unlikely friendship had mutual rewards, Jen was able to improve her English and Patricia had a loyal friend who was good at maths.

* * *

The bell sounded for the morning break.

'Hey Jen, want to borrow my mirror?' Meena asked rather loudly in her shrill voice.

'Yeah Jen, want to borrow my comb as well?' Bee Bee joined in the teasing.

'Ignore them,' Patricia pleaded as Jen made her way towards Meena with fists clenched. 'They're just jealous because you have beautiful long hair.'

'It's not beautiful, just long and untidy,' Meena jeered.

'And dirty too,' Wei Wei chipped in.

Jen felt tears stinging her eyes and a lump in her throat,

but her voice was steady. 'Why don't you all go and play your silly games somewhere else.'

'Ooh, look at our Miss Clever,' Meena taunted.

'She thinks she is sooo clever,' Bee Bee intoned.

'Little Miss Perfect, what are you going to do when you leave school? Be a hairdresser?' Wei Wei joined in and all three girls laughed and giggled at their jokes.

'Jen is not leaving school yet.' Patricia tried to defend her best friend.

'Why, are you paying her school fees?' Meena asked sarcastically

'She is going to win the scholarship. You just wait and see,' Patricia answered, her face red and her eyes blazing.

'How is she going to do that? She can't even get to school on time,' Meena continued.

'Patricia,' Jen tugged her friend's arm, 'Don't, don't answer them. They are spiteful and hateful.' Jen almost spat the words out.

'Here Jen, have this.' Meena threw a half-eaten apple at her. It landed on her lap. The three friends ran off to the other end of the playing field.

Patricia picked up the offending fruit and dropped it in the bin. Sitting in the sunshine on the soft green grass with her books on her knees, Jen remained quiet and glum.

'Don't let them get to you,' Patricia consoled.

'They have a point. What if I can't win the scholarship?'

'You will. You work hard, you deserve it more than anyone here.'

'It's not about deserving,' Jen looked at Patricia intensely, 'I'm not sure I could get top marks. I don't have enough time to study in the evenings. Tam and Lee are always playing noisy boys games. I have to look after Min too.' Jen sighed loudly and hunched her shoulders.

'Why don't you come to my house at the weekend?' Patricia asked helpfully.

'I can't.'

'Why not? My mum won't mind.'

'Mine does. I'm supposed to help with the sewing and washing and the ironing.' She felt angry at the world; her voice grew quieter and quieter as she listed the things she had to do.

'Are you okay?' Patricia was concerned. Jen looked tired, her long hair lay tangled and dank around her oval face.

'I'm okay. Just thinking about things.'

'Stop thinking and try some of these.' Patricia took some sweets from her bag.

'Thank you. I'm sorry I haven't got anything for you.'

'You're silly you are. They're only sweets, besides you are my best friend.'

'It's a Chinese custom, to exchange gifts.'

'I'm not Chinese, well, only half.' They looked at each other and burst into fits of laughter.

Jen nudged Patricia and said,' That half doesn't even speak Chinese,' and they laughed even more.

Jen and Patricia's friendship stirred and aroused admiration and irritation in equal measure. There were those who envied their camaraderie for each other, and in the opposite camp stood those who were irritated by their audacious show of kinship.

In this small town of small-minded people Jen's family was a constant reminder of bad karma. Jen's mother; a young widow, was feared by other young women. They believed that she brought misfortune on herself by some bad deeds committed in her previous life, and as an act of punishment she was widowed young. Jen, being her child must necessarily carry some of the dark influence of her mother's bad karma. Superstitious belief was part of everyday life in this small town and Jen knew better than to fight it in the school ground.

Patricia with her fair complexion and brown hair was a reminder of her mother's brief but unwise liaison with a British soldier. She was looked down upon as a half-caste with tainted blood, and this was her *sin*. Her friendship with Jen developed through their shared sense of sardonic disregard of the playground gibes and cruel remarks.

Out of the corner of her eyes Patricia saw a pupil taking several wild swings with a hand bell to announce the end of their morning break.

'What have we got after lunch break?' Patricia asked.

'Don't tell me you've forgotten.' Jen jokingly prodded her friend in the back of her head, 'What do you have in there, cotton wool?'

'It's not art again is it? I hate all that painting and drawing stuff, it's alright for you, you can draw and paint. I just make a mess.'

'Stop worrying! There's no art this afternoon. It's your favourite day though, it's sports day today, remember?' Jen teased.

'That's even worse!' Patricia didn't like sports either.

'That's not so bad. I don't like the hurdles mind. The last time I tried it I knocked them all down.' Jen laughed.

'You're supposed to jump over them you know,' Patricia said mockingly.

'They should make them this high,' Jen held up her hands to indicate what she meant, 'if they want me to jump over them. But the relays and the hundred metres are alright,' Jen said wrinkling her nose.

'It's your favourite subject Jen, maths!' Patricia teased as they took their seats in class.

For the rest of the morning the two friends worked quietly alongside each other. But for the occasional fly buzzing around in the sticky heat of the classroom, the atmosphere was calm and congenial.

* * *

It started with the intermittent rustling of papers and scraping of chairs on the concrete floor. Low mutterings and whispers became more insistent. Miss Chan checked her watch. She stood up and addressed the class just as the bell went off for lunch break.

'Listen class, as you may or may not remember it's sports day today, so there will be no lessons this afternoon.' A muted cheer went up. Miss Chan smiled and continued, 'You may put your books away and go for lunch. I hope you'll all have a great afternoon and win lots of prizes.'

'I wish,' Mei Fong commented as she turned to Jamalah who was standing behind her. Mei Fong loved her food; thus she was as wide as she was long. She hated sports with a passion but her PE teacher insisted that she joined in the various sporting activities. Her lack of enthusiasm was often matched by her flawed co-ordination.

Jamalah was Indian, a sweet, gentle girl who had a squint in her left eye. Unlike Mei Fong she was quick on her feet and she excelled in sports.

'I know!' Mei Fong had a sudden brain wave, 'you can do the running for me and I'll do your homework. That's fair.'

'You can do my homework if you really want to, but I can't run for you.'

'Why not?'

'Because…you're fair skin and I'm dark. We'll get caught.'

Mei Fong laughed and said, 'I'm also much bigger than you as well.'

Jamalah shifted uncomfortably and avoided looking her friend in the eye. 'It's all right, I know I'm fat,' Mei Fong replied.

'You're …a little bigger than me, but it's just that…that I don't think we should cheat,' Jamalah stuttered.

'It's okay,' Mei Fong tried to reassure Jamalah, 'I'm only joking. Let's go for lunch, I'm starving.'

Jen waited in the back of the class till all her classmates had left the classroom before she got up from her chair. Miss Chan was putting some books away in the cupboard with her back to the class and hadn't noticed Jen.

'Miss Chan,' Jen addressed her teacher tentatively. Her heart was pounding rapidly and her throat felt dry and her voice sounded hoarse.

'Oh! Jen! You made me jump.'

'Sorry.'

'Aren't you going for your lunch?'

'I need to speak to you, please.'

'Of course.' Miss Chan walked up to Jen who appeared rooted to the spot.

'What's the matter? Is something wrong?'

Jen hesitated and stammered, 'I'm…I'm…its school, no…I mean school work-homework.'

'Why don't you sit down and tell me all about it,' Miss Chan said, her voice gentle and soothing. She took a chair next to Jen and smiled encouragingly. 'Are you having problems with your homework?'

'I'm sorry I didn't finish my essay. I didn't have enough time last night. I can finish it now if you let me.'

'What's wrong Jen, it's unlike you not to complete your homework. You know your exams are coming up soon. You do want to continue your schooling don't you?'

'Miss Chan I really *really* want to stay in school, but…' Jen's voice quivered to a halt.

'But?'

'I'm not sure if I will be able to…allowed to…' Jen replied. She stared hard at the ground to stop her tears escaping down her cheeks.

'Whose stopping you from coming to school? Miss Chan was calm and matter-of-fact.

'No one is stopping me, but…my mother isn't able to pay my fees. My brothers are in school too, and there isn't enough money for all of us…for all our school fees.' The defeat in Jen's voice was palpable.

Miss Chan was aware that Jen's mother was widowed and her only means of income was from taking in sewing and doing the laundry for her better-off neighbours. Though education was subsidised, parents had to pay a nominal fee per month per child. They were also required to buy all the books stipulated by the education system and kit their children with the regulation uniforms. More importantly, education was not compulsory, so each child was educated according to the financial ability of her parents.

After a long silence Miss Chan spoke again, 'You are doing so well in school, I'm sure you'll pass your entrance exams to secondary school.' She looked at Jen thoughtfully and, 'Will it help if I speak to your mother?'

Jen shook her head and replied, 'My mother needs my help at home. If I help her with the sewing she can earn more money, then my brothers could finish their schooling. It's more important for them to be educated. It's the tradition, boys are…well…that's what is expected of boys, they go out to work and girls stay at home,' Jen trailed off.

'Jen, if your mother knows that you are going to do well I'm sure she will keep you in school. Besides, if you complete your schooling you'll get a better job, then you'll be in a better position to help your family.'

Jen listened and pondered for a few minutes, she took a deep breath and said cautiously, 'I've thought of a way to stay in school but I'm not sure if I can do it.' Jen's voice became more animated as she continued, 'If I can win the scholarship then my school fees and books will be paid for till I leave school, is that right?'

A slow smile played on Miss Chan's lips when she replied, 'Yes, that's right. Once you win the scholarship, the school will pay for all your books and your monthly fees. Why haven't I thought of that before…and you can do it too.'

'Do you think so?' Jen asked excitedly.

'I'm positive you can, but you need to work very hard though, more homework, extra homework even.'

Jen nodded. She felt a shiver of excitement ran down her spine.

'Could you ask your mother to come and see me one day next week. I'll explain things to her.'

'I'll ask tonight, but I'm not sure she'll come. It's not that she doesn't want to, its just that she's busy,' Jen replied, but she wasn't convinced by her own words.

'You had better run along to get your lunch now, I'll speak to you again tomorrow.'

'Thank you Miss Chan.' Jen walked out into the dazzling sunshine feeling tingly all over. She strode purposely towards a hidey-hole behind a hedge on the edge of the school ground adjacent to woodland. Patricia was waiting for her.

Jen sat down beside her friend; took out her sandwiches, peered into the soggy mess and took a bite.

'Come on, I'm waiting, tell me what Miss Chan said,' Patricia questioned impatiently.

Jen took another bite of her sandwich, licked her fingers where the condensed milk had seeped out and was making a gooey mess on her hands. She took her time and then said, 'She said…she said that she wants to see my mum.'

'Is that all? What about your exams, the scholarship, and…and your homework?' Patricia was getting a little impatient.

'She said that with extra homework I could get good marks, and…it would be possible to get the scholarship.'

'I told you so,' Patricia replied excitedly.

'I still have to compete with the other girls to get it, and if I can't finish my homework it's not going to look good, is it?'

'That's why Miss Chan wants to see your mum, she'll tell your mum to let you off the housework, then you can

19

spend more time studying,' Patricia added encouragingly.

'Why is life so complicated?' Jen asked. It was more of a statement than a question. Jen didn't fair too well for the rest of the afternoon either. She dropped the baton in the relay; then she knocked over most of the hurdles much to the amusement of the crowd. The jeering from Meena and her cronies went up each time she made a mistake. In between each event she kept out of their way and insisted on helping the teachers to tidy up the equipment room. As soon as she finished her last race she snatched up her bag and ran to the toilets.

She leant against the cool brickwork to catch her breath, after a few minutes her eyes adjusted to the dim interior. She turned on a tap and drank deeply from it and then she splashed the cold water over her face to cool off. From where she stood she could still hear the shouting and cheering coming from the school fields. Jen stared at her reflection in the mirror above the hand basin, she saw a flushed face, long, straggly hair, almond eyes, and lips firmly pressed together. After a few moments she picked up her bag and slipped out of the school by a side gate.

As Jen walked to the bus station she passed dozens of rickshaws waiting by the main gate to pick up their charges. There were a few cars about; they belonged to the rich and titled. She wondered what it was to like to be taken to and from school in a rickshaw. But for now to have a seat on a bus would be a luxury.

Chapter Three

Jen had just come through the front door; the smell of caustic soda and soap filled the house. She walked through to the kitchen and saw a mountain of dirty linen on the floor. Her mother was standing over the stove, a big sturdy stick in hand, stirring the bubbling soup of bed linen in a large kerosene tin. The white linen had come from the local hotel. Lian charged the hotel a good price for washing and ironing them. It was Jen's duty to collect and return the linen three times a week; they were paid according to the number of items laundered. The money from the hotel formed the bulk of Lian's income.

'Aah, there you are, hurry and change out of your uniform. I need a hand here,' Lian said as she continued stirring. Her face was flushed; damp hair clinging to her temples, she looked older than her thirty years.

'Yes mum, I won't be long,' Jen answered and took the stairs two at a time.

'Big sister,' Min called out excitedly, 'you're home.' She was huddled in a corner of the bedroom

'Hello Min, what are you doing?'

'I'm studying of course,' Min replied. She had an exercise book and an old textbook of Jen's on her lap and a pencil poised in her left hand.

'What's that you're studying then?'

'Just studying…I'm learning how to write my name, like this.' Min scribbled a little bit more to make her point.

'Can I have a look, what are you writing on?' Jen asked hoping that Min had not written all over her geography book.

'Mmm, that's very good, you do write well. Can you write with your right hand as well as your left?'

Min held up the pencil in her left hand and said, 'Like this?'

'No, the other hand.'

'I can't.' Min tried, but the pencil kept slipping off. 'I do it better with this hand.'

'When you go to school,' Jen said quite seriously, 'you'll have to use your right hand.'

'Why?'

'It's…just rules I suppose.'

'Do you write with your right hand then?'

'I didn't used to, but I had to.' Jen remembered her first day at school when she was told that she had to learn to write with her right hand. She wasn't told why. The teacher walked around with a ruler to tap on the knuckles of any child caught writing with her left hand.

'Do I have to? Write with my other hand?'

'Probably. Why don't you try using your other hand now, you'll get used to it, I did,' Jen answered.

'*Je..n*, are you still up there?' Lian called from the kitchen.

'I'm coming Mum. Here Min, I've a sweet for you.'

'Thank you, when I go to school I'll save you some sweets too.' Min was delighted with the mint Jen gave her.

Jen hurried into the kitchen where her mother was trying valiantly to hook the boiling hot sheet from the cavernous tin with a stick.

'Could you steady this please, use that cloth, now grip the sides while I pull.' Droplets of boiling water splattered on to the burning coals causing them to hiss and spit. 'Now can you top it up with cold water,' Lian instructed.

She took the lid off the water urn and saw that there was hardly any water left in it. She sighed and wearily went outside to fetch some more. The water from the well had a reddish tinge that would dye all whites into a dirty pink, so before she could use the water, it had to be filtered first. That took time and energy, both of which Jen felt could have been better spent on her books.

Sitting next to the well on a wooden platform was a large ceramic urn with a hole in the base. Inside the urn were layers of grit and sand. As water from the well was bucketed into the urn, the grit and sand miraculously removed the muddy deposits from the water. The water that trickled from the hole into a bucket was now clear and deemed suitable for cooking and washing white linen. This crude method of water filtration was cheap and efficient but extremely hard work.

In between topping up the water, Jen had to help her mother wash and rinse the linen and put it out to dry. The clean laundry from the day before was then ironed and returned to the hotel.

Jen had been trying all afternoon to speak to her mother about the scholarship, but the moment kept evading her. Just as she started on the subject of school, her brothers Tam and Lee came in through the back door. They were covered in mud. Tam had a couple of cabbages and two large sweet potatoes in his arms. Lee was nursing a paper bag.

'Where have you two been?' Jen asked.

'Working of course.' Lee said importantly.

'Farmer Choy asked us to help him on the farm,' Tam answered.

'Yes…it was fun. He's got two fat pigs,' Lee interrupted.

'Did he give you those?' Lian asked pointing to the cabbages and sweet potatoes.

'Yeah, he said we worked very hard. He also said we could go again if you agree.' Tam placed the cabbages and sweet potatoes on the table with such care that it almost brought tears to Lian's eyes. He turned around and put his hands out to Lee, but Lee snatched his hands away and nearly dropped the parcel he was holding.

'What have you got there?' Jen asked.

'Eggs! Six big brown eggs,' Lee replied with glee.

'Be careful,' Lian put a hand out to restrain her younger boy. She took the bag off him and gave him a brimming smile. 'You must have been very good. Farmer Choy is very kind.'

'I prefer money, but he's too stingy,' Lee said.

'Lee, you mustn't be rude about your elders,' Lian admonished.

'What did you have to do then?' Jen wanted to know.

'Its dirty work, the pigs' sty stank, and…and the chickens won't go into the coop…' Lee as usual was making the most of it.

'Why don't you boys go and wash…and change. Jen and I will cook the tea soon.'

'Mum, can I have one of those eggs for my tea?' Lee asked.

'Of course you can. There are six there so we can have one each.'

'Can I have two instead; there's five of us so there is one left over. It might go bad tomorrow, and I worked the hardest.'

'I'm sure you worked very hard, just like Tam, and Jen too. Now run along and wash the mud off you. And Lee, no jumping around the well.'

'Okay.' He was off like a bullet through the back door with both hands flapping like a bird. 'I'm an aeroplane,' he said and clipped Tam's ear with his out-stretched hand.

Lian looked fondly at her boys through the window. Tam, he was tall for a eleven-year-old, so sensible, like his father. Lee two years younger was high spirited, excitable and a bit of a rascal. He reminded Lian of her own father. She was grateful that she had a daughter as her firstborn. She looked at Jen, still bent over the table ironing and there was a pile of crisp white sheets neatly folded beside her. Min, her baby was a pretty and gentle child. Daughters were loyal and dutiful, Lian thought.

When the main meal of the day was over, Jen cleared up and did the dishes. Tam, Lee and Min were sent upstairs with a small kerosene lamp. They were allowed to read or play quietly for an hour and the lamp had to be extinguished. The kerosene in the reservoir of the lamp had to last the week.

Jen lit a candle and placed it on the table. The candles were free; they came from the temple in the village. Lian was hunched over some delicate fabric, her hands worked quickly and deftly.

'Could you put it closer this way please, these beads are so tricky to sew on,' Lian spoke without looking up. Her hands were working feverishly, needle and cotton going in and out, up and over the cloth, which was now studded with beads.

'Mum,' Jen's stomach did a somersault.

'Mmm, did you...?'

'My teacher wants to see you,' Jen spoke with more haste than she had intended.

Lian paused. She looked at Jen in the shadowy light with raised brows. 'Who is your teacher? Why does she want to see me? You've done something wrong?'

'Miss Chan, that's my teacher. She wants to speak to you...about my studies...my schooling.' Jen's voice was shrill.

'Why does she want to see me, you know I'm very busy...is it very important?'

'She said there's no hurry, sometime next week will be...fine.'

Lian sighed. 'I suppose I might as well, you're leaving school soon and it's only polite I speak to your teacher. Did she say what time?'

'No...she didn't. I'll ask her tomorrow.'

Jen took her mother's continued silence to mean the subject was now closed. She had hoped to explain about

25

the scholarship and why she wanted to continue her education. She was resigned to the fact that her ambition would not be encouraged. She was a girl.

Feeling deflated and exhausted Jen took her books out from her school bag. She sat across the table from her mother, deep in thoughts, her essay only half-finished. Lian lived in one world, Jen in another; divided by ignorance.

* * *

Lian had taken care to put on her best clothes, a short-sleeved, pale blue, floral blouse with dark trousers that billowed in the afternoon breeze. Her face was scrubbed; there was not a trace of powder or cologne on her, she considered them frivolous and unnecessary. The new black sandals drew attention to her cracked and callused feet. She had arranged with a neighbour to look after Min before she set off.

On her way to the village bus-stop she popped in to see Farmer Choy and his wife, Mei Ling, she was due to have her fourth child in a few months time. Lian had heard that she was looking for a helper to do the housework and look after her three other children when the new baby was born. Lian decided that as Jen was leaving school soon, it seemed an ideal opportunity to approach her about employing the services of Jen. Farmer Choy had always been kind and generous to Tam and Lee, she was sure that he would be equally considerate towards Jen.

Her mind made up, Lian approached the farmer and his wife in their farmhouse.

'Good afternoon Mr Choy, Mrs Choy,' Lian smiled and made a bow with palms together.

'Good afternoon Madam Lau,' Farmer Choy and his wife replied in unison.

'Please call me Lian.'

'Please take a seat,' Mei Ling waved a hand towards the dining chairs. 'Do excuse the mess…the children…you understand.'

'I'll go back to my duties and leave you ladies to talk business,' Farmer Choy said cheerfully as he left the house.

'Sorry, I forgot my manners,' Mei Ling said, 'Would you take a cup of tea?'

'Thank you, tea would be very nice.'

'To what do I owe the pleasure of your visit?' Mei Ling inquired as she placed a cup of tea in Lian's hands.

'I hope you don't think me rude coming to see you without prior warning.'

'I'm not offended, please do continue, I'm very pleased to meet you. I've heard a lot about you from Tam and Lee.'

'I hope they haven't given you any trouble.'

'Not at all. They are such good boys. You must be very proud of them.'

'Thank you. You're so kind,' Lian paused, 'I am wondering if you would be needing someone to help in the house when you…when the baby is born'

Mei Ling blushed. 'I am looking for a helper, but it's hard to find someone who is good with children and not afraid of hard work. Young girls these days prefer to work in an office or in a shop. It's more glamorous than being a mother's help.'

'I know what you mean,' Lian sympathised.

'Do you know someone, can you recommend someone perhaps. I'd be most grateful.'

'I'm wondering if you would consider my Jen. She's good with children, she's used to looking after her brothers and sister.'

'Isn't she still in school?'

'Yes, only for now, she will be leaving at the end of the year. She'll be thirteen then.' Lian answered confidently.

'I see. I'm sure my husband will approve. He has often

27

said that Tam and Lee are such well-behaved children. I'll speak to him about it and I'll let you know,' Mei Ling said after some thought.

'Thank you, I won't keep you. I'm just on my way to see Jen's teacher about her leaving school.'

Mei Ling nodded as she escorted Lian to the door. After a moment's hesitation she added, 'Why don't you ask Jen to come round on Saturday to see us. We can talk to her about it, she may not like this kind of work.'

'Yes, that's a good idea. I'll tell her tonight.'

Jen's fate was sealed in an instant.

It was arranged that Lian was to meet Miss Chan at two o'clock. Jen was restless in class.

'What's the matter with you today?' Patricia asked during their lunch hour. 'You looked like you were in a trance all morning.'

'Huh! Oh…that. I was just thinking.'

'Are you going to tell me then?'

'What's there to tell? My mum's seeing Miss Chan later.'

'Oh! Do you think your mum…' Patricia started waving her hands about like a music conductor.

'What did you say?' Jen sounded distant and distracted.

'Do you think…what do you think?'

'Think what?'

'You know…'

'No I don't know what you mean.'

'Are you going to stay in school next year?' Patricia was losing her patience.

'How should I know?' Jen almost shouted.

'Miss Chan will convince your mum that you must, you'll see.'

'That will be a miracle,' Jen's tone was scornful.

'Do you believe in miracles then, being a Buddhist?'

Jen smiled in spite of herself. 'We call them by a different name. We believe in fate.'

'Is that good or bad?' Patricia wanted to know.

'It's just it, not good, not bad.' Jen answered remembering a conversation she had had with an elderly neighbour.

It was two o'clock. Jen sat on the step outside the teacher's office waiting for her mother. Her palms were damp with perspiration; she played with the straps of her school bag nervously. Every now and then she got up and paced the corridor. She sighed with relief when she saw her mother emerge from the office. Lian kept her gaze in the middle distance.

'Good-bye Madam Lau. Thank you for coming,' Miss Chan said as she stood at the door of the office.

'Thank you Miss Chan, I will certainly think about what you've said.' Lian replied with an effort.

Jen searched her mother's face for clues. Finding none she walked alongside her like a soldier going to war, brisk, head up, shoulders back and her school bag pressed against her chest like a weapon. Lian was deep in thought, a knot of anger clutched her chest, and sadness squeezed from every pore. Most of all she felt the sorrow of being a single mother and a widow stung her deeply. If her husband had been alive she would not have had to make all the decisions herself. She wanted a better future for her children, but her present did not allow her the freedom to make that choice. Was it better to sacrifice one child for the good of the others, she asked herself? What was she to think of that child? Should she not value each and every one of her children? And what about her boys, she was brought up to respect the traditional view. Boys inherit their father's land, and carry his name for posterity. The fact that there was no land to consider made no difference.

Jen followed her mother up the steps of the bus and sat down next to her. Not a word passed between them. The ride home seemed endless. The views out of the windows did little to distract her. She felt sick, rumblings in her stomach threatened to erupt and engulf her guts.

The familiar landscape of rubber plantations interspersed with narrow, dusty tracks came into view. Jen wandered how much the rubber-tappers got paid. She knew that they had to start work at four in the morning, but that was not a problem, it would still leave her time to go to school she thought.

Like an automaton Jen stood up and rang the bell. She got off the bus ahead of her mother. They walked in silence all the way home. Once indoors Lian appeared to drop her shoulders like a deflated balloon. She sat down and looked about her. Tam and Lee were already home. There were trails of biscuit crumbs on the floor, the larder door was ajar, and the top of the flask was askew.

Jen was just about to join her brother upstairs when her mother spoke, 'Jen come and sit down. I need to talk to you.' Her voice was grave.

Jen's stomach lurched and her eyes went into a squint. She sat down.

'I've had a long talk with your teacher; she said you're a good pupil. She's very pleased with your work.' Lian said.

Jen hung on to every word. She pleaded with her eyes but remained silent.

Lian continued, 'She said you'll do well in your exams.' Silence, deep sigh, 'She said something about a scholarship...but I'm not sure...it's a long way off anyway.'

Jen jumped in, 'But Mum, if we apply now... when I sit for my exams...the marks...they require...I know I can do it. At least I could try, please Mum.' Jen took a deep breath. 'If I...if I ask for the forms next week, you can sign them and then...and then I will be registered as a candidate.' Jen stood up to give more emphasis to her words.

Lian listened. She felt that she was taking food away from Jen, depriving her of hope, of sustenance for the future...Lian felt wretched. She wanted to tell Jen about her conversation with Farmer Choy's wife, about how her financial contribution to the family would put more palatable food on the table, would provide books and shoes for her brothers, and uniform for Min when she started school in the new year. She didn't say any of those things, instead she said, 'It's late. We'll talk again tomorrow, could you please collect Min from number 46. I'll cook something for us for tea, and don't forget to thank Mrs Ong for having Min.'

Jen went out through the back door, she told herself she wasn't going to cry and she didn't.

Chapter Four

The following day was Saturday. Jen stayed in bed till seven o'clock, it was a weekend luxury. By the time she came downstairs her mother was already up. Lian was busy finishing off the ironing from the day before.

Jen washed, and dressed hurriedly. She picked up the coffeepot that was sitting by the stove and poured herself a cup of strong, sweet coffee. There were some cream crackers in a tin on the table, she picked out a couple and dunked them in her coffee. That was her breakfast.

Lian had finished her ironing. She wrapped the pile of freshly ironed laundry in a white rectangular cloth and tied the corners together to form a parcel. She looked in her purse and found a couple of coins, which she gave to Jen.

'That's for your bus fare, you'll have to take your return fare out of the laundry money,' Lian said to Jen.

'All right Mum,' Jen replied flatly. She picked up the bundle of clean linen and left the house. Jen walked to the village to catch the bus that would take her past the hotel.

As she stood waiting in the marked square, listening to the hustle and bustle of the market, she noticed the steam rising from the food stalls that flanked both sides of the walkway. She leant against an old, gnarled tree and watched the comings and goings. The aroma of spicy roast pork, steamed buns, fried noodles, banana and yam fritters and lots more that she could not identify wafted pass her nose. She longed to be able to sit down on one of those stools scattered around little, circular tables and to be served a steaming bowl of soup noodles with bits of succulent chicken on top.

Jen watched as families arrived for their breakfast, fathers, mothers and their noisy excitable children who took their places among the stalls. In an adjoining compound were farmers and their wives setting up shop in their allocated space on the concrete floor. Fresh fruit and vegetables were arranged on circular bamboo baskets, and every so often water was sprinkled over them to stop them drying out in the blazing sun. Loud bartering could be heard as the early morning shoppers clamoured for the fresh produce.

In the next compound was the meat market. Mutton and beef were on display on raised concrete slabs. After that came the livestock, mainly chickens, in large wicker baskets. The chickens were pecking each other and making a racket. The pork market was at the very end of the building. The owners of the pork stalls were all Chinese unlike the beef and mutton sellers who were either Indians or Muslims.

Jen was immersed in deep thoughts, mainly about food and rumbling stomachs when the bus arrived. Reluctantly she got on the bus and took a seat in the back. The bundle of linen occupied a seat next to her. The journey only took ten minutes but it gave her time to work out a plan.

The stonemason's yard came into view, Jen rang the bell and the bus juddered to a halt. As she got off the bus Jen followed her customary habit of standing for a few minutes and watching the men at work. She marvelled at the beautifully cut grey granite stacked in rows against a very old coconut tree. There were a couple of men at work, hammer and chisel working in tandem with bits of stone and dust flying off everywhere. Jen saw a headstone engraved with Chinese characters. She wondered whom it was meant for. Her dad had the same kind of headstone to mark his grave.

'Hello Jen, you're early,' Mrs Lim the hotel manageress said with a bright cheery smile.

'Good morning Mrs Lim.'

'How much do I owe your mum for these?' Mrs Lim asked as she put her arms out to receive the bundle from Jen's arms.

'There are five sheets and six pillowcases.'

'You're the clever one, how much do I pay you?'

Two dollars and ten cents,' Jen answered easily.

'That's right. Come along with me to the desk and I'll get you the money.' Mrs Lim pulled out a key from her pocket; it was attached to her trousers via a long piece of string. She opened a drawer with the key. The draw was divided into sections; each section had coins of different denominations in it. And in a separate compartment there were bundles of one-dollar bills and five-dollar bills held together with rubber bands. Jen had never seen so much money in one place before.

'There you are, two dollars and ten cents.' Mrs Lim handed over the money, she paused and studied Jen's face and then she put her hand back into the drawer and picked up another coin saying, 'And this is for you.'

'Thank you, thank you Mrs Lim,' Jen could hardly contain the thrill in her voice.

'You're most welcome child, don't forget now to pick up the dirty laundry on your way out!'

'I won't.' Jen almost skipped to the door. She scooped up the bundle of dirty linen tied up in similar rectangular piece of cloth like the one before. With one swing she had the bundle over her shoulder. She checked the clock on the way out; the bus was not due for another twenty minutes.

Jen walked steadily along the grass verge in the direction she had come from on the bus. She decided to walk the two miles back to the village. The money she had saved on the bus fares plus the extra money that Mrs Lim had given her would buy her a temporary dream. A steaming bowl of noodles with shreds of chicken breast and maybe a few rings of crispy fried shallots to add flavour. It was even better then her original plan, which was to walk, and save the fares for a spicy steamed bun.

She walked and ran some of the way, dodging bicycles that came too close to the verge. Every time a bus or lorry came by, she breathed in a lung full of smoke and fumes. The soya factory looked large and imposing, very unlike the view from a moving bus. The stench from the fermenting soya beans stung her eyes and burnt her throat. The heat of the morning sun was hot and uncomfortable. Beads of perspiration ran down her face and neck. Every now and then she put the bundle of laundry on the ground and took a short rest, but she never stopped long. Timing was important if her mother was to be kept in the dark about her little gift from Mrs Lim.

The village came into view; the diesel fumes from a passing bus momentarily blinded her. That was the bus she was supposed to be on. She ran the rest of the way to the market-square. Her heart was beating wildly, her mouth watered at the sight of the food on sale. Jen walked gingerly between the stalls gawping at the plump cooked chickens hanging on iron hooks, their heads were still attached. The money was burning a hole in her hand. She stood by a noodle stall, staring and wondering.

'Do you want to eat or what?' The stallholder asked; not a flicker of a smile crossed her face.

'How much is a bowl of those noodles please?' Jen asked timidly, and pointed to the mound of egg noodles on the serving counter.

'Ten cents.' She barked.

'How much is it if I have those chicken pieces as well.'

'Twenty cents.' Her face as mean as a hungry dog.

'Okay, can I have noodles with some chicken, please?' Jen perched herself on a stool and carefully laid her bundle of laundry on the ground between her feet. A bowl of steaming noodles in clear soup was plonked in front of her. White strips of chicken breast nestled in the centre of the golden yellow noodles that glistened in the sun. Jen picked up a spoon and selected a matching pair of chopsticks from the container that was sitting in the middle of the table.

Eyes shut, chin tilted forward and mouth open, Jen tasted the first morsel of her special treat. Droplets of soup splattered her chin. Working the chopsticks into the crunchy bean shoots and soft noodles she brought them to her mouth to savour the contrast in textures. She was saving the chicken till last; but like everything in Jen's life it was spoilt.

Meena and Wei Wei, two of the three musketeers from school happened to walk by. 'Look whose here!' Meena's voice rang out in the open air.

Jen's back stiffened, she sat bolt upright, 'Hello,' Jen feigned interest.

'I didn't know you breakfast here on Saturdays?' Meena said looking at Wei Wei meaningfully.

'Yes, I didn't think you have the money.' Wei Wei came out in support of Meena.

'Well I do…I come here every Saturday,' Jen lied.

'What's in that bundle?' Meena wanted to know.

'It's her swag bag,' Wei Wei answered on Jen's behalf. After having their fun they walked off laughing.

Jen looked at what was left of the noodles and ate them quickly. They no longer tasted the same; the chicken might as well have been pieces of rubber.

On the walk home she consoled herself that Meena and Wei Wei were unlikely to tell her mother that they saw her eating at a market stall. If they did Jen would have to explain where the money had come from which in turn would earn her a telling-off for having been extravagant. Her mother would then have gone on to lecture that the money would have been better spent on proper food for the whole family.

* * *

As Jen neared her house she heard her mother's raised voice through the open window.

'Tam! Lee! If you two carry on, I'm going to have you both adopted…sold even. Tam, make yourself useful and get those shoes off the chair,' Lian scolded.

'But Mum,' Lee was heard to protest.

'I don't want to know, just do as you're told. And you, Lee! Get up those stairs and take that kite of yours with you…if I hear one more word from you… you are in for it. I mean it.'

Jen pressed her wobbly body against the wooden wall just out of sight of the window to compose herself. It was unusual for her mother to be so vociferous. Money was usually the cause of much anxiety in the home and Jen knew much better than to walk in when her mother was in an agitated state.

The sound of the back door creaking open and then slammed shut told Jen that her mother had gone into the backyard. She crept in through the front door and walked silently into the kitchen. Tam was squatting by the stove. He was blowing air through a hollow tube into the smoking fire. His face was red from the effort, and his eyes watered copiously. But he wasn't winning. The damp coal refused to burn.

'What are doing?' Jen asked, her voice full of concern.

'I'm trying to keep the fire going,' Tam answered in between coughing and puffing to stop the fire dying out.

Jen picked up a pair of tongs. 'Move out of the way and let me do it. You're never going to get that to work.' Jen kept one eye on the back door for her mother's return.

With the tongs she removed the large lumps of coal from the fire and set them on the fringe of the glow. She then stoked the dying embers dislodging the ashes through the slatted grid allowing air to circulate through the bottom. The smoke cleared and the coal began to burn again. Tam watched with relief.

'Now you have to brush the ashes out from the bottom,' Jen said to Tam.

'What with? This?' Tam asked pointing to a brush and makeshift dustpan.

'No, don't use the brush; you'll end up burning it. Use that metal spoon and scrape the ash out into the dustpan. Remember to empty it outside…away from the washing line.'

'Thanks. Where were you this morning? Mum's in a bad mood,' Tam whispered.

'Is she?' Jen feigned ignorance. 'Why's that? What did you do to upset her?'

'Don't know,' Tam shrugged. He was busy cleaning up the ashes he had spilt over the floor. He even managed to smudge his face and sprinkle his hair with them.

Jen untied the bundle of dirty laundry she brought home from the hotel. She decided the best way to keep her mother happy was to make a start on the laundry.

Lian meanwhile was busying herself by the well. Before her were two large basins full of dirty washing waiting to be scrubbed, rinsed, starched and put out to dry. She had meant to ask Jen to pay Farmer Choy and his wife a visit that morning, but after her conversation with Jen's teacher she became confused and distracted. Her thoughts swung wildly between extreme annoyance with Miss Chan for putting ideas in Jen's head, and pride that Jen had a gift. Her father would have been proud of her, Lian thought. Her religious beliefs added to her confusion, and that was that a gift was given for a reason and it would be a sacrilege not to embrace it. It was a sin to go against the Gods. But time was not on her side and she had to make a decision soon.

Later that day Lian decided to broach the subject with Jen.

'Jen, I've been thinking, about what you've said…and what your teacher said.'

Jen waited for her mother to continue. She was in the middle of rinsing one of those large sheets. Her back was sore and her dress was soaked from the effort of bending over the large shallow basin of water and agitating the sheet with both hands to get the soap out.

'It's up to the Gods and the ancestors what happens in the future, but that doesn't mean that we have to wait till then. As you know, we need to eat, and your brothers and sister have to go to school…we don't know how well you'll do in your exams anyway,' Lian paused.

Jen was dying to interrupt, but felt that her plea would have sounded hollow. She had to appear to be on her mother's side to gain her trust.

Lian continued, 'You may do well and gain the scholarship you wanted, but what if you don't.' A long pause followed, Lian was thinking hard. 'This is what we'll do…it's only a temporary plan you understand. I spoke to Farmer Choy and his wife yesterday, they are looking for someone to help them with the children and do some housework.'

Jen felt like she had been punched in the stomach. She stared at her feet. A slight twitch appeared in the corner of her mouth, but she remained silent.

'Mrs Choy asked if you could go and see her today. Maybe you could…perhaps you might want to discuss it over with her yourself. You're old enough to know what you can manage…' Lian stopped in mid sentence, she felt awkward and uncomfortable.

'And how much is she going to pay me?' Jen asked, her voice laced with fury.

'It's not polite to talk about money like that,' Lian tried to placate Jen. 'She'll give you what she sees as fair I'm sure.'

'What if it's not?' Jen barely concealed her anger.

'What do you mean?'

'What if the pay is not fair? How do I know if I'm being paid for how much work I do, or if she pays me according to whether she likes me or not?'

'Jen! Why are you being so difficult?'

Jen wanted to shout, rage and scream, but instead she said, ' Sorry. I'll go and see Mrs Choy when I'm finished with the washing.'

Lian relented, 'I'm sorry things are…like this,' she spread her hands out indicating the mess in the kitchen, but really she meant the mess in their lives. 'When you go to school on Monday, ask your teacher for those forms, the ones about the scholarship. We might as well be prepared.'

Jen took a deep breath. Her knees knocked and her stomach felt like a squeezed lemon. She looked across the kitchen. Halfway up the wall above the stove was a small shelf. On the shelf was a small urn. Sticking out of the urn were stubs of joss sticks that had burned out. They were offerings for the kitchen God. Jen reminded herself to burn a few more joss sticks that night to give thanks. At least one God was listening to her she thought.

For the second time that day Jen walked to the village. As she reached the square she took a right turn. A further ten minutes walk took her over a railway line that ran parallel to another road that led to the north of the village. Once she was on the side of the railway track the landscape changed dramatically.

Closely packed wooden shacks and little redbrick cottages were replaced with dense cultivation. Tropical fruit groves and vegetable gardens stretched as far as her eyes could see. Winding dirt tracks straddled and separated the different varieties of leafy vegetables, tubers, gourds and legumes. Hues of green, yellow and brown carpeted the loamy soil that sucked and pulled Jen's feet as she walked on them.

The barking of dogs and the stench of pigs slurry told Jen that she was near the farmhouse. Farmer Choy's house was much bigger than the other farmhouses and it had a thatched roof. The less prosperous farmers had corrugated iron sheets on their roofs, the same as Jen's home.

One of Farmer Choy's sons came out to investigate the din their two dogs were making. Jen noted that they were tied to a tree with ropes that threatened to strangle them if they moved too suddenly or strayed too far. When the boy saw Jen standing just beyond the reach of the dogs, he ran indoors again without acknowledging Jen's greeting.

'Hello, you must be Jen,' Mrs Choy came to the door and greeted Jen warmly.

After a moment's hesitation Jen replied nervously, 'I'm Jen…my mum asked me to come to see you…'

'Please come in, don't mind the dogs, they are not as fierce as they look.' She beckoned Jen to step inside and told the dogs to stop yapping in the same monotone.

Jen liked Mrs Choy's sing-song voice. Her face was less wrinkled than her mother's and she walked a little awkwardly due to the bump on her front. Her clothes were more colourful than any Jen had herself.

'Would you like to sit down. Don't be shy,' Mrs Choy encouraged.

Jen sat on a kitchen stool instead of one of the chairs with a high back and arms. She saw three children peeping at her from behind the door, two boys and a girl. The boys were giggling and the little girl who was about three was sucking her fingers.

'Children, come and meet Jen,' Mrs Choy coaxed them out of hiding. Jen was solemnly introduced to the children. The boys, Siu Min and Siu Wah were aged six and four respectively. They were outgoing and chattered to Jen amiably but Wan Yin the youngest hid behind her mother and refused to speak.

Mrs Choy turned out to be a star. She seemed very interested in Jen's likes and dislikes. She asked questions about her friends, her favourite subjects at school and she wanted to know what hobbies Jen had. Fuelled by the home-made biscuits and lulled by the warmth and encouragement of the farmer's wife Jen told her all about the scholarship, her hopes and her ambitions.

Dusk was gathering in fast when Jen made her way home. Her conversation with Mrs Choy had emboldened her desire to make a better future for herself. It also diminished some of her guilt to put herself before her brothers.

Jen slept fitfully that night. Every time she shut her eyes images of wingless birds and fire-breathing monsters fought each other to take over the peaceful village in a land that Jen was not familiar with.

Chapter Five

Over the next few weeks Jen's life was filled with the usual round of school, housework, playing mother to her brothers and sister, being her mother's right hand, and worrying about her schoolwork. The weekly discussions she had with Miss Chan on Friday afternoons became a familiar routine. She loved and feared those talks where they both explored the possibilities of Jen's academic prospects and her likelihood of a professional career.

Jen hung on to every praise and criticism her schoolwork invoked. She never failed to bank all the praises and criticisms and reflected on them when she was feeling particularly disenchanted with life. She dealt with criticism in a stoical manner; she knew her life was never going to be a bowl of agar-agar, Jen's favourite sweet.

She was always able to rely on Patricia to be an ally, a cheerful and funny one at that. But her friend was inclined to be impractical. Being an only child, Patricia's daily living was unhindered by such unimportant things as housework; she had running water straight from a tap, and electricity to light the house. Jen doubted her friend knew what it was like to eat and read by candlelight or go to bed hungry after struggling to sew by candlelight till midnight.

One such Friday afternoon Jen was invited to Patricia's home for tea. It was a rare treat for Jen to be allowed an evening to spend as she wished. As it was Patricia's birthday the following day, she had asked her mum to be allowed to go home with Jen in a rickshaw instead of being picked up in her car. Jen had seen the car waiting by the school gate many times before and often thought that it looked like a frog waiting to pounce on its prey. It was pale blue in colour and purred noisily leaving a trail of fumes as it travelled along the road.

As Jen and Patricia climbed into the rickshaw it started to rain. The rider put the hood up and a waterproof canvas was clipped over the foot-well and the front leaving only a small gap for them to see out. Jen was really annoyed to have her rickshaw ride spoilt.

' I hate the rain. Why does it have to rain now!' Jen complained bitterly.

'It has to rain sometime,' Patricia was pragmatic.

'Why now? Why can't it wait till we get home? It's hot and sticky with this hood and…and this thing over us,' Jen grumbled.

'He has to put it on or we'll get wet,' Patricia answered and nodded to the man cycling at the back.

Jen looked behind her. Two muscular legs in shorts were cycling furiously. The rider had no hat or shelter from the rain. His grey short-sleeved shirt was wet with raindrops and perspiration. His hands were fully occupied trying to manoeuvre the rickshaw through the school rush hour traffic. Every so often he rang a bell that let out a shrill peal to warn other road users when they got too close, and at the same time he gave a running commentary of how bad other drivers were.

Jen was contrite seeing the rider slowly being drenched by the persistent rain. 'Sorry, I was rude, wasn't I? Thank you for inviting me to tea and sharing your rickshaw.'

'You're welcome. I wish you could come to my house more often. Maybe when we've finished our exams,' Patricia said.

'Maybe,' Jen said but her voice was far away.

'It's boring at the weekends in my house,' Patricia said.

Jen looked at her friend surprised. 'You visit your aunts and uncles and cousins, don't you?'

'I do, they are boring too. All my aunts moan about my uncles, my uncles grumble about their work, and my cousins complain about their clothes, their spotty faces, and their school friends' Patricia pulled a face.

Jen laughed. 'You should come to my house. My brothers argue, fight and do things I cannot describe. My mum nags sometimes, a lot of the time in fact. My sister is the lucky one, she is allowed to play and get in my way…'

'What about you? What do you do?'

'Do you really want to know?' Jen was teasing.

'Yes I do, all of it. What will you be doing tomorrow?'

'Well, I get up, collect the laundry from the hotel, and help with the washing and the ironing. Then I do some shopping, help with the cooking and in the evening I do some sewing, the easy bit that is, I'm not allow to touch the sequins but I can do the buttons. My schoolwork comes last, usually.'

'You are lucky, I'm not allowed to go anywhere on my own,' Patricia complained. 'You go on the bus to town, you do the shopping for your mum. I don't even know which bus to catch and if I went to the market on my own I'm sure I'll get lost.'

'I can tell you which bus to catch,'

'That's not what I mean…You're so grown up and I'm…I'm thirteen tomorrow and all my aunties and uncles and cousins will be there singing happy birthday…and treat me like a child,' Patricia was almost breathless when she finished and looked close to tears. Frustration was written all over her face.

Jen was astonished at Patricia's outburst. She had always assumed that her best friend was happy with her pampered lifestyle. She was surprised at how little she knew of the real Patricia, and her next comment shocked Jen.

'I don't have a Dad either.'

Jen thought for bit and asked cautiously, 'What happened to your dad?'

'He went back home…to England when I was baby.'

'Does your mum have a photograph of him?'

Patricia shook her head and said emphatically, 'No.'

'Did she say what he looked like?'

'It was a long time ago, she can't remember.'

'It's only thirteen years!' Jen was surprised at her own audacity.

'I'm going to be a teenager tomorrow, I wonder if he remembers me,' Patricia sounded sad.

Jen wanted to put her arms around her friend but felt uncomfortable at the thought. She was not accustomed to hugging people. She swallowed hard and listened intently to the rain pummelling the canvas, it made the pain in her chest go away.

Patricia's mother Suzie was waiting for them when the rickshaw stopped outside a brick-built single storey house with red tiles on its roof. Ornate metal grills shielded the louvre windows on the front of the house. The wooden front door was similarly protected by a collapsible metal door.

Patricia removed her shoes and left them on a rack on the front porch, Jen did the same. As Jen entered the sitting room she was surprised by the absence of an altar like the ones she and all her neighbours had. The room was comfortably furnished with rattan armchairs with soft cushions; a ceiling fan was whirring gently overhead. There was a dark, polished bookcase full of books and a brown, shiny radio sat proudly in the midst of it. The marble-effect floor was gleaming and cool under her bare feet.

Patricia dropped her school bag on to one of the armchairs. Jen slipped her bag under the same chair. Patricia gave her mother a peck on the cheek while Jen smiled awkwardly and followed them in to the kitchen.

'Did you both enjoy the rickshaw ride?' Patricia's mother asked.

'Yes, thank you,' Jen answered but was unsure how to address her host, 'Auntie Suzie,' she finally said.

'But it was raining, and the rickshaw man had to put the covers up so we couldn't see where we were going,' Patricia told her mum.

'The rainy season is here again. I was wondering whether it was a good idea for you both to come home in a rickshaw, I don't find them very safe. There is so much traffic on the road these days. Perhaps I should have picked you up in my car,' Suzie said to no one in particular.

'It was fun though wasn't it Patricia?' Jen turned to her friend for assurance.

Patricia was busy looking in the fridge, 'Orange juice?' she asked Jen.

'Yes please.'

Patricia nudged the fridge door shut and opened the food cupboard next to it. She brought out a biscuit tin, a cake tin, a packet of dried cuttlefish, and a jar of pickles. She handed half of them to Jen who was standing there with her mouth opened. On the way back to the sitting room Patricia grabbed a bowl of fruit as the walked past the dining table.

'Are you allow to eat like this every day?' Jen asked.

'These are snacks, that's what they're for, eating,' Patricia rolled her eyes.

Jen felt the aches on the sides of her jaw where she was salivating generously as she chewed the cuttlefish. Patricia's mother appeared at the door and smiled indulgently at them.

'Tea will be ready in a couple of hours. Not too many biscuits Patricia, you'll spoil your appetite.'

'Okay Mum,' Patricia answered nonchalantly.

'What do you eat for tea?' Jen asked puzzled. She had never given much thought about what other people eat.

She knew Indians and Malays have their way of cooking. But Patricia was Catholic and half-Chinese and half-English.

'What do you mean what I eat? I eat the same as you.'

'No you can't do. How do you cook your food?'

'I don't know. My mum does all the cooking. I don't even know when the kettle boils. I'm not allowed in the kitchen when mum's cooking.'

'So you don't have to make a fire in the morning, then?'

'What for?'

'Well, I have to start a fire in the morning and boil the kettle and make the coffee…'

'Mum makes the coffee in the morning. We've got a gas stove, I think, and you just turn a knob and light a match to it. My mum will tell you if you want to know,' Patricia spoke matter-of-factly.

'Have you got a well in your backyard?'

'No, but we have got a tap. My mum uses it to water her flowers.'

'How many taps have you got…in the house I mean?'

'Erm…m…two, three..! One in the kitchen and one in the bathroom…and a shower, I suppose that is a bit like a tap.'

'What does that look like…the shower?'

Patricia got off the chair. 'I'll show you, follow me.' They walked down a short corridor into a small room in the back of the house. The floor and walls were overlaid with blue mosaic tiles. The room echoed and shimmered in the afternoon sun that filtered in from a small window. A large tub stood beneath a tap and next to it was the shower-head towering above both their heads.

Jen stood in the doorway and watched fascinated as Patricia stepped forward and turned the shower on. Sharp arrows of cold water spurted through the pin-sized holes of what looked like an inverted lotus fruit. They each stuck out a foot under the cold running water. Their laughing and giggling reverberated around the little room.

'That's enough now,' Patricia's mother had to raise her voice to get herself heard. 'Here's a towel. Is your uniform wet, Jen?'

'Oh, sorry, it's a little bit damp, but it doesn't matter. Sorry about the noise,' Jen was embarrassed. She couldn't remember being so boisterous before.

'Come on, I'll show you my room,' Patricia offered.

Jen was envious. Patricia had a bed all to herself. The mattress was soft and bouncy even with both of them jumping on it. The patchwork bed cover was delicate and light, and the pillow was encased in white fine cotton with lace edging.

Patricia opened her wardrobe doors. Her clothes were neatly hung up on proper wooden hangers. Her shoes were lined up on the bottom shelf, all cleaned and polished. Sitting alongside it was a chest-of-drawers that had an oval mirror anchored to it by two wooden arms and a couple of nuts and bolts. There was not a chamber pot in sight.

Jen ran her hand over the furniture, her eyes were bright and the corners of her mouth curled upwards with pleasure.

Patricia interrupted her reverie, 'Can you come to my party tomorrow?'

Jen shook her head sadly and said, 'I can't. I've told you that last week. I'm sorry, I would like to but Saturdays and Sundays are working days in my house.'

'I just thought… Maybe just this once…'

'Do you know what you're getting for your birthday?' Jen asked hoping to change the subject.

'It's a secret,' Patricia sighed. 'I know mum's bought me a new dress for the party. There will be a cake with candles…the usual.'

'I have never had a cake for my birthday.'

'I'll save you a piece, a big piece.'

'Thanks, I'm sorry I haven't got any money to buy you a present,' Jen was apologetic.

'You've given me the best present already.'

Jen looked quizzically at Patricia.

Patricia continued, 'you've never laughed at my curly brown hair, or my white skin like some of the other girls. You never call me names because of my funny teeth.'

'You haven't got funny teeth,' Jen protested.

'They stick out too much, I don't like them myself.'

'You don't want to listen to Meena and her friends, they are nasty…there is a word for them but I cannot remember it now.'

Patricia nodded, and they smiled knowingly at each other.

Just then they heard Patricia's mum call from the kitchen. 'Tea's on the table girls.'

Jen was mesmerised by the variety of food on the table. East and west came together in delicious harmony. Braised pork, spicy chicken wings, crispy fried noodles jostled with little roast potatoes, and crunchy salads in little bowls to bring out the flavour of the ginger dips.

Patricia used a knife and fork; her mother had a spoon and a fork. Jen decided that chopsticks were the safest option.

Patricia's mum joined in their conversation. At home Jen's mother rarely engaged in dialogue at mealtimes, she generally discouraged too much joviality.

Jen was served a sweet after her main meal. She wasn't sure what it was called, but she certainly enjoyed the thick creamy texture with the thinly sliced fleshy fruit. She was encouraged to have seconds and she accepted it happily. The funny bloating feeling in her stomach didn't deter her.

After their meal Jen was offered a choice of coffee, tea or juice. She chose the tea with a dash of milk, but after a sip she decided she wasn't cut out for the rich lifestyle. She asked for a drink of water instead.

As they got up from the table Jen started to stack up

the crockery out of habit. Patircia's mother smiled.

'Thank you, Jen. Just leave them on the side, I'll do them later.'

'It's alright. I'll be careful.'

'I'd better take you home; it's getting late. Patricia, could you please put the lights on.'

Patricia flicked a switch on the wall and the room lit up. Jen was hypnotised by the illuminated white tube in the middle of the ceiling. It was much brighter than a candle or the kerosene lamp she had at home, Jen thought.

Sitting in the back of the car on the way home Jen was silent. She had had a wonderful day and didn't want it to end. She remembered to thank Patricia and her mother as the headlights of the car picked out the lopsided, wooden house Jen called home.

* * *

Sleep came easily to Jen that night. The hearty and heady meal she had had at Patricia's home was like a sedative. Rhythmic drumming of rain drops on the corrugated iron roof only added to the familiarity of her surroundings.

In a dreamlike state Jen wiped droplets of water from her face. She rolled over to her side and went straight back to sleep. But the intrusion followed her. Now the dripping of water became more persistent, drip, drip, drip, she woke with alarm. Her hair and pillow were damp. In the darkness Jen stretched her hands out, she felt Min's sleeping body close by. Waving her arms in front and around her she felt nothing but empty air.

Jen heard the howling and lashing of the strong wind that shook the house and rattled the trees outside. Every now and again she could hear the loose corners of the roof lifting and settling back down again. A few more drops of water landed on her forehead. Jen sat bolt upright clasping her pillow to her chest and waited. The soft thuds of water on the wooden boards could be heard clearly now, she fumbled in the dark to trace the spot. Moments later her hand touched a little puddle. She sat in the dark numbed to the bone trying hard to work out what was going on.

A bolt of lightning lit up the room and she heard branches snapping off followed by the deep rumblings of thunder. It then dawned on her that the water was coming from a leak in the roof.

Jen moved swiftly out of the bedroom, down the stairs and into the kitchen. She felt her way to a storage space where her mother stored necessities for such emergencies. Jen dived into a bag full of rags and dragged out a handful, next she stretched further into the shelf until her finger gripped the edge of a round tin. With both items safely in her hands she quickly ran back upstairs. Once she was back in the bedroom she went down on all fours and swept both hands around to locate the puddle. By now the puddle had spread, she hurriedly mopped up the water with the rags and then stuck the tin under the dripping roof. Immediately the room became vibrant with the pinging of raindrops as they hit the bottom of the empty tin.

Lian and Min slept on. Jen gently pushed Min's sleeping form away from the musical tin. She turned her own pillow over and tried to get back to sleep. She wondered if there was a leak in her brothers' room, but decided there couldn't have been or they would have woken up by now. Jen thought she could hear more dripping in her bedroom, or was it coming from somewhere else, but with the roar of the wind it was hard to tell. She finally fell asleep still wondering.

When she woke in the morning the rain had stopped and the sun was out. Her mother was not in the room, neither was the tin she left to catch the drips. She got dressed promptly and went downstairs to talk to her mother about visiting Patricia that day.

At the bottom of the stairs she saw the telltale signs of muddy imprints on the floor. All the shoes and clogs were mud-stained too. She realised that the rain must have been heavy and the kitchen had flooded in the night. She put on her pair of muddy clogs and went into the kitchen.

Her mother was trying to start the fire without much success as the kindling and charcoals were waterlogged. Lian sighed.

'Shall I do that?' Jen asked her mother.

'Everything's wet! We must remember to store the coal somewhere else,' Lian 's voice was taut.

'I'll go outside to see if there's any dry wood...'

'How can there be, everything's wet indoors,' Lian snapped.

'The sun's out, maybe I could find some dry twigs...' Jen tried to remain optimistic.

'Sorry, I didn't mean to snap. Yes, you are right, see if there are any dry twigs outside.'

Jen went out into the backyard. She found the broken half of a tree which had landed squarely over the well. There were lumps of wood and broken branches scattered all over the ground. The latrine door was hanging askew and the metal buckets from the well were smashed into the concrete step. One of the buckets was badly dented and the other had lost its handle and the rope that was attached to it. There were puddles everywhere, but she knew that in a few hours they would have disappeared into the soil. She also knew that they would appear again and again over the next few weeks until the monsoon months were over.

She suddenly remembered why she was out in the yard; quickly she picked up several lumps of wood, they were partially dried from the morning sun. Going indoors for the axe she noticed her mother was still desperately blowing into the smoking coal. Jen hurriedly went outside again and systematically splintered the wood she had collected. Soon she had a fair-sized pile of kindling. Jen had the fire going within minutes though it was smoking rather more than usual.

Lian decided to do the shopping before she tackled the laundry, as there wasn't enough water in the house. Before she left for the market she called over her shoulders, 'It's time Tam and Lee are up, it's nearly nine o'clock. Ask them to help you clean up the yard. The urn needs topping up with clean water too and tell Tam he needs to chop up more wood…'

Getting Lee to help with any work in the house was a joke. He was inclined to be dramatic and his idea of work always involved plenty of fun and danger. Tam was a better bet, but Jen needed both of them to help her shift the big log that was firmly wedged over the well.

Lee began work by walking gingerly on the log lodged over the well. He stuck out his arms to keep his balance. Tam watched terrified, he held his breath, afraid that Lee might fall into the well if he called out to him to get off. Jen standing some distance away sucked in her breath to stop herself shouting at him. When Lee got to the end of the trunk he jumped off proudly. Jen grabbed him.

'If you do that again, I'll kill you,' she spoke sharply.

Lee looked up in surprise, 'I wasn't in your way. You told me to get out of your way, and now you tell me not to do that. I can't win.' He was most indignant.

'You!' Jen's voice was shrill, she stopped and said more calmly, 'And now you can help Tam pick up all these branches and stack them over there.'

'Why are girls so bossy?' Lee asked Tam.

'You shouldn't have done that,' Tam replied, 'it's dangerous, you could have fallen into the well.'

'I can swim.'

'No you can't.'

'Can.'

'How would you get out? The well is very deep.' Tam was trying to reason with Lee but being reasonable was not part of being Lee.

''You throw that bucket in, then I can hold on to the rope and then you pull me out.' Lee was not put off.

'What if the rope breaks?'

'Get another rope then…'

Tam decided the argument was not going anywhere and turned his attention to Jen. 'That tree trunk is too heavy for us both to move, do you think we could chop off some of the branches first?' Tam asked.

'That's a good idea Tam. Be careful with the axe though. Whatever you do, don't let Lee get hold of the axe.'

'Why don't you give him something to do indoors, that way he won't…'

'I have to keep any eye on him,' Jen sighed. 'When he's indoors he only upsets Min.'

'Yeah, you're right. He's a nuisance sometimes.' He looked at Jen and they smiled conspiratorially.

Tam hacked at the tree trunk with all the strength he could muster. Showers of wet leaves and bits of wood chippings flew in all directions. Every few minutes he stopped to take a rest. His shoulders ached; his arms started to cramp up, his knuckles were white where he gripped the axe handle so tightly.

'Take a break Tam, I'll have a go at it,' Jen said.

'It's alright. I can manage.' Tam was reluctant to hand over the axe; he didn't think that chopping a tree was a girl's job.

'Let me have a go,' Lee jumped in between them.

'NO!' Tam and Jen answered together.

'I'll be quicker than you two,' Lee replied aggrieved.

'If you're so quick why aren't those branches cleared up yet?'

'Cleaning up is girls work,' Lee answered cheekily.

Jen wanted to put her hands round his neck till his face turned blue. She ignored him instead and picked up a broom to sweep the debris lying around the yard.

After an hour of hard work Jen and Tam with some verbal help from Lee managed to lever the tree trunk off the well. With much pushing and rolling the offending tree trunk was now safely in the far end of the yard waiting to be chopped up to make more firewood. By this time the rain had started again, it fell in sheets and showed no signs of stopping.

The damp hung around the house. By the afternoon the rain was easing off, but there were already several inches of water lapping around in the kitchen and the sitting room area. The concrete floor of the sitting room was awash with the muddy slush from the kitchen. A ring of muddy grime could be clearly seen on all the walls. Plimsolls, clogs and bits of wood and papers floated around the room like puppets.

Lee and Tam made paper boats to sail around the house. Min sat on the stairs shouting encouragement as the competition heated up. Jen sat further up the stairs trying to do some revision for her exams. Lian was sewing quietly by the window in the

bedroom.

By five that evening the rain stopped as suddenly as it came. The sun came out and the floodwater receded. The kitchen was now a slippery quagmire, and the sitting room floor was covered in black scum.

After their evening meal the boys and Min were sent upstairs. Jen and her mother began their one of many cleaning up sessions. Jen's task was to fetch fresh water from the well to sluice the floor as her mother swept with a stiff broom. Muddy water from the sitting room was channelled out into the streets via the front door. The kitchen floor was left to dry on its own accord as the excess water found its own way into cracks that augmented the inadequate drainage system under the hardened mud. They worked quietly and companionably in the kitchen storing firewood on a makeshift platform to prevent further drenching from another flood. Jen ached all over, her stomach grumbled from lack of food. Her clothes were wet and they stuck to her slight body.

'Where should I put these?' Jen asked lifting a basket full of charcoal. 'The bottom half is already wet.' She continued as drips of blackened water splashed her feet.

Her mother sighed, 'Just leave it somewhere off the floor to drip-dry. We better take all the other stuff upstairs.'

'What stuff?' Jen asked rubbing her aching arms.

'All the dried food of course,' Lian answered with an edge to her voice. She had looked into the rice urn earlier and noticed that it was only a quarter full, there were a couple of dried salted fish wrapped up in newspaper, a few sweet potatoes and a yam in a basket that was all the food in the house. With the heavy rainfall she was unable to do the laundry for the hotel, and that in turn reduced her income even further. By the time they went to bed Jen had an aching body and her mother had an aching heart.

Chapter Six

The next day, a Sunday, was marked with sporadic showers. Jen and her mother were able to get most of the washing and ironing finished and delivered on time. But the extra work had left little time for Jen to revise for her exams or complete her homework. Looking through her timetable it suddenly occurred to her that she would be thirteen in three weeks time and her school examination was scheduled for the week after her birthday. The thought of both events made her heart flutter uneasily.

Getting ready for school on Monday morning Jen noticed that her school plimsolls were damp and there were two small holes on the soles of her right shoe. Dare she ask her mother for a new pair of plimsolls, she thought, but she brushed the fancy idea aside. There were more important things like getting to school on time, passing exams and wiping the smiles off her bullies' faces but to name a few.

The long grasses growing on both sides of the dirt track were wet and alive with leeches. Jen and her brothers were careful to avoid them, though Lee enjoyed speculating about them.

'Do you know how to remove a leech if you find one sucking blood from your leg?' Lee asked Tam.

'I'd just pull it off,' Tam replied.

'No, you shouldn't do that.'

'Why not?'

'Because you'll break its neck and the head will stay inside your leg,' Lee explained, bunching his fingers together to demonstrate the headless leech sucking blood from its victim. 'And it will carry on sucking your blood.'

'Alright clever, how do you do it then?'

'You burn its bottom with a cigarette end,' Lee replied triumphantly.

'Who told you that?'

'Farmer Choy. He said that's what he did when he found several leeches on his legs.'

'That's cruel, burning it with a lighted cigarette.'

'Well, if a leech sucks my blood I'm not going to kiss it. I'll burn its bum instead, that's seems fair to me,' Lee laughed.

Jen was approaching the ditch when she saw the level of murky water stagnating in the deep end; it had risen several feet and looked quietly threatening. As she walked across the makeshift footbridge she called back a warning to her brothers.

'Watch out, you two! This plank is wet and slippery. And Lee, please don't mess around, there's lots of water in the ditch. I don't want to dive in there to get you out.'

'I don't want to fall in there either,' Lee replied indignantly.

'You go first,' Tam said to Lee.

Reluctantly Lee stepped on the long wobbly plank. He looked into the murky water curiously noting the intermittent croaking and leaping of frogs on the embankment. He couldn't help but bounced up and down a few times to test the veracity of Jen's warning.

Tam looked on in exasperation. Jen walked purposely towards the bus-stop. The arrival of the bus concentrated Lee's mind and he swiftly walked across the plank without further ado and raced down the track to where Jen was boarding the bus.

Patricia was pleased to see Jen in class. She had a lot

of news for her about her birthday party, the treats and surprises. So eager was she to speak to Jen that Miss Chan had to throw her a couple of warning looks to remind her that they were there to listen and learn and not chatter unnecessarily. It was such a relief for Patricia when the bell sounded for morning break.

Jen got in first, 'Sorry I couldn't see you on your birthday, I tried but…'

'Oh that, I'm sorry too, but it's okay, I don't mind…'

Jen interrupted, 'Did you have a good time?'

'Wonderful time!' Patricia said. She was all smiles and seemed in such good humour. Patricia continued, 'It was the best birthday ever. And I've still got more surprises to come.' Patricia's big brown eyes became even rounder and bigger. 'You'll never guess who is coming to see me in a few weeks time!'

'Another auntie?' Jen asked.

'Nope, you'll never guess,' Patricia's smile was broad showing off her protruding front teeth.

'Go on then, tell me,' Jen pleaded.

'Have another guess,' Patricia teased.

'Some relations from Singapore? You said that your mum has a cousin there, is she coming to see you?'

'No, no, no…someone more important than that!'

'I give up, please tell me who this mysterious person is,' Jen grabbed Patricia by the arms and gave them several rigorous shakes.

'MY FATHER, of course!' Patricia said; her voice shrill and she started dancing around like an excited puppy.

Jen was speechless for several minutes, and when she recovered she muttered, 'Your Father!'

'That's right, my father. MY DAD!' Patricia emphasised the word 'Dad' as if to familiarise herself with the sound of the word.

'Tell me some more about your…er…father. How did you find out? I thought…?' Jen seemed to have caught some of the excitement that Patricia was feeling. She was really pleased for her friend, but there was something else she was feeling but was unable to define.

'Well, it was my Uncle Tom, he knew my father when he, my father was a soldier over here.' Patricia wasn't making much sense to Jen.

'Who is Uncle Tom?'

'He's my mum's eldest brother. We call him Uncle Tom but he is not a real uncle really, my grandmother adopted him when he was a little boy. What was I saying? Oh, yeah, when my father went back to England he started writing to Uncle Tom to ask about me. He sends money on my birthday and at Christmas to Uncle Tom. Uncle Tom then buys me the presents, that's why I always get lots of present.' Patricia was breathless when she finished explaining.

'Did your mum know that, that it was really your dad that paid for the presents?'

'No she didn't.'

'Why didn't your Uncle Tom tell her, I mean before?'

'Uncle Tom said that my father asked him not to.'

'Why?'

'I don't know, maybe he will explain himself better when I see him.'

'When is he coming to see you?'

'Soon. I think he said six weeks time. I'm meeting him at Uncle Tom's house.'

'We'll have finished our exams by then,' Jen said but Patricia didn't appear to hear her. Jen prodded her in the ribs.

'Huh! What?'

'Where do you go when you're not listening to me?'

'I was just thinking. SIX WEEKS! And I'll see my DAD!'

'I'm really happy that you've found your dad. What does your mum think about it?'

After some thoughts Patricia said quite sombrely, 'My mum's been rather quiet. I think she's angry with Uncle Tom for not telling her about my dad.'

'I suppose she's upset,' Jen said with feeling.

Patricia was thoughtful, she had been so excited about meeting her father that she hadn't realise what a shock the return of her father must have been to her mother. As to her mother's real feeling Patricia had no idea.

'I forgot,' Patricia said as she delved into her school bag and brought out a small squashed parcel. 'I've saved you a piece of my birthday cake.'

'Thanks, thank you very much.'

For the rest of the day Jen's mind was like a whirlpool. Thoughts and fancy ideas chased each other around in her head, sometimes they agreed and sometimes they quarrelled. One moment she was pleased for Patricia and in another instant she became extremely worried for her.

It was in this frame of mind that she arrived home from school. She recalled her father's coffin in the sitting room and everyone present wearing black and crying. She was eight years old, frightened and bewildered. She had lots of questions and nobody to answer them.

Later that evening Jen was sitting at the table doing her homework when she decided to share some of her thoughts with her mother.

'You know my friend Patricia,' Jen started with trepidation.

'That half-caste girl?' Lian asked without looking up from her sewing.

'Why do you call her that?' Jen's voice was louder than she intended.

'She is half-caste isn't she?' Lian looked up at Jen, the creases in her brow stood out in the dim light.

'Yes, but it sounds…so rude.'

'It's just a way of identifying her that's all, it's not meant to be rude. What were you saying about this friend?'

'She's seeing her father for the first time...soon.'

The creases in Lian's brow became even more pronounced as she studied Jen's face. She had no previous knowledge of Patricia's family history apart from the fact that she was Eurasian. 'How do you know that?'

'She told me today. It was her thirteenth birthday on Saturday, and her uncle told her that her father was coming to see her all the way from England.' Jen's voice quivered with excitement.

'That's nice for her.' Lian replied in her laconic tone.

'I think it's exciting. Fancy seeing your father for the first time and she's thirteen,' Jen continued. She hadn't noticed her mother's pursed lips and stiffened back.

After a minutes silence Jen started again, tentatively this time, 'It's my birthday soon, I'll be thirteen like Patricia. Mum, do you think I could have another pair of plimsolls for school...as a present.'

Lian stopped her sewing. She looked at Jen from across the table, her expression remained bland. 'You need a pair of clogs for wearing indoors; the ones you've got on are paper-thin. I'll get you a new pair of those instead. The school shoes...we'll wait and see. You've only got another four or five weeks before the term ends...'

Jen didn't argue the point. She knew what her mother meant. If she was unable to qualify for the scholarship she would not be going back to school anyway and therefore a pair of plimsolls would not be a necessity. And if Jen did receive the scholarship she could then apply for financial assistance through the welfare fund. She had another agenda to pursue and felt the time was right to make a peace offering to her mother.

'When my exams are over I've got to wait for four weeks for the results, do you think I should go to see Farmer Choy's wife? About the helping round the farm and looking after the children.'

'That's a good idea; their baby is due anytime now. How

long is the school closed for at this time of year?' Lian could never work out the different holiday seasons.

'I do my exams at the end of November, and the school is closed for the whole of December. The results of my exams will be sent out at the end of December and if I pass I'll go back to school in January.' Jen felt as if she was reciting from a book, there was a tremor in her voice.

It was well past midnight before they both went to bed. The candle had long burnt out.

* * *

One wet day merged into another soggy night and the whole cycle would start again. In between the sun shone, the wind blew and life went on, shaped by routine and hard work.

Jen went to school with papers stuffed in her shoes. There were holes in both her shoes now. Sand and grit worked their way into them as she walked. They chafed and rubbed the bottom of her feet. Each evening she rummaged in the bin for scraps of newspapers to replace the torn and inky pulp. Sometimes when she was really lucky she even managed to find some cardboard pieces. They made better insoles and gave her feet better protection and they lasted more than a couple of days before they needed replacement.

Some mornings when the rain had been particularly heavy and the tracks to the bus-stop were covered in countless puddles, the paper insoles became sodden, and she ended with dirty imprints on the bottom of her feet. Wearing wet shoes had also encouraged fungal growth between her toes that itched like crazy.

In class Jen was careful not to remove her shoes, and she sat with both feet firmly planted on the floor. Exposing the holes in her shoes to her classmates especially Meena and Bee Bee would have earned her endless teasing and name-calling.

During the wet seasons Jen became rather adept at predicting sudden downpours. Dodging into shop doorways to get out of the rain became almost a routine, but she was caught out several times and arrived in school looking rather like a wet rag. She was then further humiliated by having to change into some dry clothes loaned by the school until her own had dried.

It was on one such day when Patricia spoke to her as she made her way to change back into her own uniform.

'Jen, wait for me! I want to ask you something,' Patricia said as she looked around her to see if anyone was listening.

'What about?'

'Promise you won't get offended.'

'I can't promise if I don't know what it is,' Jen replied a little impatiently. She was anxious to get back into her own clothes, the ones loaned to her were too big and too long and she felt silly in them.

'I was… I was talking to my mum last night about a present for your birthday. I …we were wondering if you'd like a new school uniform.'

Jen felt her face flush and her throat close up and she was unable to answer.

'I'm sorry, I thought you wouldn't mind…but it's alright if you don't want it,' Patricia was flustered.

Jen managed a weak smile and said rather hurriedly, 'Of course I'm not offended. I don't know what to say, you're very kind and your mum too. But…I'm not sure. I may not be coming back to school in the new term.'

'You will! I insist you do,' Patricia gave Jen one of her big encouraging smile.

'I wish I were sure. A new uniform is too expensive. I can't accept such an expensive present. I didn't give you anything for your birthday…'

'Why do you have so many rules? I want to give you a present, you always say that a present must be useful, and when I thought of a useful present you said you couldn't accept it.' Patricia was now getting annoyed with Jen and her strange ways.

'I'm sorry, I don't mean to be ungrateful.'

'And stop saying sorry,' Patricia was putting on a good show of being indignant.

'Ss...h.. okay...I have a better idea, promise you won't get offended.

'How come your ideas are always better than mine?' Patricia couldn't help smiling.

'I'm smarter that's why,' Jen gave Patricia a push and then linked arms with her to walk the rest of the way to the changing room.

'Are you going to tell me your good idea, then?'

'Oh yeah. Why don't you give me your old uniform and you have the new one for yourself, that way we'll both benefit. My mother cannot object to that as I'm always wearing hand-me-downs from our neighbours anyway.'

'That's not a present, and my uniform wouldn't fit you anyway. If you hadn't noticed I'm a lot bigger than you.'

'They won't be when I've unpicked and sewn them together again,' Jen reassured Patricia.

Patricia looked doubtful, 'I don't know, it's mean to give you my old clothes as a birthday present.'

'But it's what I want,' Jen argued.

'Okay, I'll speak to my mum again, but I still want to buy you a birthday present, a present from me.'

'If you insist, but only a teeny one,' Jen said holding up forefinger and thumb to emphasise the size.

'What would that be, one that size?'

'Finger and thumb?' Jen said raising her eyebrows.

They burst into fits of giggles as they arrived at the changing room.

'Shush...!' Jen held a finger to her lips just as a teacher walked by.

'I'll wait outside,' Patricia said.

'You can come in, I'll let you if you promise not to look.'

The changing room was hot and the air stale. Jen's blue pinafore was hanging stiffly by two hooks against a wall. Her white blouse was draped over a line strung across a window latch and a nail on the opposite wall.

When she was dressed in her own clothes again Jen took off her plimsolls to smooth down the paper insoles that had wrinkled up. Patricia saw the holes in her shoes and the paper insoles. Jen put her shoes back on and they left the changing room, not a word was said about the state of her shoes.

The Friday before Jen's birthday Patricia had walked to the school gate with her after school. She asked Jen to wait while she collected a brown paper bag from her mother's car. As she handed it over she said, ' Happy birthday, and my mum said happy birthday to you too. Oh, there is…there's a pair of my old plimsolls for you in the bag, they're too small for me now, mum asked if you would like to have them.'

'Thanks, thank you very much.' Jen looked up and waved to Patricia's mother who was waiting in her car.

Just then Meena came through the school gate with BeeBee and Wei Wei.

'Hello Jen, Hello Patricia,' Meena greeted them pleasantly. But Jen noted that she had nudged her two friends and made some comments and they all laughed till their eyes disappeared into their faces.

Patricia looked flushed, and was about to say something but then changed her mind. Instead she whispered to Jen, 'Go quickly, go and catch your bus, they won't say anything, my mum's here, she'll tell them off.'

Clutching the paper bag in one hand and her school bag in the other Jen hurried off to the bus station. As she rounded the corner she looked back and waved to Patricia who was waiting by her mother's car. Patricia waved back and shouted, 'See you Monday.' Before she got in the car she turned and glared at Meena and her friends who were waiting for their respective transport to arrive.

Once safely seated in the bus Jen peered inside the brown bag. There was a home-made card, a rectangular package that looked suspiciously like a book and a pair of plimsolls. Jen examined the plimsolls carefully; they didn't look like they had been worn before. She suspected that they were brand new. She tried them on and they fitted perfectly. Jen decided to keep them on and dirtied them a bit on the way home.

It was a face-saving exercise for her mother's sake. Lian had always impressed upon her children that they must not accept any presents unless they were able to return the compliment, which of course they couldn't. Jen felt torn between receiving tokens of her friendship from Patricia with grace or accepting her mother's code of etiquette without rancour.

However, Lian's etiquette did not extend to hand-me-downs. She considered it a sign of humility and good manners to accept second-hand goods whether or not they served the purposes they were intended. At times Jen found her mother's view on life confusing. So it was with a clear conscience that Jen scuffed the new plimsolls on her way home from school that day.

Jen's thirteenth birthday was on that Sunday according to her birth certificate. But according to her mother her birthday was another week away. Lian only remembered the date in accordance to the cycle of the moon as stated in the Chinese calendar. Jen was never sure if she should accept that her birthday was on the date as decreed in her birth certificate or surprise herself every year with a new date.

What was even more puzzling was that her mother had told her that she was fourteen on her birthday and not thirteen. Lian had explained that according to tradition when she was born she was already one year old. Neither Jen nor her mother could satisfactorily explain the logic but her mother was adamant that she was fourteen on her next birthday, which was the following Friday and not that Sunday.

So it was that that Sunday passed as all Sundays did for Jen. Her mother made no acknowledgement that it was a special day for her, neither did her brothers or sister.

Chapter Seven

On the morning of her exams Jen had woken up earlier than usual after having slept fitfully. It had rained the best part of the night, so when she waded into the kitchen her spirit was as heavy and damp as the muddy floor.

She took a gulp of water to quench her thirst and soothe the lump in her throat. The churning in her stomach gave her hiccups and her racing heart made her gasp for air. She made an attempt to eat some dry biscuits and drink her morning coffee but they refused to go past her throat so she spat them out and drank more water instead.

In a daze she got Tam and Lee out of bed, presided over their morning ritual of play-fighting, arguing and haranguing each other over breakfast and getting ready for school. Out of habit she straightened Lee's clothes and smoothed his hair down, but she didn't notice he was ducking out of the way as each stroke of the comb came his way.

The smell of burning rubber assailed their noses as Tam and Lee watched in amazement as Jen's shoes took on a yellowish tinge as they were drying over the embers of the stove. Jen was standing by the window reading a book. Lee shrieked with laughter; Tam was suddenly moved into action when he saw smoke rising from the stove. He took a lump of firewood and knocked the shoes off the stove, they plopped on to the muddy floor.

Jen spun round just in time to see Tam with the lump of wood in his hands and her shoes lying on the wet muddy floor. She yelled at him, 'Why did you do that? Look! They are dirty now.' She bent down to pick up her shoes and saw the dark smudges over the yellow tinge.

Tam was extremely put out by Jen's shouting, and after a few moments of silence he replied sharply, 'I was only trying to help, next time I'll let them burn. It was a stupid place to put them anyway.'

Jen was equally frustrated. 'I left them there to dry out!' she shouted. 'They were wet. Someone must have knocked them off the stairs last night. They were on the bottom of the stairs this morning and they were soaking wet.'

'Well, it wasn't me,' Tam retorted.

'It wasn't me either,' Lee bellowed when two pairs of eyes glared at him.

'I'm going to school,' Tam said as he grabbed his school bag and left the house by the back door. Lee followed and slammed the door behind him.

Standing in the kitchen alone with her wet and stained shoes in her hands Jen allowed the tears to cascade down her face. Her legs felt heavy. The thoughts in her head whirled and twisted as if caught in the eye of a storm. The rapid pulsing of her heart spiralled out of control and threatened to burst through her chest.

The sound of her mother's footsteps on the stairs stirred her into action. She wiped her face with the back of her hand, jammed her shoes on to her feet, they were still damp, picked up her bag and slipped out the back door.

The smell of burnt rubber followed her up the wet and squelchy track. She could see Tam and Lee ahead. They were standing by the ditch where the makeshift bridge was, but neither of them made any attempt to cross it. As Jen neared the bridge she couldn't see the plank that straddled the narrowest part of the ditch. The overnight rain had weaken the muddy embankments and swept the plank off its anchor.

'How are we going to get across?' Tam asked.

'We can swim across,' Lee as usual had an answer to their problem.

'We'll have to take the longer route round,' Jen said as she gestured in the direction they had come.

'But we'll miss the bus,' Tam argued.

'We haven't got much choice,' Jen answered impatiently.

Lee standing dangerously close to the muddy edge of the ditch butted in, 'I think we should swim.'

'Don't be stupid,' Jen snapped, with that she snatched at Lee's arm and dragged him away from the water's edge.

Tam followed. They walked in single file back on to the main road that was really a wide track of hardened mud studded with stones of various sizes. The bumps on the track were hard on the shoes and cruel to their feet. The route took them past their house again and when they came to a crossroad they took a right. The road climbed gently and after fifteen minutes they found themselves on a tarmac road with a railway line running parallel to it. The bus-stop was on the opposite side of the road, it was deserted, and they had missed the school bus.

'We're going to be very late,' Tam said, hunching his shoulders and staring into the distance.

'At least you don't have exams to do,' Jen replied dejectedly.

'What time does it start?' Tam asked feeling contrite.

'Eight o'clock, I think.'

'Let's start walking, we'll be late but you'll still be on time to do your exam,' Tam was trying his best to be optimistic.

'I don't want to walk. It's too far and I'm already hot and bothered,' Lee complained.

'Who asked you?' Tam rounded on Lee.

'I'm sorry Lee, but we can start walking or we can just stand here until the next bus comes but we'll still be late,' Jen tried to placate Lee.

'I'll wait for the next bus, you two can walk if you want,' Lee was adamant.

'I can't leave you here on your own, Mum will kill me,' Jen said.

'I'll stay with him, you go ahead,' Tam offered.

Jen stood there uncertain what the best course of action was. It was true that if she walked the two miles to her school she would still be on time to start her exams, but that meant leaving her brothers to fend for themselves. She had promised her mother when Tam and Lee started school that she would see them to the school gate each morning and she hated breaking her promise.

The occasional car went by and Jen followed its progress down the road with mixed feelings of envy and anger. After a few minutes of anxious waiting she spied a couple of rickshaws racing each other on the other side of the road and Jen recognised the riders as regulars who did the school run. They were on their way back to the village to pick up the morning shoppers having dropped their charges off to school.

Jen made a snap decision at that moment; her future depended on it. She shouted and waved frantically with both hands. Tam and Lee watched stupefied. It was so out of character for her to be so bold and loud especially in public.

The rickshaws stopped, the riders made two perfect U-turns and came to a halt on the grass verge where they were standing.

'I'm sorry to interrupt your work, but I'm- my brothers and I are very late for school. Could one of you please take us there?' Jen asked, her voice was shrill and she spoke rapidly. Her face was hot and the palms of her hands were sticky with trepidation.

'Got out of bed late did you?' One of the riders teased.

'No we didn't,' Lee bellowed. Jen put a hand on his shoulders to restrain him.

'Sorry, my little brother misbehaves sometimes. We missed the bus because of the flood, the bridge was washed away, and we had to come this way- the bus had gone by then.' Jen tried to explain but by the look of the two riders she wasn't making a lot of sense.

Tam whispered in her ear, but she ignored him.

'We only need one rickshaw, if you drop my brothers off first and…'

The two rickshaw riders chattered to each other and one of them rode off towards the village. Jen and her brothers climbed into the rickshaws and made themselves comfortable. The seat was only meant for two medium-sized passengers so Lee was squashed between Tam and Jen. He started protesting loudly but they ignored him. Tam muttered something into Jen's ear but she didn't catch it.

'What did you say?'

'We don't have enough money to pay the man,' Tam spoke softly in Jen's ear.

Lee opened his mouth to say something, but Jen and Tam put out a hand each to clamp it shut.

'Shut up,' Tam roared into his ear and at the same time pushed him into the foot-well of the rickshaw. 'Stay there, there isn't enough room for three of us on the seat.'

'That's not fair,' Lee complained.

'You can walk or sit there, it's your choice.' Tam was firm and he kept a hand on Lee's head to stop him bobbing up again.

Jen whispered in Tam's ear, 'Give me your bus fares and I'll pay him when I get off.'

'But that's still not enough,' Tam spoke under his breath.

'I know, I'll have to tell him when we get there.'

Tam looked at Jen as he had never looked at her before. There was fear and admiration in his eyes. Their attention were temporarily diverted when they saw two boys of

Tam's age cycling ahead of them. They were going to be late for school as well. Tam felt relieved, a burden shared, he waved to them as the rickshaw overtook the bicycles.

When the rickshaw stopped outside the boys' school gate Lee jumped off nearly knocking Tam off balance. As they hurried into the school ground Jen noticed the orderly lines of boys walking out of the large hall towards their respective classrooms. From that she deduced that the bell had not long been sounded and if she walked very quickly, and took the back streets, she would make it to her school by eight o'clock. Without a word of warning Jen jumped off the rickshaw causing the rider to swerve and brake suddenly. He was not pleased and gave Jen a dark look with knitted brows and clenched jaws.

'What are you doing, young lady! Trying to kill yourself?'

'Sorry Mister, I've decided to walk from here. How much do I owe you?' Jen asked with as firm a voice as she could muster.

'Sixty cents,' he replied and put out a hand to receive the coins.

Jen fumbled in her school bag for ages before she pulled her hand out in triumph and pressed a few coins in his hand.

'There's only twenty-five cents here,' he said giving Jen a quizzical look.

"I'm sorry Mister; I haven't got enough money. I'll pay you the rest by the end of the week.'

'You're not trying to cheat me now are you?'

'No Mister, honest I'm not trying to cheat you. I'm really sorry to put you in any bother. You see I've got an exam this morning that I must get to… Please Mister could I pay you on Friday, I'll have enough money by then.'

'If you are already late why did you get off here, why not…'

Jen interrupted him. 'I'm trying to save some money,

if I get off at my school you'll charge more, but if I get off here to walk the rest of the way…' Jen felt the tears stinging her eyes.

'How are you going to pay me the rest of the money if you have no money now?'

'I'm going to walk home every day after school for the rest of the week and save the bus fares to pay you.' After a pause she continued, 'I'll wait for you at my school gate this Friday afternoon and give you the rest of the fares. You know what school I go to by the colour of my uniform, and my name is Jen… Lau Li Jen.'

The rickshaw rider's face softened, he was a man of little means and knew how hard he had to work to put food in his stomach and a keep leaky roof over his head. 'I'll take you to your school and I won't charge you extra for it. You can pay me the rest of the money on Friday like you said.'

Jen stood and reflected for a moment and then said, 'Thank you very much Mister, and I will keep my promise to pay you.' She climbed back into the rickshaw and sat in the middle of the seat.

It was a quarter to eight when they went past the clock tower that was part of the post office building and a couple of minutes later the school came into view. Jen hopped off as the rickshaw stopped by the gate, there were a couple of prefects standing guard to write down the names of late arrivals.

'I'll meet you here with the rest of the fares on Friday, and thank you again Mister,' Jen said as she ran off to her classroom.

She arrived at her desk gasping for air and collapsed into her chair from fear and relief. Miss Chan was busy writing on the blackboard giving the time and the order of the examination papers. She twisted round when she heard Jen entered the room.

'I'm sorry Miss Chan, the…I…'

Miss Chan shook her head and said, 'I'm glad you've made it Jen. I thought you'd changed your mind.'

Chapter Eight

Jen was standing before the kitchen god with lighted joss sticks held aloft. She prayed that she be forgiven for her wicked thoughts, she argued that she deserved the scholarship more than anyone did in her school. She asked for blessings for her family and just before she placed the joss sticks into the compacted ash in the urn she asked for one more favour. 'Please may Mrs Choy pay me well, I need new books when I go back to school.'

Jen meditated for a long while with the kitchen god, her eyes were tightly shut, palms together with the tips of her index fingers touching the tip of her nose.

Her exams were now over and the school holidays had begun, but for Jen that particular break from school was a double-edged sword. Everyday she worried about the outcome of her exams and everyday she made the long trek to Farmer Choy's home to help his wife in their busy and noisy household.

As she let herself out of the back door she glanced at the red paper with Chinese lettering stuck on the wall. She wanted so much to believe that her prayers were being heard and in due course answered. Each morning as she left the house she looked for clues, like if the joss sticks stopped burning halfway through, or the smoke rising from them formed a shape or a coded lettering but each day the joss sticks burned all the way down to the wooden stubs. She even wondered if the perhaps the gods spoke in a different language to humans and if so what could she do about it.

It was her second week working at the Choys' farmhouse. She enjoyed the company of Mrs Choy who treated her like a friend and confidante. The children adored her and she was even allowed to sit and read to the children. She didn't mind that the books were old and grubby and that several pages were missing. The pleasure of sitting down with a book reading to an eager audience was a luxury. They all called her 'big sister' except for the baby who was only four weeks old and spent most of the time sleeping.

Whilst the children were noisy and boisterous, the house and the farm around it were hypnotically tranquil. Jen spent most of her time between the kitchen and the garden, she concentrated on keeping the children amused, fed and occupied. She was as excited as the children whenever she accompanied them to the chicken run to look for freshly laid eggs.

Jen was amply rewarded for her hard work and diligence. Each day she made her way home laden with fresh vegetables, eggs, and bags of rice, and on one occasion she was given a live chicken. She felt enormously proud bearing the fruits of her labour which offered her family a substantial meal. It was agreed that she would be paid some money at the end of her month of service, but most of her payment was in fresh produce. Jen was more than happy to see the cheerful faces of her brothers and sister when they tucked into their evening meal that she had brought home.

In spite of her work outside her home Jen continued to help her mother with the washing, sewing, ironing and returning the freshly laundered linen to the rightful owner. Being kept so busy helped to take her mind off her exam result; the worry of failure plagued her day and night.

The Chinese New Year was only six weeks away and in every household preparation was in earnest to welcome a new beginning. This was the most important festival of the Chinese calendar and every family rich or poor, sad or happy, big or small made enormous efforts and sacrifices to follow the tradition handed down by their ancestors.

Jen's mother had consulted a village elder about the best date to clean her spartan home. When the day arrived she woke the children up early to help her carry the task of ridding the house of cobwebs, year-old solid particles of dirt and dust that had made their home in very nook and cranny.

Lian went out of the back door with the axe in her hand, the children followed. The chicken that Jen brought home from the farm threw them a look of terror; it then ran to the far corner of the yard to scavenge for more worms in the long grass.

'I'll help you catch it,' Lee said. He was jumping up and down with excitement.

Min, unsure of what was going on, stood behind Jen sucking her fingers.

'What are you going to catch?' Lian asked Lee.

'The chicken of course!'

'I don't want the chicken, we're fattening it for the New Year celebration.'

'Why...why have you got the axe then?' Lee was disappointed. He had been salivating for a chicken leg since the day he saw Jen came home with the chicken tucked under her arm.

'I want to cut some branches from that tree, that's what the axe is for,' Lian answered as she surveyed the tree for a foothold.

'Is the tree getting too big?' Lee asked spreading his hands out wide.

Lian couldn't help smiling at the remark, Tam giggled and Jen teased him, Min took her fingers out of her mouth and joined in the merriment.

'No, I'm not trying to cut the tree down, I just want some leaves, I need some of those thicker branches growing out of the sides…' with that Lian lopped off a couple of branches from the lowest side shoot.

Tam, Lee and Min watched as their mother trimmed some wayward shoots and shorten the main stem. Jen went indoors and came out with a long piece of string and a bamboo pole. She gave these to her mother. Lian tied the branches of leaves to the end of the bamboo. When she was satisfied that they were secured by giving it a few tugs and shakes, she made her way indoors closely followed by Lee and Min.

The house cleaning started in the boys' room. Lian was poking around with the homemade broom in the rafters to dislodge the cobwebs. Big blobs of dead insects entombed in dust, fell off their perch straight onto Tam and Lee's bedding. It earned them a scolding. They had been told to put them away in the cupboard when they got up, but in their scramble to get to the lavatory first they had forgotten.

Min got in her mother's way when she tried to help, picking dirt with her fingers, and talking to the dead insects were not her mother's idea of help. Lee was crouched on the floor with a hairpin doing battles with the bed bugs that were hidden between the cracks in the floorboards. He upset Tam by stepping on the piles of dirt that he had swept into little mounds to be collected into the dustpan. Jen kept out of the way by cleaning the kitchen on her own.

As Lee watched his mother tickling the ceiling with bunches of leaves, showers of dust and broken branches came tumbling down. He watched and puzzled as only Lee could. When he could not contain his curiosity any longer he blurted out, 'Mum, why don't you use the broom instead? That thing is no good, the leaves keep falling off.'

Lian stopped what she was doing, cocked her head and spoke sombrely, 'It's unlucky to hold the broom upside down in the house. A broom must only be used to sweep the floor; you mustn't lift it over your shoulder.'

'Why is it unlucky?'

'It just is. You ask too many questions. Stop getting in my way and make yourself useful. Why don't you go and help Jen in the kitchen.'

'Jen won't let me help her,' Lee complained.

'You can help me,' Tam piped up, 'You can sweep up, ...sweep the piles of dirt into the dustpan instead of stepping on them.'

'That's boring, that's your job anyway.'

'You can get a bucket of water and a rag to clean the floorboards when Tam has finished sweeping,' Lian tried to win Lee over.

'I don't know how to, I'll go and help Jen instead.' He left the bedroom and half walked and half jumped down the stairs making the steps creak and squeak in protest.

Jen meanwhile was intent on coaxing a spider out of a crack in the wall and didn't notice a cockroach scuttling across the floor behind her, but it caught Lee's eyes. He pounced on it with a vengeance and the ensuing din startled Jen. She stepped backwards and tripped over him. He shrieked as she landed on him and she screamed as she thudded into a heap on the mud floor.

'What did you do that for?' Jen was furious

Lee was equally mad, 'You fell on me and you blame me!'

'What were you doing on the floor you stupid boy!'

'You're the stupid one, don't you call me stupid, you stupid girl!'

Tam came running down the stairs. He was sent by Lian to investigate the commotion. When he saw Lee's smudged face nursing a bump on his forehead, and Jen's naked broom, the end had broken off when she fell, he laughed and laughed.

'Shut up Tam,' Jen glared at him.

'Mum wants to know what's going on?' he asked when he finally stopped laughing.

'Nothing, I fell over that's all,' Jen replied.

'Yes, over me,' Lee complained.

'You should make yourself useful sometimes.'

'I was…I was trying to catch the cockroach…now its escaped.'

Tam left them to it and went back upstairs for the peace and quiet.

Later in the afternoon when most of the cleaning had been done, Lian gave the boys a couple of coins to buy a treat for being so helpful round the house.

Lee wanted to buy a sweet bun from a hawker who came round the house but Tam said that they should combine their money to buy a bag of broken biscuits from the village shop to share with everyone. Lee felt that it was unfair that he had to share his treat, but Tam pointed out that it was also unfair that Jen and their mother did most of the work. Lee finally agreed to Tam's request on the promise that he got the biggest share of the biscuits.

In the weeks running up to the New Year, Jen stayed up most nights helping her mother with the extra sewing for the neighbours. It's traditional to wear new clothes to welcome the new year and the extra money that Lian earned at this time of the year helped her buy a few lengths of cloth to make new clothes for her children. The additional income also enabled her to buy more sugar, flour, rice, oil and charcoal; these were also necessary ingredients needed to make biscuits and cakes that were traditionally eaten at this festival. What she couldn't make she traded with her neighbours and in this way she had always managed to give her family a good feast on a par with her next door neighbours.

Lee and Min were excited and high-spirited about the forthcoming festivity. When Lian measured them for the new clothes she was going to make, they posed and preened happily. Tam on the other hand was subdued when his mother fussed around him with the measuring tape. He would have preferred to have his clothes bought from the shop like his friends from school. Jen however, was only too happy to have some new clothes, as most of her dresses were hand-me-downs from her neighbours.

Lee boasted to Min about how much food he was going to eat and how much money he would get in his red envelopes on New Year's Day. Min was too young to appreciate the value of money and said that she wanted a big new shiny coin. Tam told her that there must always be two coins as it was unlucky to have a single coin. Min thought that meant she was getting two new shiny coins, and jumped up and down in anticipation.

Lian listened silently to her children's mounting excitement and worried she may not have enough money to buy sufficient material for the new clothes she intended to make for all of them. She was also concerned that she may have to forgo their presents of 'lucky' money in the red envelopes she had saved from the year before.

Jen worried the most. Her exam result was due the following Tuesday.

* * *

Tuesday morning loomed dark and thundering. It matched Jen's mood. She had been awake before dawn, but fear and trepidation held her to her space on the floorboards next to Min. She envied her sister's peaceful sleep and even breathing.

She had informed Mrs Choy the day before that she would not be going to the farm that day, but her mother had made a fuss when Jen told her of her plans. Lian didn't understand why Jen needed the day off work just because she was getting her exam results, but for once Jen was adamant.

Several times that morning Jen stood outside her house anxiously looking for the postman. It wasn't often that a postman came that way so she left the door open. The creaking of the ancient lock attached to the lopsided door jarred her nerves. Every time she heard the ringing of a bicycle bell she would rush out of the house, heart thumping, hair flying and scattering clothes all over the kitchen floor.

By eleven o'clock she was feeling sick. Her temples felt hot and her palms were damp. She tried to concentrate on the ironing but several times she nearly lost her grip on the wooden handle of the iron. Lian cast her disapproving looks whenever she made any sudden movements.

When the letter was finally delivered Jen nearly missed it. The postman flung the letter through the open doorway as he cycled past without stopping. It landed with a soft thud on the concrete floor. Jen momentarily stopped her ironing and looked up at her mother, and suddenly realising what had happened she slammed the iron down and dashed off to the sitting room. She retrieved the brown envelope from the floor and then stood looking at it, her fingers trembled and she licked her lips in anticipation.

Lian meanwhile stopped her sewing and waited. Silence filled the air.

'Jen,' pause, louder, 'Jen, are you still there?'

'Yeesss, … I'mm still here.'

'Have you passed your exam?'

No answer came from the sitting room. Lian was moved into action, she stood up quickly, knocked her stool over and pricked her finger with the needle she was threading. Min chose that moment to run in through the back door with an egg cradled in her hands.

'Look, mum look, the chicken laid an egg,' she screeched.

'Oh! That's good. Just put it away,' Lian answered distractedly and walked off.

Min stood looking confused and disappointed. The egg was still warm and she studied it with great concentration. She had been chasing the chicken round the back garden when she found it among some long grass. Tracing a finger round the shell of the egg she spoke to it soothingly.

'Jen, what are you doing? Lian asked when she saw Jen holding the letter up to the sunlight as if she was reading it through the envelope.

'Huh! …I'm…I'm' Jen stuttered.

'Are you going to open it? The envelope…' Lian's eyebrows seemed to have moved to the centre of her forehead where she was frowning so much.

'Yes, I am,… I am going to,' Jen said waving the envelope in the air. With fingers still trembling she tried to unseal the flap and ended up making a jagged tear. A white sheaf of folded paper fluttered out and she caught it in mid-air. Jen read the printed words, her face a mask of emotions. She read it twice more. Realisation dawned on her. She clapped a hand over her mouth and with the other she handed the paper to her mother.

Lian hesitated, took the paper carefully off Jen and looked at it. The words

and lettering didn't make any sense to her. She couldn't read in English having only attended night school to learn the most basic Chinese characters. She stared at the sheaf of paper for some minutes.

'What does it say?'

Jen's eyes were brimming with tears, she was unsure what to do or say under her mother's scrutiny. A thousand thoughts went through and round her head and back again.

Lian became worried, she didn't know if she was to console or congratulate her daughter. Jen burst into tears.

'Jen, what does this say?' Lian asked once more.

'I've passed, I've passed...'Jen bawled, with tears streaming down her cheeks. And suddenly she broke into a beaming smile and ran past her mother. She whipped the paper out of Lian's hand and rushed upstairs taking the steps two at a time.

Lian was bewildered by Jen's sudden rush of energy and activity. She followed her up the stairs.

'Why are you changing your clothes?' Lian asked.

'They are wet, I can't go out with wet clothes can I?'

'Why are you... where are you going?'

'To school of course.'

'There's no school today. It's shut...for the holidays.'

'I know.'

'You do!' Lian was seriously worried.

'I'm going to school to look at the notice board.'

'If the school's shut...what notice board?' Lian looked confused and a little annoyed.

'I've got to see Patricia,' Jen interrupted her mother as she dashed round the room looking under the wardrobe and behind the door. She picked up a pile of bedding and dropped them back into an untidy heap in the corner of the room.

'What are you looking for?' Lian couldn't help asking.

'My shoes, Min was trying them on yesterday. She is always trying on my things,' Jen complained bitterly.

Lian put a hand out and caught Jen's shoulder, 'Now tell me why you're going to school when the school is shut. I know you've passed your exam, but you don't have to go back to school till next week.'

Jen sighed, heaved her shoulders and sighed again. She felt ten feet tall and her mother appeared very small and childlike to her.

'I have to go to school to read the results of the other people, that way I'll know.'

'Know what? You've already passed, and...you've not finished the washing yet, we need the money... can't you wait...?'

'Mum!' Jen snapped. In a softer tone she said, 'I know we need the money, that's why I have to go to school to check. If I've come top of the class, that is if I've the highest mark then I will get the scholarship. The school is opened today, just for us to check our results.'

Lian was shocked into silence. She had never seen Jen so purposeful in her manner.

'I'll finish the washing when I come home,' Jen said as she left the house.

She ran all the way to the village bus-stop and when she got off at the station she ran all the way to the school. By the time she arrived at the school gate she was coughing and panting and her legs felt like jelly. She walked quickly across the playing field and as she entered the hall the noise that met her was deafening. There were groups of girls huddled together whooping with joy and congratulating each other on their mutual successes. Jen also saw clusters of girls sobbing in the background being comforted by their friends.

With her heart thumping madly she pushed her way through the tight knot of girls standing in front of the notice board. She scanned the list pinned on the board from the bottom up, reading the names to herself. She heard a familiar voice call her name, but she could not take her eyes off the board. As she neared the top of the list her heart was kicking into her ribs, she momentarily shut her eyes and then opened them again. She swallowed hard several times, the writing appeared blurred as tears pricked the back of her eyes just as a hand came to rest on her shoulders.

'Jen, I've called and called, why didn't answer me?' Patricia was breathless and excited.

Jen didn't speak. Her eyes were fixed on the board. She felt proud, excited, sad, happy, and lots more besides.

She read her name out loud, again and again. It sat proudly on the top of the list.

Patricia gave Jen's shoulders a squeeze, she was crying too.

PART TWO

Chapter Nine

TUESDAY 30TH DECEMBER 1958

The tears pricked the back of her eyes like sharp pins. She bit her lips to stop them cascading down her cheeks but with little success. 'Lau Li Jen,' she repeated her name quietly for the third time. Blood rushed to her head. She felt an arm round her shoulders but ignored the intrusion.

Her heart beat furiously in her tight chest, her vision blurred by the salty tang of her tears. Jen stood transfixed, seemingly lost in disbelief that her name sat proud and solid on the top of the list.

The names of all the other pupils who had also passed their exams were also on the same list, but she was only vaguely aware of them. The scholarship was hers. If her name had appeared anywhere else on that list it would have been the end of her school life and with it the one friendship that had meant more to her than food.

Another list was affixed to an adjoining board; it gave the names of those pupils who didn't make the grade. They would not be returning to the school, not that school in any case. There were no second chances and Jen knew how fortunate she had been to pass her exams, and gain entry into secondary education. The scholarship was a bonus that she had not dared to think of until that moment.

Patricia, standing next to Jen, gave her shoulder another squeeze and said, 'Let's go outside.'

Reluctantly Jen took her eyes off the board and looked at Patricia for the first time. Her lips twitched but the smile never came, she saw Patricia's beaming face through misty eyes. The two friends stepped out into the sunshine leaving behind them the murmurings and snivelling reverberating from wall to wall in the large hall. Both their faces were red and tear-stained. Patricia had hold of Jen by her elbow and guided her towards their hidey-hole by the hedge on the far side of the field. Jen, deep in thoughts and breathing erratically, was staring at the ground. Patricia searched her friend's face for clues as to how she was feeling, she also wondered if she should tell her best friend her own good news.

As they neared their favourite spot Patricia tugged at Jen's arm and said, 'Let's go to Church.'

Jen jerked her head up and looked Patricia in the eye for the first time, 'Why? It's too late now! The exams are over!' she exclaimed.

'I don't mean that, we can sit in the church to talk. Come on, I want to tell you something, something very important.' She grabbed Jen's arm and lurched across the field in a sprint. Jen followed reluctantly.

The church was right next door to the school. Patricia and her mother regularly attended the morning service on Sundays for as long as Patricia could remember. As Patricia led the way up the steps to the large wooden door Jen stopped and muttered, 'No, not in there.'

'It's all right, I come here often, nobody will mind,' Patricia tried to reassure her.

'It's not that!'

'Then what?'

'I just... can't we just sit here? On the steps?'

'I know you're not Catholic, but you can still go in, don't be scared,' Patricia said soothingly and touched Jen's arm lightly to coax her through the door.

But Jen was insistent, 'I prefer to sit out here, it's cooler out here.'

'Okay. We'll sit here,' Patricia agreed, she was surprised at Jen's sudden stubbornness but didn't pursue the matter, besides they had more important things to talk about.

They sat quietly for a few moments facing each other. Jen with her head down, arms folded and knees together cut a pathetic sight. Her hair fell forward and hid her face, but her eyes were studying the cracks in the concrete steps and her mind was caught in a whirlwind. Patricia was anxiously twisting the strap of her wristwatch and watching Jen's every move.

'Are you all right?' Patricia asked gently, she was worried and fearful of Jen's calm and distant behaviour.

Jen took a deep breath and drew her shoulders up, the corners of her mouth twitched; her chest rose and fell in waves. To Patricia's alarm she burst into hysterical laughter. Jen rocked herself back and forth. Her inane laughter continued for several minutes and became more and more rapid and high pitched.

Patricia's concern turned into fear. She grabbed Jen's arms and shook them gently. Jen ignored her and continued to shriek uncontrollably.

'Jen! Jen... stop it, you're frightening me. Please, please stop,' Patricia pleaded, and shook Jen's arms more vigorously.

It had the desired effect. Jen's laughter slowed and eventually turned into loud hiccups with intermittent gasps and prolonged exhalation. She opened her mouth to speak several times but no words came, she continued to gasp for air. Patricia sat and held her friend's hands. She watched as Jen's breathing slowed and became more even after a while. A trickle of tears ran down Jen's face, the salty tang caught the corners of her mouth, she licked them off, more tears fell, and this time she ignored them.

Some minutes passed, calm had returned to the steps of the church. Patricia fished out a handkerchief from her skirt pocket and gave it to Jen. She took it, wiped her face and blew her nose into it. Jen inspected the handkerchief and said, 'I can't give it back to you now, it's dirty. I'll wash it first,' with that she screwed the handkerchief into a ball and tucked it into the waistband of her skirt.

Patricia let out a deep sigh, she felt the knot in her stomach loosen, 'Are you okay?' she asked, and momentarily felt the knot tighten.

'I'm sorry. I'm fine now. I'm so sorry…'

'Stop saying sorry, I was worried when you wouldn't speak to me.'

'I'm… sor… okay; I won't say that word again. I forgot, I meant to congratulate you but I…' Jen smiled feeling embarrassed. Crying wasn't something she did and to do so in public only added to her discomfort.

'Congratulations to you too,' Patricia replied, 'I forgot as well.'

'Now you'll have to put up with me for at least another five years,' Jen said.

'I don't know about that, we'll have to wait to find out if we are going to be in the same class,' Patricia remarked feeling sure that they won't be in the same class again. Class, money, religion, creed and points scored in exams divided and defined a person's status, both Jen and Patricia were aware of that.

'I'm sure we will,' Jen sounded less confident than she intended.

'Let's not think about that, we still have another week of holidays.'

'Only six days.'

'Stop being so… so…'

'Pedantic?' Jen asked with raised brows and a cheeky smile.

'What did you have for breakfast? A dictionary?'

'No! An En… encyclopaedia!' Jen replied hesitantly and they both broke into convulsive giggles. 'It's your fault you know, the dictionary you gave me for my birthday; I've been reading it everyday. I try to learn ten new words a day, but I keep forgetting.'

Patricia clapped both hands to her face as her jaws were aching, 'I can lend you some story books, it's less boring than the dictionary,' she said trying not to laugh again. 'Come home with me and you can choose what books you want, my mum's picking me up.' Patricia checked her watch and jumped off the steps, 'Oh... no! My mum's going to go mad, I was supposed to meet her at the gate ten minutes ago.'

'Quick, this way, round the back, there's a hole in the fence,' Jen said dragging her friend after her.

They both emerged from the side of the school walking gingerly alongside the monsoon drain just in time to see Patricia's mum, Suzie, getting out of her car.

As they approached the car she frowned and asked, 'Where have you been? I've waited for ages.'

'Sorry, Mum, I forgot the time, it was busy in there. I had to... we had to wait for our turn,' Patricia replied and looking at Jen for support.

'Yes, we had to wait for our turn. I'm sorry, Auntie Suzie, it was my fault.'

'It's all right Jen; you're here now. Come on then, tell me the good news,'

Jen became all shy and coy about her achievement. She spoke quietly into her chest, just to confirm that she had passed her exams.

Patricia, impatient and excited for her friend jabbered and danced wildly around the car interrupted, 'She's passed, Mum, she's come first, she's staying in school.'

'Patricia! Act like a lady,' Suzie chided her daughter.

'Sorry... sorry... I'm going to act like a lady,' she winked at Jen, and tried to stop laughing by clamping both hands over her eyes but her protruding front teeth were in full view.

'Ignore her, Jen. Tell me about your results. Have you got the scholarship?'

'I think so, Auntie Suzie. Miss Chan, our teacher, told us that our names were put in the order of our marks, and whoever scored the highest will be on top of the list,' Jen answered.

'Well done, congratulations. Your mum must be very proud of you,' Suzie commented with a kindly smile.

'Thank you... I must go home now, I've got to finish my work,' Jen suddenly realised that she hadn't thought of her home or family since she left it earlier that morning.

'I'll give you a lift home. Get in the car, Patricia, and stop behaving like a tomboy,' Suzie was shaking her head. Since Christmas Patricia had been very excitable and misbehaved more often than normal.

Patricia decided to sit in the back of the car with Jen. 'Mum, can Jen come to our party tonight?'

'Of course,' Suzie looked into her rear view mirror and caught Jen's eyes, 'If your mum agrees.'

'That's settled then, you can come to my party, Jen,' Patricia said, nodding her head at Jen.

'What kind of party is it?' Jen wanted to know.

'My party of course! To celebrate... I've passed my exams too, remember!' Patricia cocked her head at Jen with her nose almost touching her friend's.

'Oh! Yes! I like to... but...'

'I want you to come, please!'

'I'll ask my mother when I get home,' Jen said looking doubtful.

'Oh goody! Come early if you can,' Patricia was smiling and pumping Jen's hands. 'We have another party tomorrow night too! Do you want to come to that party? We'll have to take you in the car, because it's a long way from here...' Patricia wasn't paying any attention to what her mother was saying.

'Patricia!' Suzie tried again.

'Yes, Mum!'

'Let Jen talk to her mum first.'

'So why are you having two parties?' Jen asked.

'Tonight we are having the party in my house and tomorrow's at Uncle Tom's house. We always have a New Year party at Uncle Tom's.'

Jen looked puzzled, 'Do you celebrate New Year in December then?'

It was Patricia's turn to look puzzled. 'Yes, don't you? Tomorrow is the 31st and at midnight it's the 1st of January, and that's New Year's Day,' she explained nodding her head.

'That's your New Year? I… my family only celebrate Chinese New Year,' Jen said.

'So when is your New Year?'

'Erm… sometimes it is in January and sometimes it is in February.'

'That's silly,' Patricia said, 'so how do you know when is your New Year?'

'Well…' Jen smiled, 'I look in the calendar of course.'

Patricia playfully boxed Jen in the arm. 'Mum! When is Chinese New Year?'

'The Chinese New Year follows the lunar cycle, and it falls anywhere between the 21st of January and the 19th of February in any year,' Suzie explained.

'That's silly, how do you know when to have a party?' Patricia was warming to the argument.

'We don't have parties,' Jen said.

'That's boring.'

'We have reunion dinners instead.'

'So you do have parties,' Patricia shot back.

'Sort of.'

'When is your new year then?'

'A few weeks' time,' Jen answered but not confident of the date.

'Mum, do you know?' Patricia asked.

'I'm not sure. I think it's the 8th of February.'

'Are you coming to my party tonight?' Patricia was impatient. She lowered her voice and whispered, 'My dad's here and he is coming to our house tonight and I'd like you to meet him,' she said earnestly.

Jen had completely forgotten that Patricia's father had come all the way from England to see her. She was curious about this stranger who was her best friend's dad. She looked at Patricia's flushed face and bright eyes and said tentatively, 'I'll ask my mum. If I finish all my housework early she may let me come to your party.'

Suzie kept both hands on the wheel and her gaze ahead. Her neck was sore and she sat stiffly upright. She wasn't sure if the party was going to be as much fun as the years before. The sudden appearance of her ex-husband had given her a few sleepless nights.

Chapter Ten

It was nearly three o'clock when Jen entered the house by the opened back door. Lian was sat on a stool hunched over her sewing; she looked up on her hearing Jen's footsteps, 'There you are. You've been gone a long time.'

'Sorry. I'll finish the ironing now and return them to the hotel later. Is there any more washing to do?' Jen asked, feeling guilty that she had not helped with the washing that morning.

Her mother shook her head, 'They're out on the line. Bring them in later, they need ironing too.'

Jen waited for a few moments and then said, 'I've passed my exams.'

'You told me this morning,' Lian answered without taking her eyes off her sewing.

'I think I've also got the scholarship too, but the school will have to confirm that when I go back on Monday,' Jen added.

Lian stopped her sewing momentarily and said, 'It's good you've passed your exams. The water urn is almost empty.' Lian went back to her sewing.

'I'll see to that later, Mum,' Jen answered with a sigh.

Jen had to re-fire the iron. The cast iron was a triangular caged-like receptacle with a hinged lid and slits in its sides to allow air circulation to keep the charcoal burning. Jen picked it up and rested it on a heavy metal ring next to the stove. She removed the kettle and prodded the embers with a pair of tongs. Very carefully she pinched the tiny fragments of burning coals with the tongs and piled them into the iron, and over these she placed handfuls of fresh coal slivers. She fanned it gently with a piece of cardboard; sparks flew everywhere as the slivers of coal caught alight. As they burned she added several lumps of charcoal to fill the entire cavity of the iron, this was left sitting on the floor while she prepared the table for ironing.

There were several sheets and pillowcases sitting stiffly folded on a stool. She arranged two old and tattered blankets on the table and then meticulously smoothed down all the imaginary creases. Then she placed a double layered sheeting over it; the sheeting was once pristine white but was now almost bronze in colour through frequent use. Next she filled a tin with cold water and placed it on a corner of the table; then she picked up a clean sheet and smoothed it out on the makeshift ironing board. She picked up the tin of water with one hand and with the other she dipped it into the water and flicked it all over the sheet. When she was satisfied that it was sufficiently damp she rolled it up and put it in a clean basin. She gave the rest of the sheets and pillowcases the same treatment.

The popping and crackling sound of the charcoal burning drew her attention. She flicked some water on the opened lid of the iron; it hissed, sizzled and formed minute bubbles that evaporated rapidly with the heat. With two rags in her hands she lifted the iron and its metal rest and placed them on a stool by the table where the ironing began in earnest. The secret was to do the job quickly before the iron cooled down when she would need to re-fire it again.

Lian, sitting in the same hunched position, hands moving fluidly over the cloth, deep in thoughts, gave Jen a cursory glance every once in a while. Jen looked up several times trying to make conversation, but her mother's stillness stopped her. The silence was only broken by Lian's coughing every so often.

A dragonfly lost its way and darted in through the back door, Jen caught sight of it as it flew out again. That fleeting interruption gave her courage to grasp the moment, and she found her voice and asked, 'Where's Min?' She knew that her brothers Tam and Lee were working in Farmer Choy's farm but was surprised that Min wasn't in either.

'She's with Mrs Ong,' Lian replied.

Mrs Ong, a neighbour, had no children of her own. Over the years she had babysat for all of Lian's children and she could remember when each of them was born. She lived with her husband in a big cluttered house of brick and timber further up the lane where it didn't flood when it rained. Mr Ong was a market trader, selling cooked and dried food, most of which was made and prepared by his wife.

For as long as Jen could remember Mrs Ong spent most of her time in her big kitchen presiding over a very large brick-built stove that had three cavernous chambers for wood burning. From the back the stove looked just like a platform, four feet high, and eight feet long resting on three solid concrete legs. The spaces between the legs acted as storage for the firewood. The front of the stove was very different, it had two levels, the first level was set back to half its depth where the holes were made for the wok and cooking pot to sit on. The second level was the entry port for the firewood; this level was deeper than the first to ensure that the burning firewood was contained in the portholes. Sometimes a brick was placed in front of the porthole to support the firewood especially if it was longer than the depth of the stove.

When Jen was younger she used to help Mrs Ong prepare, cook, steam and deep-fry a multitude of food for her husband to take to the market each morning. The weeks running up to the Chinese New Year were particularly busy and Jen knew that Min was doing the job that she used to do. It had been her duty to keep the fire burning with lumps of firewood, and every so often she had to poke around with a pair of tongs to dislodge the ashes and re-arrange the burning wood. Jen remembered the smoke getting into her eyes, and when she got too close to the stove the fire scorched her face and made it red and hot. Her efforts were well rewarded, she was allowed to eat as much as she wanted and any food not sold in the market she was given to take home to her brothers and sister.

Jen's mouth watered thinking about all that food, and it reminded her that she hadn't asked her mother about Patricia's party.

'Ma, Patricia has invited me to her house tonight – can I go?'

Jen saw her mother's brow furrowed and her lips moved forward and then back over her front teeth. 'It's not convenient, visiting so late.' It was a statement and not an answer.

'Her mother has invited some relatives over for dinner to celebrate Patricia passing her exams. Her mum asked if you would let me join them,' Jen said lowering her gaze.

Lian shifted in her chair and stopped her sewing. She seemed to have gone into a trance, not speaking for a long while and then suddenly asked, 'What time are they eating?'

Jen stared at her mother for a few moments, startled at her response she stuttered, 'Ah... I don't know, but her mum said she will bring me home when it's over.'

'How you getting there?' Lian asked; her tone had lost some of its edge. She felt a little ashamed that she had not thought of celebrating Jen passing her exams, but then she had never celebrated anything in her life. Not even when she married or when each of her children were born. To her a woman's life was one of duties, supplications, sadness and pain. And if she did want to celebrate where would the money come from? As it was it took all her strength to ensure her family had one hot meal a day.

Jen had already decided how she was getting there. 'After I've delivered the laundry to the hotel, I'll catch another bus,' she answered. A bubble of excitement ran through her spine as she visualised the party and meeting Patricia's relatives.

'You better be quick, and finish, those too,' Lian said nodding to the dwindling pile of laundry.

Jen checked her iron and tutted; wisps of white ash escaped from the side slits of the iron and were marking the white sheet she was ironing. She immediately lifted the iron off the table and took it to the backyard. Holding the iron firmly with both hands she gave it a few vigorous shakes, scattering puffs of white ash on the ground, and in their descent some were borne away by the afternoon breeze.

Jen decided to have a bath after tying her bundle of ironed laundry in a faded blue sarong. She went up the rickety stairs and hunted in the drawers for something suitable to wear. Pulling out a plain green dress, she saw that it had a tear on the hem but was mended with a green flora patch, a cut-off from another dress. She dropped that back into the drawer and picked up another, a pinkish floral frock with a rounded neck. She tried it on but the buttons had been wrenched off through repeated washing, and it left a ragged edge under her left armpit. She folded her second choice and laid it back in the drawer. Jen stood for a minute mentally ticking off what other choices she had before she opened another drawer. She reluctantly pulled the vermilion dress out of the drawer and held it to the light to check for any obvious mended patches or missing buttons. The dress appeared to be whole, if a little long. The smell of mothballs followed Jen down the stairs. The hot iron took out all the creases but not the odour.

Jen looked at the dress as it sat limply on the table, she

argued with herself whether she should go to Patricia's party or stay at home. The dress looked awful and she didn't have a decent pair of shoes to wear. She was on the point of changing her mind about going when she saw her mother bending over the stove. Lian was stirring a pot of rice porridge with one hand and in her other hand she had a bowl of chopped-up sweet potatoes. Jen made up her mind that she was going to the party, she couldn't stomach another meal of rice porridge flavoured with sweet potatoes.

She picked up the dress, the communal towel, and the soap tin. The few bits of soap were swimming in a slimy soup; she drained the water off and went into the bathroom. She decided a bath was what she needed. She stepped into the dim interior of the bathroom and had a quick look around for anything thing that moved. Rats often came out in the dark to drink from the puddles in the pitted floor.

The bathroom was neither a room nor was it suitable for a bath. It was just a box with a door made with corrugated iron sheets nailed together on to a wooden frame. It was seated in a corner of the kitchen. There was no lighting and the concrete floor was slippery and had no proper drainage. A bath for Jen consisted of scooping cold water from the petrol drum and throwing it over herself. To get the water out of the drum she used an old biscuit tin that had a wooden handle crudely wedged in under the rim of the round tin and held into place by two nails, one on each end.

She peered into the drum and noticed that it was only half full; she sighed and came back out. There wasn't enough water for a bath. To top up the drum she needed to draw water from the well, a quart at a time into a two-gallon bucket and then haul it though the kitchen before tipping it into the drum. It was another ten minutes before she had enough water to bathe herself.

Jen shivered as the cold water hit her face and ran down her small frame. Getting the soap to lather proved difficult as the bits of soap kept slipping off between her fingers. As she soaped herself down she remembered how over the past few weeks she had noticed the changes in her body. She decided that she would ask Patricia about them, after all Patricia had been wearing a bra for the past few months.

When Jen left the house around six o'clock carrying her large bundle of laundry, the smell of soap and mothballs accompanied her to the village bus stop. On her feet was the pair of white plimsolls that Patricia had given her for her birthday.

She was just in time to catch the sixty-thirty bus to the hotel. When she got off she spent a few minutes looking into the stonemason's yard, as was her habit. It was quiet as a grave; there was no one about chipping and hammering like on the other occasions when she had stopped by. But there were plenty of granite slabs leaning against the trunk of the coconut tree. She always felt closer to her father whenever she saw those granite slabs. A car hooted as she attempted to cross the road, she barely gave the driver a glance and kept on walking.

Mrs Lim the owner and manageress of the hotel was waiting for her when she entered the hotel by the side door. 'You're later than usual, Jen,' she said.

'I'm sorry, Mrs Lim, I had to go to school this morning,' Jen replied.

'Oh, I thought you're still on holiday.'

'No, yes I am, but I had to go back for my exam result,' Jen said and tried desperately to suppress a smile breaking out. The memory of what occurred that morning amused and embarrassed her.

'I'm sure you've done well. Did you?' Mrs Lim asked.

Jen smiled and nodded.

'Well done, are you pleased? I'm sure your mum must be very pleased.'

Jen nodded again, though what her mum thought of her success she could only guess at.

Mrs Lim handed over the money and another bundle of dirty laundry and then she pressed another two coins into Jen's hand. 'This is a present for passing your exams. Keep working hard in school, then you won't have to wash laundry for a living.'

'Thank you, thank you, Mrs Lim,' Jen dipped her head and backed out of the door feeling hot and flushed.

She walked briskly to the town's central bus station half a mile away. At the station she walked around the hawkers' stalls looking at all the fruits on sale. She stopped at one that had a large mound of oranges. She picked one up, checked it for firmness, put it to one side and selected four more. The hawker dropped them into a brown paper bag and Jen paid for them with the money that Mrs Lim gave her. She knew that Patricia loved oranges, besides she was always taught that it was rude to visit a friend empty-handed. For a very brief moment she though of handing over the bundle of dirty laundry to Patricia and imagined her face thinking that it was a present, but it was only a very brief thought.

Jen walked into the waiting area to check the timetable. She had never taken a bus to the village where Patricia lived though she had visited once before. She remembered that occasion well, it was Patricia's birthday and she had asked her mum for a very special treat – a rickshaw ride home with Jen.

As Jen got on the bus it was getting dark. She took a seat at the front and placed her bundle of dirty linen next to her. She looked out the window, the station was buzzing with activity; the night market had opened for business. There were people milling around looking at all the wares on sale. Further along were the food stalls, rising heat and steaming vapours mingled with the people hovering around the stalls ordering their supper. Dozens more were seated around little round tables eating bowls of noodles and sipping drinks and some were simply chatting to each other. There were agitated young children squirming in their chairs and squawking toddlers spilling food and drinks and harassed parents mopping brows and spillages. A few beggars were about chancing their luck; there was a young man in rags standing on bended knees at a table of young people, they ignored him and he moved on to the next table.

A tapping sound and a pungent smell distracted Jen. She looked around and saw a man trying to get on the bus. He was wearing a wide-brimmed hat that almost obscured his face. In his right hand he had a walking stick. He tapped his stick to guide him along the aisle of the bus, and as he did so he also chanted a kind of mantra. He put out a hand in Jen's direction. She looked up at him and shrank into her seat. The man had no nose and he was also blind, and the whites of his eyes were staring at her. Where his nose had been there was a hole instead. A liquid was dripping from the hole onto the front of his singlet. She felt pity and repulsion at the same time. He was a beggar, and Jen had heard of him in the school playground. She had been told from a young age that lepers were defined by missing digits and other body parts. Jen turned her head away and folded her arms tightly across her chest. The beggar moved on to the next passenger, and when he finished begging from every passenger he got off the bus. Jen watched him tapping his way across the tarmac and got on another bus.

By the time the bus left the station, Jen's sides were aching from holding herself in and her fingers had gone quite numb. Several minutes into her journey she found herself rubbing her nose just to check that it was still there.

Chapter Eleven

The route the bus took was unfamiliar to Jen. Suzie had told her to get off at the stop directly after she passed a temple on her right. She peered through the opened window, anxious not to miss her stop. It was dusk and the light was fading. The warm evening air whipped her hair back into her face and blew dust into her eyes and nose. She blinked and wrinkled her nose as a mosquito was momentarily blown up her nostril. She jerked her head back, snorted fiercely and expelled the offending insect. It flew off in disgust.

Jen saw the large urn sitting in the front porch of the temple when the bus was still a long way off. The smoke from the many bunches of joss sticks and the flames from the lighted candles stood out in the evening gloom. She felt a flutter of excitement and nearly lost her balance as she got up to press the bell. With both arms clasped around the bundle of laundry she hauled it off the bus. She hadn't realised that it was quite as heavy as it felt then.

As she landed on the verge she dropped the bundle on the ground beside her and looked around to get her bearings. There were no street lights but she could just pick out the houses by the shafts of light through the opened doors and windows. With a mighty effort she heaved the bundle over her shoulder; steadying it with both hands she crossed the road. She followed the lane into a large housing compound.

Patricia and her mother lived in a single-storey brick-built house that had running water and electric lighting.

Jen, remembering her last visit, shivered with pleasure and anticipation. Conversations in Cantonese and Hokkien filtered through the opened doorways as she walked past. A barking dog charged through an open door and went smack into the closed garden gate of its front porch. It stood growling at Jen with its muzzle poking through the metal grill. She instinctively pulled back and walked over to the other side of the lane.

By the time she arrived at the row of houses where Patricia lived, she was out of breath and her shoulder was aching. Dropping the bundle of laundry to the ground she rubbed her shoulder and smoothed her dress down. Her heart was doing kung-fu kicks to her ribs; she swallowed hard and took a few deep breaths. She mustered all her strength together and dragged the bundle of laundry to the gate of the house and pushed it into a corner. She stood for a few minutes unsure what to do next.

Jen waited for a while leaning on the gate, lost in thoughts. She faintly heard a car turn into the lane, the beam of its lights threw a long shadow of her outline on the porch floor. She turned around and was dazzled by the light. Unfamiliar voices came from the car as the light was switched off and two men got out. At the same time Patricia's raised voice could be heard from the house. Jen watched in the shadows as Patricia came running from the house calling excitedly, 'Uncle Tom, Uncle Tom.' She threw open the gates and gave Uncle Tom a hug. So, that was Uncle Tom, Jen thought, Suzie's adopted brother, the man who kept in touch with Patricia's father all those years after he left Malaya to return to England.

When she disentangled herself from Uncle Tom Patricia stepped back and trod on Jen's foot, she jumped and Jen yelped.

'Sorry. Sorry. Oh, Jen! I didn't see you,' Patricia apologised and took Jen's arm. 'This is my Uncle Tom,' she gushed clumsily.

'Hello, you're Jen, I've heard a lot about you,' Uncle Tom said to Jen.

'Hello, how do you do,' Jen replied nervously. Patricia had told her that was what people said when introduced to someone new. Jen shook Uncle Tom's hand. She noticed the other gentleman standing next to Uncle Tom. He hadn't said a word but Jen could see that he was smiling.

'Jen, this is my dad,' Patricia introduced the tall gentleman.

He stepped forward and shook Jen's hand, 'Hello Jen, very pleased to meet you,' he said.

Jen looked up at him, he was much taller than Uncle Tom and he didn't speak like any of them. He had a thick accent that Jen found difficult to understand. She muttered 'Hello' as she shook his large and warm hand.

'Let's all go inside. The mosquitoes are having a feast out here,' Uncle Tom said as he smacked his face and checked his palm for the dead insect.

The ceiling fan was whirling merrily and the curtains flapped gently, wafting the smell of cooking around the sitting room. Jen sat down on a hard-backed chair while Uncle Tom and Patricia shared the sofa; her father sat in a rattan armchair.

Uncle Tom like Patricia's mum was Chinese, but Patricia's father wasn't. He was from England, so Jen assumed that he must be English. She told herself that she must check out in the world map where exactly England was. From where she was sitting Jen studied his face and listened in on their conversation. She could pick out what Patricia and Uncle Tom were saying, but not what Patricia's father was saying. Jen couldn't remember his name, it sounded like 'Reg... something' but she was fascinated by his enunciation.

Besides being very tall he was also very fair, much fairer than Patricia. His brown hair was generously streaked with grey. There were fine lines etched around his grey green eyes. His nose was perhaps a little too big for his face Jen thought. Reg was what Jen's mother would call a 'white devil'. All foreigners from the West were called 'white devils' mused Jen.

The room suddenly became quiet as Suzie walked in with a tray of drinks.

'Good evening to you, Suzie,' Reg smiled showing his even white teeth.

'Good evening, Reg, is Tom looking after you?'

'He's doing a grand job is Tom,' Reg answered nodding at Tom.

'Hasn't got used to the heat though,' Tom laughed, 'But the mosquitoes think he is good company. Foreign blood you see, taste better.'

Patricia joined in the merriment.

As Suzie returned to the kitchen Jen slipped off her chair and followed her. 'Can I help you, Auntie Suzie?' she asked.

'You're my guest,' Suzie replied but the rest of her protest died on her lips. The look on Jen's face stirred something inside her, she looked at Jen again and realised that in their different ways they were spectators for the night. 'I could do with a hand. Could you keep stirring this while I lay the table?' she asked kindly.

'Can I use this?' Jen asked picking up a ladle.

Jen stood over the stove giving the chicken curry a gentle prod as small bubbles popped and burst sluggishly. She watched Suzie as she padded quietly between the table and the cupboards. Jen looked up at the ceiling aimlessly, there were moths and other flying creatures dive-bombing the strip lighting. The white light made Suzie's face look strangely pale. Jen checked her own arms, they were a garish green, unlike the warm golden glow from the kerosene lamp she used at home.

'Auntie Suzie.'

'Huh! Yes, Jen?'

'I just want to say thank you for inviting me to your party.'

'You're welcome, Jen,' Suzie continued counting the pile of plates she removed from the cupboard. Jen noticed that she had done that twice already.

'Auntie Suzie.'

'Yes, Jen?'

'I also want to thank you for paying my rickshaw fare.'

'What rickshaw fare?'

'You know, the one I took to school. I was late that day for my exams... I was very worried I might not be allowed to do my exams if I got there late.'

'Oh, that rickshaw fare, that's nothing, Jen. He overcharged you anyway, I told him too.'

'Thank you for doing that; Patricia shouldn't have told you. I'll pay you back when I've saved enough money.'

'You don't have to pay me back, think of it as a present. Patricia thinks you are the best friend in the world,' Suzie said, smiling for the first time that evening.

Just then they heard more voices coming from the front of the house.

'That'll be Bridget and her family,' Suzie left the kitchen to greet them.

Jen took the opportunity to check out the food sitting invitingly on the table. The centrepiece was an elaborately decorated plate of fried vermicelli. Shredded scallions and red chillies were generously sprinkled over the golden filigree of noodles and bean sprouts. A plate of king-sized prawns, with their heads and tails still attached, were half submerged in a golden brown sauce that had a strong aroma of tamarind lingering over it. A fried fish, a pomfret, the size of a dinner plate, lay crisp and aromatic on its side. The eyes were white and half out of its sockets. It had several slashes on its flank exposing the white tender flesh; a garnish of sliced red and green chillies were sprinkled around it. Beside it sat a white china plate labouring under an abundance of mixed vegetables, glistening pods of mangetout lying cheek by jowl with thinly sliced carrots and slender chunks of cauliflower. Alongside this was a whole braised chicken. It had been chopped up and carefully re-arranged to its original form.

She was still standing by the table admiring the arrangements when Suzie returned to the kitchen with her sister Bridget and her two children. Embarrassed at being caught drooling over the food, Jen quickly returned to the stove where the curry had gathered momentum and was bubbling over.

'Hello, you must be Jen,' a plump friendly face smiled at her. Jen surmised that she must be Bridget, Suzie's sister, though she was twice her size.

'Hello, pleased to meet you,' Jen replied, aware that she was picking up the custom of her present company fairly quickly.

'Meet my niece and nephew, Mary and Sebastian,' Suzie introduced her teenage relatives. Patricia had spoken about them often in school. Mary was tall, slim, and pretty, with her long black hair swept up into a ponytail she looked haughty and proud. For a Chinese girl she had very large round eyes Jen observed. She was fourteen, a year older than herself. Sebastian was fifteen. He was shy, spotty and he wore dark-rimmed glasses that made him look older. His short jet-black hair was flicked back with a parting on the right. Jen took an instant liking to him.

'Hello,' Jen smiled weakly at Sebastian as she continued mopping up the spilt curry. She felt the heat spreading from her face to her neck, aware that he was watching her. He leant against the wall with his hands in his pockets trying to look nonchalant.

More raised voices erupted from the sitting room. Mary, Sebastian, Bridget and Suzie left the kitchen in a rush to welcome the newcomers. Jen, left in the kitchen on her own again, hurriedly washed her curry-splattered hands before going back to watch the pot simmering and spitting. From where she stood Jen could hear snatches of conversations. She decided to take a peek at the new arrivals and moved herself into position behind the connecting door.

She worked out that David; another Chinese gentleman was Bridget's husband. There were four more strangers by the front door, two adults and two children. The two children must be Patricia's nieces, Cicely and Betty, whose mother was Suzie's youngest sister Annie. Patricia had shown photographs of them to Jen before but that was the first time she had seen them in the flesh. Cicely was six and Betty eight, and according to Patricia they were a pair of little monkeys. Jen thought they looked really pretty in identical pink dresses with matching ribbons in their pigtails. Jen liked their pretty names and wondered if she had to become a Catholic like Patricia's family in order to give herself a foreign name.

She was still standing behind the door when Suzie walked in closely followed by her two sisters. As they pushed the door back it caught her squarely on the forehead and threw her against the wall.

'Oh, Jen! I'm sorry. Did I hurt you?' Suzie helped Jen to straighten up and examined her face for injury, 'I'm really sorry.'

'No, I'm sorry. I was just...' Jen stuttered.

'Why don't you go and join the others. Annie and I can help – you're a visitor, you shouldn't be working in here,' Bridget said.

'No, I... I really like to help,' Jen protested.

Suzie came to her rescue, 'You can help me lay the table Jen. Bridget, I think the curry's ready, why don't you dish it up for me. Annie can keep an eye on the rice, I think it's nearly ready.'

For Jen the rest of the evening became a feast for all her senses. The food filled her stomach and the company and lively conversations enthralled and entertained her. She was captivated and charmed by Patricia's father. He told wonderful tales of life in England. Jen found his accent difficult to comprehend. Sandwiched between Patricia and Suzie, Jen was given a double dose of translation not to mention the extra food they kept piling on her rice bowl.

All through the meal Jen studied Reg's face, fascinated by his moustache, how it moved up and down as he spoke. It tickled Jen to think that he had a caterpillar clinging on to his top lip. Patricia had to pick a few grains of rice off his bristly hair when he tried to scoop them into his mouth with his chopsticks. He held his chopsticks like a pen and when he finally managed to pick up a piece of chicken without dropping it they all clapped and cheered loudly.

It was well past midnight when Suzie dropped her off on the dusty track leading to her tumbledown home. She knocked on the front door and waited. All was quiet in the neighbourhood. The waning moon cast eerie shadows all around her. The night air was still. The trees and their branches leaning every which way reminded Jen of ghosts and demons of the night. She knocked on the door again, still no answer. A breeze swept past her neck and lifted the hem of her dress. She took off in an instant and ran round the back of the house and knocked frantically on the door.

'Whose that?' Jen heard her mother asked.

'It's me – Jen,' Jen answered breathlessly.

Lian lifted the wooden latch and opened the door a fraction. Seeing Jen's face she opened the door wider to let her in. Disapproval was written all over her tired face. 'You very late!' she said sharply.

'I'm sorry, I had to wait for Patricia's mum to bring me home.'

'Dinner can't take that long. You've been gone six hours,' Lian's voice was taut.

'But...' Jen decided silence was preferable to an argument. She didn't know how to explain to her mother that she couldn't leave in the middle of her meal, besides she didn't want to. She had taken home with her many happy memories of the evening and refused to allow her mother to spoil it. Instead she said, 'Can I help with some sewing?'

Lian didn't answer immediately. Jen stood defiantly opposite her mother and waited. Finally Lian said, 'I've finished for tonight, you go to bed. There's lot of washing to do in the morning.'

Jen lay in her space on the floorboards next to her sister, writing herself a mental note – do the washing, the ironing, speak to Mrs Choy about her job, write a letter to thank Patricia's mother... just before she fell asleep she remembered that Patricia's father was called Reginald.

Chapter Twelve

Jen felt a tap in her side, she rolled over and went back to sleep. Another tap. Thick with sleep she yanked her pillow and wriggled away from the tapping.

'Big Sister! Big Sister,' Min whispered loudly in the darkened room.

Jen slept on.

'Big Sister!' Min got up and sat down by Jen's prone body. 'Sister,' she whispered loudly into Jen's ear and poked her in the chest for good measure.

'Mmm. Oh Min! Go away. I'm tired, it's too early,' Jen muttered.

'It's late already. Look!' Min lifted a corner of the curtain to prove her point. The sun was out and the rays of light filtering in exposed the drabness of the room and the paucity of its contents.

Min let the curtain go and cast the room back in a cocoon of stale sweat amongst the gloom. 'Did you bring us some food from the party? I waited for you. You were very late, I was very tired and fell asleep,' Min complained.

Jen was suddenly wide-awake. Guilt washed over her. She forgot to bring any food home from Patricia's party for her brothers and sister. She didn't go to work the day before, so she hadn't brought any fresh vegetables home from Mrs Choy's. She promised to do the washing this morning and she had overslept. And, oh, what did she do with her bundle of dirty linen? It came to her very slowly; she had left it on the other side of the front door when she ran off in a tearing hurry.

Jen jumped up quickly and knocked Min in the chin with her elbow.

'Ooowoo,' Min cried out rubbing her chin.

'Sorry, Little Sister,' Jen apologised, as she dressed hastily. 'I'm sorry, I didn't bring any food home last night.'

'But why not?' Min wanted to know. Her stomach was rumbling.

'Because I couldn't,' Jen was getting impatient.

'But why?' Min persisted.

Jen sighed. She didn't know how to explain to a five and a half-year-old that it wasn't the done thing. For a moment Jen imagined herself asking Suzie for leftovers, and having to explain that her brothers and sister were always hungry because there was never enough food in the house. Jen felt sad and ashamed. She shook her head and bit her lips. When she spoke again her voice was steady, 'I'm sorry Min, I didn't bring you any treats. When I go to see Mrs Choy today I'll bring you something nice. Okay?'

Min smiled, showing the gap where one of her front teeth was missing. 'Can I come with you to Mrs Choy's house?'

'Maybe, but now I must do the washing,' Jen said as she dashed down the stairs.

When Jen got downstairs Lian had already started work, she was stooped over the table cutting a length of cloth. The measuring tape was wrapped around her neck like a tether, and as she cut the slippery material she moved her tongue side to side as if it was following the path of the scissors.

Jen slipped past her mother noiselessly to the front room and opened the door. She let out a sigh of relief when she saw the bundle of washing balanced precariously on the step. The bag of oranges she bought for Patricia was still tucked down the side of the dirty laundry. For a few seconds she stood staring at the knotted bundle chiding herself; and when she heard her mother clear her throat she hurriedly picked up the laundry and took it through the kitchen. Then she spent the next two hours soaking, scrubbing, rinsing, starching and hanging them out on bamboo poles to dry in the sun. The front of her dress was sopping when she finished. Her fingers were raw and she still hadn't eaten any breakfast, neither had Lian.

Lian had been up before daybreak. Most nights she managed to sleep for five to six hours, but with the increased workload she was getting less and less. The few weeks running up to the Chinese New Year were particularly busy, as more people needed new clothes. It's traditional for Chinese to wear colourful new clothes to welcome a new lunar year. It was also the only time of the year when she had the opportunity to earn a little more money to put by for leaner times.

She was known in her neighbourhood as a very proficient seamstress and she charged a reasonable price for the clothes she made. At this time of year it was a customary practice to charge more for the same piece of work, and all the dressmakers in the village adhered to this practice. But Lian didn't feel comfortable about increasing the price of her work, so she charged the same price all year round. Consequently she had more customers than most, but the extra sewing was taking its toil on her already frail health. She had frequent bouts of coughing throughout the day and night.

Jen heard her mother cough just then, a dry hacking bark that drained the colour from her face. Her loose-fitting clothes were looser than ever. The dark circles around her eyes were puffy and the fine lines around them were more pronounced, accentuating the hollows of her cheeks. Jen glanced at her mother who had stopped cutting the material and was rubbing her forehead with both hands.

Min meanwhile was sitting cross-legged on a stool

watching her mother. Every so often she would get off the stool to pick up the scraps of material from the floor and put them away in a cloth bag. Being the youngest, she didn't have any responsibilities unlike her sister and brothers, so she spent most of her time watching and imitating the other members of her family. She had asked for a needle and cotton to sew the scraps together but Lian had told her she was too young to play with needles. She tried helping Jen with the washing but was told to stay out of the way in case she got wet. She wanted to visit Mrs Ong but was told it was too early. Frustrated, she decided to collect all the leftover materials to sell them as rags, she didn't know who she was going to sell them to but that was what she was going to do.

Tam and Lee were still sleeping. All through the school holidays they had been coming in at dusk after helping Farmer Choy. Feeding pigs, cleaning chicken coops, hoeing the sun-baked earth ready for planting and watering the vegetable gardens was hard physical work. Tam did most of the work while Lee played at working. Jen had also been working in the farm, but her work was indoors, helping Mrs Choy with the housework, cooking and minding the children.

Their combined labours had ensured that they had at least one substantial midday meal at the farm, and fresh vegetables to take home every evening. Twice a week they were given eggs and bags of rice. Occasionally when the farmer had been shopping he would give Jen bags of flour, and a catty of ground coffee. There were a few fruit trees in the farm and any fruit not deemed suitable for sale in the market were given to Tam and Lee to take home to share out with his family.

Jen wondered what she could do to keep up the supply of food when she and her brothers go back to school the following week. She made up her mind to speak to Mrs Choy that day to re-negotiate her previous arrangement, which was working from ten in the morning until five in the evening. Starting at ten in the morning gave her enough time to do the washing before she left the house and when she came in at five o'clock the washing was dried and ready for ironing. But when she goes back to school the following Monday all the plans would have to change. She decided to ask Mrs Choy if she could carry on working but only at the weekends because she still had to help her mother with the laundry as that formed the bulk of her income.

Her mother's coughing interrupted Jen's train of thoughts. Min had got off her stool and was standing by her mother, her eyes full of concern.

'Is you head hurting, Mama?' Min asked in a small voice. She laid one of her little hands on her mother's arm and her head cocked to one side, looking vulnerable and frightened.

Lian was sitting down with both hands on her temples. She looked up at Min and tried to smile at her baby but failed. Min brought fond memories to her harsh life; the night before her husband died he held his youngest child in his arms and told Lian that the child was beautiful like herself and that he loved her. A tear ran down her cheek as the memory of that night knotted her stomach and squeezed her chest.

'I am fine, Little Daughter,' Lian answered softly.

Min was reassured. Her mother generally called her 'Min' if she was naughty, but when she was good she was called 'Little Daughter'.

Jen had been watching and listening to her mother's bouts of coughing and she was worried. Life had been hard having lost her father when she was eight years old; she didn't dare think what life would be like if something happened to her mother as well. A shiver ran down her spine and she momentarily folded her arms and curled her shoulders as if to fend off intruders. Being the eldest she felt in some way responsible for her mother's health.

She was standing over the stove poking around the dying embers to dislodge the ash and hoping to revive the fire to boil the kettle. An invigorating mug of coffee and a few dry biscuits was what they all needed.

'Min, go upstairs and get Tam and Lee please,' Jen spoke firmly to her sister.

'Why do I have to do it?' Min pouted.

'It's late, they have to go to the farm soon.'

'They won't get up when I call them, you do it.'

'I'm making you some coffee, go on, tell them coffee's ready,' Jen tried to cajole her sister when firmness didn't work.

Min clattered off up the creaking stairs.

When she heard Min yelling at her brothers Jen turned her attention to her mother, 'You need to see the doctor, Ah Ma, you've been coughing a lot lately.'

'I am all right,' Lian replied keeping her voice low.

'I heard you coughing last night as well. Why don't you go to see the Medicine Man in the village,' Jen spoke quietly but her eyes bore into her mother's face.

'It's only a cough. I don't need a doctor,' Lian was adamant.

'Ma,' Jen paused, 'I… Tam told me that he heard you coughing too. He is worried too.'

Lian sighed, and her eyes clouded over. After a few tense moments she said, 'Maybe you get me some cough medicine, on your way home this evening.'

'I wouldn't know what to get,' Jen pleaded with her eyes.

'Just go in and see the herbalist and ask him, he'll know what medicine I need.'

Jen looked at Lian, her thin arms jutting out from her shoulders, her hair coiled into a bun at the nape of her neck like an old lady, her woeful sight cut Jen like a knife. She appeared much older than her thirty-three years. 'I'll go to see him when I finish at the farm,' Jen knew there was no point arguing with her mother. They both knew that seeing a herbalist cost money and it would be cheaper to get some medicine across the counter.

The tension in the kitchen dispersed as Min came running down the stairs complaining that her brothers had refused to get out of bed.

Presently Tam and Lee appeared in the kitchen, dishevelled, bleary-eyed and noisy. Lee as usual was bursting to go to the lavatory in the backyard; he barged past Tam still rubbing the sleep out of his eyes. No one spoke. Lian cast her weary eyes over her sons; a warm feeling ran past her chest, her sons always had that effect on her.

Lee didn't bother brushing his teeth. He was too impatient to wait for Tam to finish with the toothbrush. Jen gave her mother a hot, strong and sweet black mug of coffee. Lian declined the dry biscuits. Tam and Lee were happily dunking their biscuits in their coffee. Min broke hers up and dropped all the bits in her coffee, and then stuck her fingers in the hot liquid trying to retrieve them with little success. Jen gave her a spoon and told her not to make a mess. Jen ate her biscuits dry between sips of coffee. She watched over her brothers and sister and cried inwardly.

Outwardly she was calm and methodical. She recalled the list of things she had to do for that day and then spoke to her brothers, 'Hurry up you two, and Lee stop making so much noise drinking that coffee.'

'It's too hot, I'm blowing on it,' Lee was indignant.

'Can you blow quietly then?' Tam asked.

'No, I can't!' Lee replied and elbowed Tam.

'Stop that, you nearly made him spill his coffee,' Jen said impatiently.

'He does that all the time, playing around,' Tam nodded to Jen.

'I don't play around, I work very hard at the farm,' Lee protested.

'Can I come? I want to play in the farm too,' Min said sitting upright and looking expectantly from Jen to Tam.

'NO! Girls can't work on a farm. They are not strong enough,' Lee said puffing his chest.

'I'm strong,' Min answered lifting both her arms in the air.

Lee gave her arm a squeeze and said, 'That's not strong. I've got more strength in my little finger!'

'Stop tickling me,' Min squealed and wrestled her arm free.

'LEE!' Jen raised her voice as Min's mug of coffee was jolted off the table. 'Now look what you've done?'

'I've done nothing!' he protested. 'It was her!' he said pointing to Min.

'I didn't do it,' Min said as tears formed in the corners of her eyes.

Tam got off the table and picked up the empty tin mug from the floor. 'It's alright, Min, you can have some of my coffee,' Tam said and poured what was left of his coffee into her mug and offered it to her.

'Thank you, Big Brother,' Min said wiping her eyes with the back of her hand.

'I'll go and get changed. Lee, you as well or we'll be late. I promised Farmer Choy that we'll get there a bit earlier today,' Tam said as he rinsed his mug and hung it on a nail.

'Wait for me, I'm coming too,' Jen called after him.

'Can I come?' Min asked.

'It's too far for you to walk to the farm, you stay here and I will bring you something nice to eat.'

'I want to come too,' Min's lips quivered. 'It's not fair, I don't want to stay home on my own.'

'You're not on your own, Mama's here,' Jen tried to pacify her sister.

Min kept her head down and refused to look at Jen.

Jen took her sister to the backyard. She squatted down and put a hand on her sister's shoulder and whispered, 'You stay here to look after Mama for me, she is sick. I have to buy some medicine for Mama this evening, so I can't take you,' Jen explained to Min.

'Why is Mama not well?'

'I… she will get better soon… so will you be a good girl and stay to help Mama in the house?' Jen asked anxiously.

Min nodded and then asked, 'Can I go to see Mrs Ong instead?'

'Not today… today you have to stay at home to look after Mama. And when Mama coughs get her a drink of water,' Jen said. Big ugly thoughts gathered like a storm cloud in her head as she walked back into the house.

Some ten minutes later Min waved Jen and her brothers off to the farm. She went back to her position on a low stool watching her mother's every move.

Chapter Thirteen

It was already twenty-five degrees Celsius when Jen and her brothers picked their way through the dusty track leading to the farm. Every now and again Lee would grab a stone and took aim at a bird flying overhead. When he wasn't doing that he was kicking up dust. And when he got bored, a bush or a tree in the middle distance would catch his attention and he would search the ground for another stone to take aim, and if he scored a direct hit he would raise his arms in the air and shout gleefully. Tam, being used to his antics ignored him and strode purposefully towards the direction of the farm. Jen however, was irritated by Lee's constant weaving and running around.

'Do you have to kick up so much dirt?' Jen asked looking pointedly at Lee.

'I'm playing a game. You try it,' Lee answered unperturbed.

'I don't want to play your silly game.'

'It's not silly, it takes skill to play my game,' Lee replied.

'Why can't you walk like everybody else?'

'I AM walking like everybody else, I'm using my legs aren't I?'

'Stop being so cheeky, it doesn't suit you.'

'Stop nagging like a mother, it doesn't suit you either,' Lee retorted.

Jen felt her cheeks burning; she also felt the tears fighting to escape from her eyes. Her shoulders felt heavy, and she wished she had wings so that she could fly away to hide in a cave. She had heard of Batu Caves – a place of worship for the Hindus, perhaps she could go there and say a few prayers. She wondered if praying to different gods would help or should she only pray to Buddha.

'What's the matter with you?' Tam asked looking concerned.

'What?'

'You didn't answer me.'

'Answer you what?' Jen puckered her brow at Tam.

'Are you going back to school on Monday?'

'I am, why?'

'I just wondered?'

'I know it will be hard on Mum, but I have got the scholarship now.'

'I don't want to go back to school,' Tam said.

Jen stared at her brother for a few moments, she wasn't sure she heard Tam correctly. His lips were pressed together firmly, his hands in his pockets and he had a faraway look in his eyes. Though he was a year younger than Jen he was a couple of inches taller. He was always the quiet and thoughtful one in the family, the complete opposite to Lee.

'What do you mean, not want to go back?'

'I'm not good at school, I'm not learning anything.'

'Of course you are!' Jen protested.

'No I'm not! I don't like school.'

'You'll be twelve next month and then you've got to take your exams before secondary school. Are you worried about the exams? You've got another ten months to go yet.'

'I know I won't pass my exams, so why bother!'

'Tam, you mustn't say that, Ah Ma will be upset if she knows about… you wanting to leave school.'

'I am… can you speak to Ah Ma… for… with me?'

'No, I can't do that. Stay for another year and see how you do in the exam, you are too young to leave school.'

'I am too young to waste my life in school,' Tam tried to explain. 'I want to be a farmer, Farmer Choy needs help on the farm, I can work… I like working on the farm.'

'Are you worried about the money? I will still be helping on the farm at the weekends and do the laundry for the hotel in the week.'

'I don't like school, I am not clever like you, but I do like working on the farm, so… I don't know why I can't just leave and do what I enjoy and maybe earn some money.'

Jen could see the logic of his argument, but their mother would not see it that way. Tam is her oldest son and by tradition he should have the best slice in every aspect of family life and that included education. Was Tam doing it because of her? Jen wondered. Being the eldest boy it was also incumbent upon him to look after the family in the absence of a father, and Tam knew that too.

'No, you mustn't do that, it would be better for me to leave and you to stay in school,' Jen said and at the same time felt a heaviness in her heart.

'Big Sister,' Tam seldom addressed Jen that way, 'I feel sad that I am not learning in school, but it makes me feel good working on the farm. You, Big Sister are clever, you must go back to school to finish your schooling. I don't mind hard work and I know it won't pay much, but one day I will buy my own farm,' Tam said staunchly. He was a boy of few words and the long speech had exhausted him. After a few moments' pause he suddenly smiled as if something had struck him on his funny bone, 'When you become rich one day you can buy me a bicycle so I won't have to walk to the farm every morning.'

Jen chose to ignore his light-hearted remark. 'Does Farmer Choy need a permanent helper then?' she asked.

'No, he didn't say so, but he said that he was thinking of buying more land to grow more vegetables. He only has two pigs left, the rest have been sold and he wants to have more piglets for next year.'

'I don't know, Tam; I don't know what to say. Let's just think about it today, okay?'

'Then will you talk to Ah Ma? I know she won't like it, but sending me to school is a waste of money. I know you and Ah Ma work hard, now I want to help too.'

'I am not promising. Ah Ma's not well.'

'I know. I've heard her coughing.'

'I'm going to the herbalist on my way home to get her some medicine.'

'Do you think it's serious? Father died of TB, so did Grandma.'

Jen felt a shiver flashed up and down her spine. 'I… don't know. Perhaps she is just tired and she is not eating enough.' Jen hoped she was right.

'Can we catch TB?'

'I don't think so, see this circle,' Jen pointed to her right upper arm, 'this is a scar, an inoculation scar, to prevent us getting TB.'

Tam lifted the sleeve of his right arm and checked for the circular patch, 'Like this one?'

'That's it, that's the one; yours is bigger than mine.'

'I don't remember getting an injection,' Tam said giving his scar a rub.

'They gave it to you when you were a baby.'

'How did you know that?'

'Mrs Choy told me; she said her baby screamed when the nurse pricked her arm with this funny needle, it's like lots of needles stuck together. They prick your arm until it bleeds…'

'Eeergh!' Tam pulled a face.

They were approaching the farmhouse. Lee was sitting on the step stroking the dog that was still tied to a tree. Jen entered the house through the back door while the boys went in search of the farmer in the farmyard.

Over the past four weeks Tam had found something that he truly enjoyed. Working with his hands gave him a kind of calmness in his head that he had never known before. In school he found it difficult to follow the lessons, he knew how to count numbers in his head, though writing it down was a bit difficult. His teacher had told him time and again that he wasn't trying hard enough, but Tam knew differently. He wasn't good at sports like Lee, as he was inclined to be clumsy. He didn't have many friends, as he preferred to observe rather than take part in the rough and tumble life in the school playground.

He felt more at home digging, planting, hoeing and harvesting on the farm. The pigs weren't interested in his general knowledge, they were happy as long as they were fed. He didn't mind working on his own, he found the solitude comforting and it also gave him time to work things out at his own pace. His chest swelled with pride when he walked among the rows of seedlings, he noticed they had grown a couple more inches. He watered them every morning and again before he left for home in the evening just as the sun was setting.

The finer points on rotational planting were explained to him by the farmer and he made a mental note of what crop went where and when to maximise the nutrients in the soil. Tam thought that was what he should have been taught in school instead of History and Religious Knowledge. As he ran his hands over the texture of the maturing marrows hidden under the enormous leaves he felt a shudder of joy, soon he would be able to harvest them to sell in the market. His only problem was Lee. His brother had an uncanny habit of being in the wrong place at the wrong time and doing the wrong thing at the wrong moment.

Tam felt that Lee was too excitable and restless to be working on a farm. He was forever chasing the pigs and grabbing their little pink tails. His raucous laughter often sent the chickens scattering all over the runs. At the end of each day he had collected more dirt on his clothes than the pigs do, and he wasn't much help to himself or the farmer either. Still, Tam thought, Lee should be going back to school on Monday, and then things would be different. He made up his mind that he would ask Farmer Choy about a permanent job once he had spoken to his mother about leaving school.

Just then Lee came crawling through the rows of vegetable, 'HELLO, TAM!' he shrieked.

'What are you doing down there?'

'Chasing a spider,' Lee answered as he continued to tunnel through the rows of vegetation.

'Leave the spider alone, you're suppose to water those plants over there,' Tam said jerking his head in the direction of the vegetable patch.

'I've done it,' Lee shouted over his shoulder as he gave chase again.

Tam rushed forward and grabbed Lee's legs, 'You go and water those plants again, you cannot have done them properly,' Tam's voice had risen an octave.

Lee shook Tam off and stood up. 'You are getting just like Jen – nag, nag, nag!' He stalked off to the well and reluctantly picked up a bucket.

Jen was having an equally fraught time in the kitchen. The baby was screaming for her feed. At nine weeks she was a bundle of wriggling frailty, and Jen was terrified of dropping her. Three-year-old Wan Yin and her four-year-old brother Siu Wah were shredding papers and fighting each other on the floor. Mrs Choy had left the house with her oldest boy, Siu Min, to catch the bus to town to purchase new uniforms. Siu Min was nearly seven and about to start school on the Monday.

'SHhhh,' Jen tried to pacify the baby cradled in the crook of her right arm. In her left hand she had a bottle of baby milk, the glass bottle was shaped like a crescent moon with a teat on each end. The feeding end teat had a hole in the centre but the other was blind.

Jen sat down and eased the teat into the baby's protesting mouth. She refused to suck and kept poking her tongue at the teat. 'Come on, little baby, you're hungry why aren't you sucking,' Jen spoke soothingly.

Wan Yin soon lost interest in her squabbles with her brother and came to stand by Jen watching the baby feed. She tried to help by pushing the bottle further into the baby's mouth and leaning on her chest. The baby stopped feeding and bawled in protest, her little face turned quite red. Jen eased Wan Yin off the baby's chest and that started her off too. She threw herself on to the floor and thrashed her legs around screaming that she wanted to feed the baby.

'Be a good girl now, Wan Yin, when I finish feeding Baby I'll play with you.'

'NO, I want to feed Baby now,' Wan hollered even louder.

Farmer Choy poked his head round the back door, saw what was going on and retreated. Crying and screaming children wasn't on his agenda as a farmer.

When the baby nodded off in her arms Jen gently placed her in the home-made cradle. The whole construction could be made in a few minutes, using a rope, a heavy-duty coiled spring, a wooden divider and a sarong with its end stitched together. A thick length of rope was secured on a beam in the ceiling; the spring was then attached to it. A shorter rope was then tied to the lower end of the spring from which the wooden divider and sarong were secured. The wooden divider splayed the gathered sarong out like a pouch and the baby is then placed in the pouch.

Jen stood by the cradle, gently yo-yoing it. When she was sure the baby was sleeping soundly she returned to the kitchen where Wan Yin had picked up the baby bottle and was sucking noisily from it. Siu Wah meanwhile was nowhere to be seen. She picked Wan Yin off the floor, removed the bottle with much struggling and went looking for Siu Wah in the back garden.

Siu Wah, unaware that he was missing, was happily chasing the chicken in the run with Lee hot on his heels. He was shrieking with delight, and with Lee's help he cornered a chicken between the coop and the wire fencing.

'Wah Wah!' Jen called as he took a dive for the chicken.

Siu Wah looked up at Jen from the ground with disgust, 'I nearly got it,' he complained bitterly.

'You are not supposed to be in there,' Jen said as she helped him up. 'When your Mama gets home I am going to tell her you've been a naughty boy.' Jen turned her attention to Lee who was standing there looking sheepish. 'You are supposed to help Tam, now go and make yourself useful.'

Siu Wah struggled free of Jen's grasp and went indoors. Jen stood for a few moments watching Lee skipping his way down to the pigsty. She shook her head and went indoors, it was time to cook lunch, and there was also a large basin of dirty washing waiting for her attention.

Chapter Fourteen

As each weary step took her nearer to the village herbalist Jen became more panic stricken. Up until that point she had not acknowledged that her mother had been ill. Like Tam she had secretly been worried that Lian might have caught tuberculosis from her father, but she had pushed that thought away. She debated with herself if she should mention it to the herbalist. Who else could she ask if she didn't ask the herbalist? What would happen to them if their mother had TB? Could she be cured? She contemplated asking Mrs Choy that afternoon but at the last moment she changed her mind.

The last time Jen visited the herbalist was to buy a small tub of Tiger Balm for her mother. This yellow waxy ointment was a cure-all for little aliments like headaches, tummy-aches, mosquito bites and it was even rubbed into bruises to relieve swelling. In spite of herself Jen had a little smile when she remembered the time when Lee rubbed some tiger balm into his grazed knee. The burning from the balm had him hopping around yelling, 'Water, water, I'm burning, I'm on fire, water, water, everybody help!' Jen, like the rest of the family, fell about laughing much to Lee's disgust. The memory of that incident lightened Jen's spirit as she entered the medicinal shop.

The herbalist was quite a distinguished looking man. He was thin and tall, and stood very erect. He had a white wispy beard that tapered into a point. His fingers were long and the nails on both his thumbs and little fingers were long and curved inwards. He had deep-set brown eyes with his bushy white eyebrows pointing skywards. His white shirt was long and loose that came down almost to his knees. He was wearing black cotton trousers that flapped about as he walked. The black sandals on his feet only added to his mysterious aura.

Jen looked up at him and made a couple of attempts to speak but her lips seemed to have stuck together and her tongue felt rough and dry like she was eating sawdust.

A flicker of a smile appeared on the herbalist's face as he asked softly, 'What can I get for you, my child?'

'Arrh… Erm… I need some medicine for my mother,' the words came out in a rush.

'What kind of medicine? What is wrong with your mother?'

'She has a cough,' Jen replied nodding her head to give more weight to her words.

'Can you describe the cough?'

Jen looked puzzled and thought for a moment. Then she screwed her eyes up, tilt her head forward and coughed several times making rattling noises in her throat to demonstrate her mother's cough. When she opened her eyes again she saw the herbalist's face was twitching with suppressed laughter and his assistant was sniggering in the corner.

'Did she cough up any phlegm, and do you know what colour was it?' asked the herbalist pursing his lips.

Jen couldn't remember, and why did he want to know the colour of the phlegm she wondered. 'I think she did cough up some phlegm but not a lot.'

'And how long has your mother been coughing like that?' he asked as he scratched the side of his face thoughtfully.

'Some time now,' Jen answered confidently.

'A few days or longer?'

'Longer. Maybe two or three weeks.'

'I will give you some cough medicine, but your mother should come to see me if she is not better,' he said as he opened a cabinet behind him. He brought out a small dark bottle of liquid, examined the writing and then handed it over the counter to Jen. 'Tell your mother to take one teaspoonful three times a day. Remember... if she is no better after a few days she should come to see me,' he said, raising his eyebrows to an arch.

Just then Mrs Ong entered the shop. 'Jen, Jen,' she called out, 'what are you buying?'

'Oh! Mrs Ong, I've just... got this for my mother, she's got a cough.'

'Wait for me I'll walk home with you, Jen.' She turned to the herbalist and reeled off a list of herbs that she wanted.

Jen watched fascinated as the assistant scribbled frantically on a large white square of paper; when he had finished writing he recited all the names of the herbs back to Mrs Ong who then nodded in agreement. Then he opened up a few small drawers from the bank of drawers behind him and from each he picked out some dried herbs and put it in the middle of that paper. Jen noticed that some of the herbs looked like red seeds or pips found in pumpkins and gourds. The dried brown bits of leaves the assistant was heaping on the mound of pearl-essence granules resembled those she had seen kicking around in the dirt in the farmyard. From another drawer he produced several tiny sheets of irregular shaped parchments and added to the herbs. He then cross-checked his list, nodded to himself, satisfied that he had made up the potion as requested by Mrs Ong, he wrapped up the herbs into a rectangular parcel and tied it with a piece of string.

'Is there anything else I could offer you?' the assistant asked.

'No, I think that's all. How about throwing in a sweet? Those herbs make bitter medicine,' Mrs Ong said.

The assistant stood back from the counter and opened a jar that was sitting in the corner. Inside the jar were packets of sweet preserved prunes wrapped in gaily-coloured waxed paper. He dipped his hands in the jar, took one out and tucked it inside her parcel of herbs. 'There, this will take the bitterness from your tongue,' he said cheekily.

'Thank you, young man. Come, let's go home,' Mrs Ong said to Jen.

They walked for a while in silence. Jen was curious about Mrs Ong's purchase, she wondered if she knew what herb to buy for her mother's cough.

'How's your mother?' asked Mrs Ong.

The suddenness of the question completely threw Jen; for a moment she thought the old lady could read her mind.

'Oh! She's fine.'

'You said she had a cough?'

'Ah yes! She got this cough; cough, cough, cough, day and night.'

'So, you've bought her some medicine?'

'Yes,' Jen showed Mrs Ong the bottle.

She peered at the writing on the label, gave it a shake and returned it to Jen and making a 'Mmm' sound in her throat.

'Is this good for cough?' Jen asked holding the bottle up to her face.

'I am no medicine doctor. I don't like foreign medicine; these new Western medicines, you don't know what's in them. Chinese medicine is what I take. My old Mr Ong is the same, he prefers Chinese medicine too.'

'What kind of medicine is good for coughs?

'You must ask the medicine man to make you one up, then when you have a cough again you can ask for the same herbs.'

'Do you think I should go back and ask again?'

'It's better if your mother ask, you're too young to know about grown-up sickness.'

Jen pondered over what Mrs Ong said. She then asked,

'The herbs you've got, are they any good for coughs?'

She smiled and said, 'No… these are for my old bones, my bones give me pain sometimes, and I think I have wind and damp in my bones.'

'How do you get wind and damp in your bones?'

'It happens when you get older.'

'Do you think my mother may have wind and damp in her chest?'

Mrs Ong gave a chuckle and said, 'You're a funny child, Jen. You're worried about your mother I can see, I'll come home with you, I haven't seen your mother in a while.' She grabbed hold of Jen's hand and led her across the road and down the lane to their homes.

Min saw them while they were still several hundred yards away. She had been looking out for Jen to claim her treat. She ran down the lane calling 'Big sister, Big Sister, you're home already!'

'Min Min, you forget to address Mrs Ong,' Jen chided her sister.

'Auntie Ong, I'm sorry.'

'That's all right, Min. Are you playing out here?'

'No, I'm waiting for Big Sister to cook my dinner.' Min turned her attention to Jen and said, 'Big Sister, what's that bottle, is it for me?'

'No, this is medicine for Mama.'

'Where's my sweet?'

'Ohoo! I'm sorry, I forgot, Little Sister.' Jen stood and watched her sister's face crease into a mask of disappointment. 'I'm really sorry…'

Mrs Ong watching the exchange said, 'It's my fault your Big Sister forgot, I was talking to her,' with that she pulled out the little packet of preserve and gave it to Min saying, 'but you can have this instead.'

Min was delighted, 'Thank you, Auntie Ong.'

'Thank you, Mrs Ong,' Jen was equally grateful.

As they walked into the house through the back door Lian looked up and was about to say something to Jen when she noticed Mrs Ong, 'Mrs Ong,' she addressed her neighbour, 'have you eaten?' Lian gave her neighbour a weak smile.

'Yes I have, and you?' Mrs Ong noted that Lian was indeed looking thin and sick.

'Not yet, but please sit down.' Lian stood up and moved a stool to a more level position for Mrs Ong. The mud floor was quite uneven and for the uninitiated it was dangerous to sit down in Lian's home.

'You look like you've lost some weight, you're working too hard,' Mrs Ong knew she was being very forthright but she had known Lian for a good many years and treated her like a daughter she never had.

'The weather is too hot, I don't want to eat much,' Lian said waving her hands about.

'You make beautiful garments. Have you put the price up this year?' she asked as she picked up the blouse that Lian was sewing when she came in.

'No... I don't think it is right...'

'You are in business, of course it is right. You don't want to kill yourself sewing for these ungrateful customers. You must charge more so you'll have less to sew and still earn the same money,' Mrs Ong was in full flow.

Lian opened her mouth to protest when another bout of coughing stopped her. Min picked up the mug of cooled boiled water from the table and held it out to her mother.

Jen was standing by the stove about to start the fire to cook their evening meal. The kitchen was quiet apart from Lian's coughing.

Lian was all red and flushed by the time she stopped coughing. 'Excuse me, Mrs Ong, I have this cough, it's very irritating. It must be something I've eaten, it didn't agree with me.'

'It's likely that you've haven't eaten enough and your

lungs are weak from all this work. Your eyes, they have dark circles around them, you not sleeping much? No, Lian, you're not well, you should see the herbalist.'

Jen felt a huge weight lifted off her shoulders when she heard what Mrs Ong said to her mother.

'It's only a cough. I have too much to do right now; I'll see him later. Jen! Have you bought me any cough medicine?

Mrs Ong knew that Lian could be stubborn when challenged. She watched as Lian took a spoonful of the dark liquid, she shut her eyes and shook her head as the liquid slid down her throat.

'How's Tam and Lee these days? I haven't seen them for weeks,' Mrs Ong said.

'Oh they are busy helping Farmer Choy, they'll be home soon. Stay for dinner then you can see them, Jen's already cooking rice now.'

'Thank you for asking. I've already eaten. I've got to get home to boil these herbs.' Mrs Ong held up her parcel, an aroma of floral and earthy fragrant wafted past Lian's nose.

'You're not ill are you?'

'No, no, no, I've just got damp in my bones.'

'Are they good, those herbs?'

'Ah yes, they work for my old man, and me,' she laughed. 'I must go now, if you have time come to see me; and the children can come over anytime you can spare them,' she said looking over to where Jen was squatting by the stove.

'Walk carefully now. I'll send Min over tomorrow,' Lian said and got off the stool. She leant heavily on the table for support as she straightened up.

Min, restless and bored, followed her mother to see Mrs Ong off at the front door.

Tam and Lee arrived home soon after with some fresh vegetables, two duck eggs, three catties of rice and half a cooked fish that was left over from lunch.

Jen immediately set about washing and cutting the vegetables while the rice was cooking. She reheated the fish by steaming it in the wok. The duck eggs she reserved for the following day. After their meal she still had to catch the bus to the hotel to return the clean linen, collect the money owed and then bring home the dirty laundry for washing the following morning.

Tam and Lee went out into the backyard to wash off most of the dirt and grime from their hands and face. Min followed them asking for any treats they may have hidden in their pockets. She patted Tam's pocket, and he turned them inside out to show her that he had nothing hidden in them. When she tried the same with Lee's pocket he dodged out of the way.

'You've got something in your pocket! What's it?'

'I'm not telling you,' Lee teased.

Lee ran off and she gave chase. Tam went indoors and left them laughing, shrieking and hollering at each other. After he had run round the yard several times, Lee decided he had teased his sister long enough, he put his hand in his pocket and brought out two yellowish-green rambutans. He gave one to Min and kept the other for himself.

'Thank you, Bother Lee,' she said biting into the hairy skin of the fruit to get to the flesh inside. She screwed her eyes up as the sharp taste hit the tip of her tongue. 'Did you buy this? Why is it not red?'

'No, I plucked it off a tree, it's a yellow rambutan and it's not very ripe yet, a bit sour,' Lee replied as he gnawed the flesh off the fruit leaving the stone clean and naked. 'Now I can plant this seed in the ground and grow my own rambutan tree,' he said confidently.

'Can you grow mine as well?' Min asked as she handed the stone from her fruit to Lee.

'I'll keep the seeds in my pockets and plant them later.'

'Can you get me some more tomorrow?'

'I don't know. The tree is in the next farm and I had to throw many sticks and stones at it to get the rambutans down, they are high up in the tree,' Lee said raising his arms above his head to show Min the size of the tree.

'Did the farmer see you?' Min asked, feeling really proud and afraid for her brother.

'No, I waited until he went to market with Farmer Choy. He can't catch me, I'm too fast,' Lee boasted and his smile stretched his broad cheeks.

'You're very clever, Brother Lee, can you teach me how to get the rambutans from the high tree with a stone?'

'When you are older I'll teach you, we better go in now, Jen's calling… Min!'

'What?'

'Don't tell Mama or Jen about the rambutans.'

'Why?'

'Because I will get into trouble.'

'Is it all right to tell Big Brother?'

'Yes, but… he would stop me getting them if he knows…'

Min's eyes narrowed as she considered her brother's words for a few moments; she smiled knowingly and shook her head vigorously. 'I won't tell,' she said.

Chapter Fifteen

The night was warm and humid. It was nearly midnight when Jen finally undressed in the dark and then crawled around the bare floorboards to feel for her pillow to rest her weary head. She felt Min's hair splayed out over her pillow and instinctively she ran her hand over her sister. She pulled the cotton blanket from under Min's feet and brought it up to her shoulders. They didn't have mosquito nets to keep the pesky insects at bay and the patchwork blanket was the next best thing. Min stirred and rolled over, throwing the blanket off her shoulders at the same time. Jen covered her up again before she herself lay down to sleep.

Sleep was slow in coming as Jen mulled over the day's events. She remembered her mother taking rather a large spoonful of the cough mixture after another prolonged bout of coughing that evening. Lian said rather stubbornly that a teaspoon three times a day must be the same as taking two big spoonfuls twice a day. Tam's decision to become a farmer and not to return to school was particularly worrying. Min had another year to go before she had to start her schooling; perhaps if Tam did leave school in a year's time it may take the pressure off their mother to find the money for four school fees every month – no, that would be three school fees, she was getting the scholarship. Was that a good thing or not Jen asked herself as she finally nodded off.

Sometime in the early hours of the morning Lian's coughing woke Jen up. She listened in the dark; the coughing and wheezing was more piercing and urgent, like a taut string pinging over a water container. Jen felt her heartbeat increase with the whooshing sound in her ears, fear gripped her young heart; she had never felt as fearful as she was then. It seemed like her mother had been coughing for a long time but it was probably a few minutes. Jen willed her to stop, and after a time only the occasional 'Ahem! Ahem!' was heard from behind the curtains that separated their sleeping space. Eventually that stopped too. It was a long time before Jen went back into a dreamless sleep.

When morning came it was the noise from the boys' room that woke Jen up. She looked around her, Min was still asleep, and the curtains across her mother's sleeping area were still drawn. Lian was usually meticulous about keeping the room tidy and each morning as soon as she was dressed she would draw the curtains back.

Jen cleared her throat, she called out quietly, 'Ah Ma,' she waited a few seconds, 'Ah Ma,' she called again. No answer came from behind her curtains. Perhaps her mother was up and at that very moment sitting in the kitchen sewing as usual. The thought didn't quieten Jen's rising panic; she sat up cautiously and surveyed her surroundings as shreds of sunlight filtered in through the threadbare curtains across the windows. Curiously, Jen also noticed for the first time how many pinpricks of light illuminated the bedroom. The tiny holes were the only telltale sign that nails were missing allowing the wooden walls to sway in the strong wind.

Jen got up and walked the two small steps to the partition curtains and stood with her face pressed against it. Her breathing was getting more rapid by the second; she took one big lungful of air and drew the curtains apart.

Lian was lying on her side seemingly in a very deep sleep. Jen squatted down and very gingerly she touched her mother's arm with a forefinger. She felt warm, Jen let out a long deep breath. Then her mother flopped over on to her back, catching Jen in the knees with her arm. Jen jumped up and screamed, flailing her arms.

Min, woken up by Jen's scream, let out a shrill wail, 'BIG SISTER! BIG SISTER! Where are you? I'm scared!'

Tam and Lee came charging into the room to see what was happening.

Lian attempted to open her eyes but felt as if someone had stitched her eyelids up and put a boulder over them. Her mouth was dry and her lips were cracked and painful. Her whole body felt heavy and lifeless. In the distance she heard four familiar voices calling her. The face of her late husband hovered and spoke to her but she couldn't hear what he was saying. The four children standing side-by-side bending over their mother watched as her lips moved but no sound came out.

Jen and Tam looked at each other. Lee, curious and confused by the spectacle lowered himself until his face was level with his mother's.

He rested one hand on his mother's shoulders and gave a gentle squeeze. Lian didn't respond; he squeezed harder, still no response. He dropped both his hands on his mother's shoulders and shook her several times.

Low deep groaning sounds came from Lian's throat. All of a sudden four pairs of hands were shaking and rocking her side-to-side accompanied by urgent cries of 'Mama, and Ah Ma'.

Lian finally managed to peel her eyelids back and looked up at her children's distorted faces. Their images kept moving left to right and back again. They were all talking at once but none of them was making any sense to her. She had this overwhelming desire to go back to sleep again, but the children's rocking and shaking prevented her from slipping back into oblivion. Vaguely she felt a cold cloth being rubbed into her face and Jen's voice floating above the others, giving out orders to her brothers. Soon there was only Min talking to her in a whiny voice, a habit she reverted to whenever she felt small and afraid.

When Jen was satisfied that her mother was not dead she gave Lee instructions to run as fast as he could to ask Mrs Ong to come over. She told Tam to get over to the farm and inform Mrs Choy that she would not be in that day as her mother was ill, but when he asked her if he was to stay at the farm or come back to the house to help Jen snapped at him.

Lee ran up the lane like a dog after a cat. He was quite breathless when he arrived at the half opened door to Mrs Ong's house. The top half was opened to let in air and light and the bottom half was bolted from the inside. He stood on the step hanging on to the top of the half-door and yelled, 'Auntie Ong! Auntie Ong! Please can you come, it's Lee!'

Mrs Ong was cleaning up in the kitchen and replenishing the firewood she had used up for her morning cooking. Her husband had long left for the market to sell the cakes and buns that she had made in the early hours of the morning. When she heard Lee calling from the front door she shouted out to him to come to the back door. Lee ran down the side of the house and through the back door, into the kitchen and nearly collided with her bulky body. She put a hand out to steady him and cast her eyes over his dishevelled figure. His T-shirt was torn in the sleeve, the over-sized shorts he was wearing hung limply around his belly and his hair was standing up in short tuffs. He stuttered and stammered to make himself understood, 'Jen... Mama... sick... please come... see Mama!'

Mrs Ong took a few moments to digest what Lee was trying to tell her. Having seen Lian the evening before she surmised that something must have happened to her. She gave him a shove towards the door back door, 'Go tell Jen I'm coming!'

Lee ran all the way home while Mrs Ong lumbered after him.

When she arrived at the house huffing and puffing she saw Jen squatting by the stove trying to start the fire, unsuccessfully. Her hands were shaking and there was a small pile of broken matches strewn over the bits of coal. As soon as Jen saw her she allowed the tears to cascade freely down her face.

Mrs Ong gripped Jen by her shoulders, hugs and cuddles were not a common practice, 'Come now, where's your mother?'

Jen wiped her eyes with the hem of her dress, 'She's upstairs. I can't wake her!' she sobbed.

'Let's go and see!' Mrs Ong commanded breathlessly, having only partially recovered from the downhill run from her home.

The stairs creaked very loudly in protest; not being used to having a heavy person treading on it before.

Mrs Ong crouched awkwardly over Lian calling, 'Lian! Lian!' her deep resonant voice fought hard to penetrate the fog of Lian's brain. When Lian didn't respond immediately she slapped her face, gently at first, then when Lian emitted a low groan the slapping became harder and louder. Jen, Lee and Min were watching on the sidelines. Lee had balled up his hands into fists, Min sucked desperately on her three middle fingers while Jen stood very still taking short shallow breaths.

'Lian! Can you hear me? Lian! Are you alright?' Mrs Ong's booming voice filled the room.

'Mmm… mm… Y-e-s… what?' Lian answered weakly. She opened her eyes very slowly and saw the dark head of Mrs Ong looming in front of her.

'Lian! It's me! How do you feel?' She turned to Jen and said, 'Get your mother a drink of water.'

'What… time… mm… is it?' Lian asked looking pale and slurring her words. Her long hair had unravelled from its anchor and stuck to one cheek and the rest was spilling over her pillow.

'It's all right! It's still morning. Did you take the medicine Jen brought you yesterday?'

Lian lay very still trying to make sense of what was going on. 'Yes… sss, I did, I think it helped my cough,' Lian said as she attempted to sit up.

Jen entered the room at that moment with a mug of warm water. She held it to her mother's lips with shaky hands. 'Water, Ah Ma!' she said as she spilt some down her mother's chin.

Lian held on to the mug with both hands and took a long drink. Mrs Ong straightened herself up, bending over Lian had given her heartburn, she rubbed her chest with her hand but she kept her eyes on Lian.

'Right children! Leave your mother to rest. Jen, bring your mother some coffee, I'll stay here a while.'

Lee tried to say something but Jen got hold of his wrist and dragged him downstairs with her. Min followed still sucking her fingers.

Jen boiled the kettle and attempted to make some breakfast. In the quiet of the kitchen she heard muffled conversations, mostly she heard Mrs Ong's scolding voice. She picked up the biscuit tin and gave it a shake, it was empty, and she sighed and looked into the flour tin. There were a few black insects moving around in the white powder otherwise it looked edible. She picked out the black bits and poured the flour into a large bowl. She added a rounded tablespoon of sugar, some water, and broke in a duck egg. Using a pair of chopsticks she whipped the mixture into a frothy sludge.

'What are you making?' Lee asked.

'Breakfast!'

'What is that?' Lee asked pointing to the bowl of frothy slop.

Jen let out a loud sigh, 'I'm making pancakes!'

'I want pancake too!' Min shouted taking her fingers out of her mouth for the first time.

'You can have a pancake, Min, go and wash your face first,' Jen spoke gently to her sister.

'I don't want that, I don't like duck egg, it smells fishy, I want biscuits and coffee,' Lee said.

'There isn't any,' Jen pointed out quietly.

Lee picked up the biscuit tin, gave it a shake and then took the lid off and peered inside it. Satisfied that even the crumbs had been eaten, he replaced the lid and sat down on a stool looking defeated.

Mrs Ong appeared in the kitchen as Jen dished out the first of the pancakes. 'That looks good, Jen. Make sure your mother has something to eat and drink, I'll come back later to take her to see the Medicine Man,' she said. As she left by the back door Tam walked in looking flushed and out of breath.

'Is Ah Ma all right?' he asked Jen.

Jen nodded. 'I'll take these to Ah Ma, you see to Min.'

Jen climbed the stairs with infinite care; the mug was full to the brim with black strong coffee. By contrast the pancake looked anaemic lying on the cracked plate and smelt strongly of pork fat. As she entered the bedroom Jen called out to her mother, Lian's weak voice answered in a monotone. Feeling reassured she entered and pulled the curtains aside.

Lian was sitting up leaning against the wall for support. Jen placed the mug and plate by her side, 'Ah Ma, I've brought you coffee and something to eat.'

Lian, feeling groggy and nauseous, picked up the mug of coffee but pushed the plate away. After a few sips of her coffee her pupils appeared more focused, she looked up at Jen and said, 'The cough medicine you buy me made me too sleepy.'

'Ma, you shouldn't have taken so much, the herbalist said to take one only teaspoon,' Jen replied. 'Mrs Ong said that you should try to eat something, do you want me to boil some rice for you?'

'I am not hungry, is there any dry biscuits?'

'There's none in the house, but I can get some later.'

'Did I hear Tam and Lee downstairs? Haven't they gone to the farm yet?'

'They are eating breakfast. Do you want Tam to go to the farm today?'

'He might as well, only a few days left before school starts…'

'I'll speak to him. Ma…' Jen stopped when she saw her mother shut her eyes and leant her head back on the wall. She left the room and went back to the kitchen and saw her brothers and sister eating at the table all quiet and gloomy. 'Tam, Ma said you and Lee should go to the farm. I'll stay to look after Min and get on with the washing…'

Chapter Sixteen

Mrs Ong talked to her bad knee as she walked home, 'You stupid knee, giving pain, I haven't got time to rest you know. One day I'll get new ones and leave you in some dust bin, so you better stop bothering me!' She chuckled to herself as she became aware that a neighbour was watching her, and hurriedly went indoors and changed into an outdoor blouse of pale grey and put on another fresh pair of loose black trousers. She only ever wore black trousers with either blue or grey coloured tops. In her younger years she favoured paler blue with tiny motifs of bamboo or spring blossoms, nothing too loud or obvious to be noticed. Now in her late fifties she felt too old to be wearing any colours but imitation of the skies.

As she walked round the kitchen checking that the fire in the wood-burning stove had died out, shutting the windows and locking the back door, her brain was racing about what she was going to do with Lian. The sight of her lying there looking like a corpse gave her such a fright, and those poor children, poor fatherless children she thought. Life was so unfair. She shut the front door with a slam and walked down the lane once more.

As she came down the side of the house she saw Jen drawing water from the well. 'Is your mother ready to go?' she asked.

'Go?'

'Yes, to the village, to see the herbalist! You go and tell your mother to get dressed, I'm going down the road to fetch a rickshaw; I don't think she should walk being so weak…' Mrs Ong said.

An hour later Lian was sitting in the herbalist's shop. Seeing that there were three other people ahead of them Mrs Ong decided to do some shopping in the market and also to speak to her husband. He was doing a brisk business in his allotted space in the covered market and was most surprised to see his wife as he normally did the shopping on his way home.

'Have I forgotten to buy something yesterday?'

'No! No, it's bad business!' she answered.

His eyes widened and he looked at his wife concerned, 'What's bad business?'

Mrs Ong shook her head and continued, 'She didn't look any fatter than my fingers.' Here she raised her right hand to demonstrate to him how thin Lian looked to her.

'Who? What are you talking about, Wife?'

'Husband! Listen when I'm talking to you. It's Lian, she is sick. Why do you think I'm standing here? Wasting my time?'

Old Mr Ong was used to his wife talking in riddles, he normally guessed at what she was telling him and answered yes and no at the appropriate moment. But on this occasion he shook his head and said, 'What? Why are you here if Lian is sick, what has it got to do with me?'

'Husband, I had to drag her to the doctor, the Chinese Doctor. There are other people waiting, I come here to tell you that, I'll be with her if you find the house empty.'

Mr Ong nodded as he tried to serve another customer. 'So, should I come to call you, at her house?'

'No need, I'll manage. I'm going back to see how she is,' she said walking away.

He called after, 'Whey! Wife! Have you cooked dinner?'

She turned round and gave him one of her dark looks and carried on walking away thinking, 'If he is hungry why can't he eat one of the cakes or buns he's selling, why does he insist on eating rice twice a day?'

The herbalist examined Lian's eyes; he pulled her lower

lids down and stared at them. He hummed and nodded and then asked her to stick her tongue out. He felt her pulse on the inside of her wrist, he shut his eyes and hummed and nodded some more. He moved his fingers to a different spot on her wrist and shut his eyes again. Lian thought that he had gone to sleep. She coughed a little and he nodded and moved his fingers further along her wrist. He muttered something but Lian didn't catch what he was saying. After several minutes of meditation he opened his eyes and looked Lian in the eyes.

'You have water in your lungs. Your meridian is not balanced, your Yin and Yang, they are out of balance. There is too much cold and not enough heat in your body... causing too much phlegm.' He paused; his fingers still on Lian's pulse he looked down at nothing in particular and then closed his eyes again for a few moments. Then he exhaled noisily, opened his eyes and said, 'I make you some potions for you to take home.'

He got up and wrote on a white square of paper and gave it to his assistant. He turned his attention back to Lian again and said, 'I've made you two potions, you boil it in a clay-pot with three bowls of water until you have one bowl left, then you drink it. Do this in the evening, and drink it before you go to sleep. You have the second potion the next night and come back to see me in three days' time.'

Lian looked into those deep wise eyes and said reverently, 'Thank you, Mr Herbalist, thank you very much.' She got off the stool and went to stand behind the counter where the assistant was busily reading the scribe, opening drawers and picking out strange and wonderful shapes of nuts, seeds, leaves and strings; that's what they looked like to Lian in any case.

Mrs Ong meanwhile, was sitting on a stool a few paces away listening to the various conversations that had taken place between the herbalist, Lian, and all the other customers. At appropriate places she had nodded her head and pulled a knowing face and stored some of that information into an obscure recess of her mind to be retrieved later and used as wisdom for the young and uninitiated.

As they both walked out of the shop Mrs Ong put a restraining hand on Lian's arm and said, 'Wait here under the shade, I'll go and find a rickshaw.'

'I feel better now, I can walk,' Lian protested.

'Even if you can walk I can't, my old bones are tired!'

Lian smiled weakly and stood under the shade of the jacaranda tree outside the herbalist's shop. She clutched the two parcels of herbs to her chest self-consciously and crunched the wrapping between her fingers; her actions released a pungent aroma from the herbs and she sniffed at them and grimaced when the bitter smell hit her nostrils.

It didn't take Mrs Ong long to find a rickshaw in the village square but the rider eyed her nervously; he would have to work hard for the fare. The combined weight of the two adults and the uphill climb had proven too much so he got off and pushed the last few hundred yards before Mrs Ong took pity on him.

'You can stop here, Mister, we can walk the rest of the way,' she said as she gave Lian a hand to get off and then handed over the correct change to the rickshaw rider's out-stretched hand.

He was tempted to ask for more money but the expression on Mrs Ong's face stopped him. He muttered unhappily and freewheeled downhill.

Jen was waiting anxiously for her mother's return as she boiled the white sheets with a handful of caustic soda in a large tin that had once held gallons of coconut oil. She then rinsed them out in clean clear water that she had painstakingly filtered through the urn of graded sand. That was after she had drawn them from the well, bucket by bucket. Worrying about her mother had quickened the pace of her work.

Even Min picked up on her anxiety and kept running out onto the lane to check that no rickshaw had called in her absence, her vigilance had earned her a scolding. Jen had asked for her help to wring the sheets; she was to hold on to one end of the wet sheet while Jen twisted it from the opposite end to get the water out, but Min having small hands and unused to such work kept dropping her end back into the basin of water. After several failed attempts Jen got so frustrated she told Min to leave it in the basin. She then put one foot inside the basin and held one end of the sheet stationary and with both hands on the other end she swirled it round and round until most of the water was squeezed out. After she had rinsed every sheet and pillowcase three times she starched them in a thick gluey paste made with corn flour.

Min watched as Jen poured some corn flour from a paper bag into a small washing bowl; to that she added some cold water and mixed it with her fingers. Using a stick she stirred the mixture and added hot boiling water at the same time. The mixture slowly solidified as she stirred. She stopped adding the hot water when she was satisfied that the right consistency was achieved. The starch was then diluted with cold water to a gluey viscous texture, and a drop of blue colour was added to make the whites whiter. The sheets and pillowcases were then put into this mixture individually to starch before they were hung out to dry under the equatorial sun.

Min followed Jen into the backyard asking, 'Why did you do that, Big Sister?'

'Do what, Min? Careful! You are stepping on my washing.'

'That thing, with hot water, and mixing and mixing,' Min said as she mimicked how Jen was stirring with the stick.

Just then they heard Mrs Ong's and their mother's voices as they came through from the front door into the kitchen. Min ran indoors leaving Jen to finish her chores.

'No more sewing today, you go and have a rest,' Mrs Ong said as Lian went towards her pile of sewing sitting neatly folded on a chair. The old hand-sewing machine sat forlornly on a corner of the table. Lian was very fond of that old relic bequeathed to her by her late mother. It clattered noisily when in use but Lian found the familiar sound of fabric sandwiched between two metal parts comforting especially when she turned out beautiful garments from that ancient machinery.

'Mama, Mama, you home!' Min ran up to her mother and held her mother's hand and swung it a few times as if to test that it was still alive and working.

'Leave you mother alone now, Little Min, she's tired. Where's your sister? Ask your sister to make your mother something to eat.' And to Min's delight she said, 'How would you like to come home with me?'

Min beamed and nodded, Mrs Ong represented food, lots of it. She ran off to tell Jen the good news leaving Lian to more ministration and advice from Mrs Ong.

Lian slept off and on in the hot and stifling afternoon. The curtains were drawn to keep out the light. Jen had brought her a light meal of boiled rice and steamed salted fish with finely shredded ginger. Ginger was supposed to be good for phlegm, so Mrs Ong said. She had managed to eat a few mouthfuls of rice when a sudden surge of sadness came from very deep within her; it rose up into her throat and stayed. It felt like a very large stone had blocked her windpipe though she was breathing quite normally. Her coughing was no worse than it had been. She put her bowl of rice down and felt her throat with both hands.

She ran her fingers around the front and then all the

way round her neck and back again. The outside felt normal but she was certain the lump was still in her throat. She swallowed hard; there was definitely something stuck to the inside of her throat. She called out to Jen to bring her a cup of water.

Jen stood in front of her mother watching her sipping from the mug; she noted the food was barely touched. 'Is the fish all right, not too much ginger?' she asked uncertainly.

'The fish is fine. Jen, can you see anything on my throat?'

Jen squatted down and peered closely at where her mother's fingers were pressing into the dry papery skin. 'I can't see anything! Do you want some tiger balm on it?'

'No, I wonder if I got a fish bone in my throat. It feels like something stuck,' Lian said as she attempted to clear her throat.

'It can't be a fish bone, you haven't eaten any fish yet,' Jen said as she lifted the plate to examine the fish more closely.

'No, you're right, it can't be a fish bone. I'm not hungry. You can have it with your rice. Is Min home?'

'Not yet, I'll collect her later.'

'Jen!'

'Yes, Ah Ma!'

'I… I'm… sorry. You have a lot to do because I've not been well,' Lian could barely get the words out.

Jen shifted uncomfortably, she didn't know how to respond to an apology from an older person, especially one from her own mother. 'I'll go and finish the ironing,' Jen said awkwardly and went swiftly down the stairs. Her heart was beating hard and fast, she remembered watching an old film once where the mother had called all her children to her bedside to apologise for some past misdeeds before she died.

Chapter Seventeen

Left alone with her thoughts Lian shivered and shook for several minutes. She drew her knees up to her chest and hugged them tightly. Snapshots of her past swirled and whirled into her thoughts unbidden and unchecked. She was too tired and sick to censor any ugly dramas that passed through her internal theatre. Her breathing became more hurried, but she felt strangely peaceful. Slowly and quietly hot salty tears rolled down her face. As the tears increased her breathing slowed and in a dreamlike state she wiped her tears with the back of her hand like a child waiting for her mother to rescue her.

There were no sound, just tears and thoughts. She was sixteen again. Her mother had called her into her room to speak with her. Old Mrs Tang was a wiry four-foot ten of nervous energy. She had a slight stoop and tottered on her bound-feet around the house like a caged animal. Old Mr Tang, her father, was an elusive and silent figure; he only came home once a week to give his wife housekeeping money to ease his conscience. The rest of his life and time was spent with his second mistress. Lian's parents had been married for nearly forty years but for thirty of those years he had lived with his mistresses. Lian had often wondered why her mother had her so late in life and, unusually for the times, why was she the only child.

Lian stepped into the dim interior of her mother's room; Mrs Tang was sitting on the edge of her bed. The smell of liniment was coming at her from every wall.

'Lian, sit down,' her mother waved her towards a chair

by the bed. 'I have something to tell you. You are now sixteen and it's time we found you a husband,' Mrs Tang said not looking Lian in the eye. 'I'm getting old and your father said he had approached a match-maker… it's been arranged for you to be married to Old Lau's youngest son.'

A shiver shot through Lian. She remained silent, too stunned and afraid to speak. She tried to catch her mother's eyes but Mrs Tang was looking at her hands that were resting on her lap, all wrinkled and engorged with veins treading an uneven path to her fingers. 'Mother,' Lian finally found her voice, 'you have not been well lately, would it not be better for me to remain with you, to look after you. There's plenty of time to find me a husband… when you are better,' Lian said with as much conviction as she could muster.

'Daughter, I would like that if I could, but your father has made the arrangement. You mustn't let your father down,' Old Mrs Tang said, her voice more timorous than normal.

A sudden surge of energy lifted Lian off the chair, 'She faced her mother, 'NO! I will not do it!' she cried.

Old Mrs Tang kept her head down. Her shoulders shuddered and she let out a long low groan like a trapped animal, it went on for ages. Lian looked on in shock. The mother she knew was a placid and timid woman not given to angry outbursts. She took a step backwards and fell back into her chair. For a long while neither spoke, the hush in the room threaten to engulf both of them.

'I'm sorry, Mother,' Lian said and slowly lowered herself down to the ground until she was kneeling directly in front of her mother.

Old Mrs Tang lifted her head slowly until their eyes met, 'Lian, I'm sorry it had to be this way,' a sob escaped from her pressed lips. 'There are things that I should have told you before… but I couldn't,' her sobbing had become more insistent and she stopped to wipe her face on a

161

handkerchief. 'You see, I… I can't have children…'

Lian thought her mother was so upset by her defiance that she was talking gibberish. 'Mother, you don't have to tell me anything, you are tired, take a rest and I'll make you some herb soup…'

'No, Lian! You must listen to me, when I am dead you will never find out the truth. You are not my daughter!'

Lian felt as if her mother had slapped her a hundred times. Numbed to her bones she sat back on her heels and put her hands out and covered her mothers'. 'I… I… I… don't understand what you are telling me, Mother!' she stuttered, tears not far behind.

The old lady seemed to have shrunk even further in those few moments; she withdrew her hands from Lian's clasp and wiped her eyes vigorously. After tucking her handkerchief up her long sleeve she stood up and turned her back on Lian. With both hands she gripped the headboard to stop herself toppling over on her three-by-two-inch bound feet. 'You are the daughter of our father's last mistress, she died soon after giving birth to you; your father said I should bring you home to live with me. I cannot have children, I have to accept that he must have a mistress to bear his children,' she sobbed quietly.

Lian was still kneeling on the floor and felt safer to remain there; her foundation in life had been severely shaken. The message her mother had just imparted sounded distant and unreal. Soon she was crying quietly too, but unlike her mother she didn't have a handkerchief to wipe her nose. Now she understood why her father rarely spoke to either of them, her mother for being barren and Lian for reminding him that she was the cause of his mistress's death.

'Mother, can't you forbid him, he cannot marry me off like a pig to market!' Lian pleaded.

'I've tried. He threatened to stop the money for our food. I have no money of my own.' She turned round to face Lian, 'Don't kneel there, I don't deserve it, sit on the chair,' her voice was broken and pitiful.

The heavy burden of knowing that the woman whom she had called Mother all her life had asked her not to kneel in her presence because she didn't deserve it, had to be the ultimate punishment for both of them. Lian got up and looked at her mother closely. Long hair pulled back into a bun and pinned into the nape of her neck. Eyes heavily lidded with hardly any sparkle in them. Wrinkles grooved her face and the corners of her mouth were turned down in a permanent disappointment.

Lian was silent, but she felt a rising rage threatening to explode. She was unsure how to comfort her mother and soothe her own anger. With great effort she spoke to her mother calmly, 'Mother, you sit on the chair, I want to talk to you before it's too late.' Lian held her elbows and steered her onto the chair. 'Please tell me everything.'

Old Mrs Tang sniffed and let out a long deep sigh. 'When I was sixteen your father came back to fetch me—'

'Fetch you from where?' Lian interrupted.

'We were both brought up in a little village in Guangzhou. My father and his father were in business together. He agreed that on my thirteenth birthday I would be betrothed to his business partner's youngest son. Your father is five years older than me. When he was sixteen he left home, joined a boat and came to Singapore. He met a man who gave him a job in his kitchen, but his boss died two years later owing a lot of money to his enemies. They threatened to cut your father up and feed him to the dogs, so he ran away to Malaya. He started his own restaurant with the money he had saved, and when I turned sixteen he came back to China to make me his wife.' Mrs Tang paused as if in a trance.

'And then what happened?' Lian asked.

'What else could I do but follow him here. I only had

two changes of clothes and no money when I left my parents' house. I thought I was lucky to be married to a man with a restaurant, I would always have food to eat. But the Gods hadn't endowed me with the gift of children. I prayed every day to have a son, but years passed and nothing happened,' the sadness in her voice was palpable.

Lian flinched when her mother said that she prayed for a son. Another hundred slaps to her face. But she couldn't be angry with her mother for she had been kind and had taught her to sew, read and write what little she herself knew. 'What... when did Father... how did he meet my birth mother?'

'After ten years and still no children, your father got impatient. He said he wanted a son to inherit his name and fortune, that was what he said,' she pulled her handkerchief out and dabbed at her eyes. 'He met her at the restaurant, she was helping in the kitchen.'

'Did she give him a son?' Lian felt her anger thudding against her ribs. It wasn't the kind of question one asked one's mother but being angry made her reckless.

Her mother nodded. 'Her first-born was a son. He was ten years old when you were born. She was in poor health and didn't want another child but to please your father she had you.'

Lian shut her eyes and imagined the horror of her mother dying soon after giving birth to her. What was her name? What did she look like? She has a brother! Where is he now?

But to her mother she asked, 'Did you ever meet my birth mother?'

She nodded. 'I saw her lying in her bed, she was very sick, she was crying when she gave you to me. You were tiny, I was so scared, you were screaming, screaming...'

'What happened to my bro... to her son?'

'The second mistress looked after him for some time. I suppose he's grown up now... I don't know where he is.'

The old lady's eyes misted over again, she put both hands over her face and pressed her fingers hard into the sockets of her eyes. Her distress wrenched at Lian's heart.

'Mother, you are tired, here, let me help, lie down and have a rest. I'll get you a cup of tea.' Lian had to get out of the room for some air. She stumbled into the kitchen and stood holding on to the back of a chair. Her legs felt like jelly and her hands shook when she poured the tea from the thermos flask into her mother's cup.

Sadly that was the last conversation Lian had with her mother. Old Mrs Tang died in her sleep that night. Six months later Lian was married to Lau Chee Kuan. He was ten years older than Lian, a kind and gentle man. For the first time Lian felt contented if not happy. He was a carpenter and he single-handedly built the house that she and her children still lived in. She never had any further contacts with her father since her arranged marriage.

Chee Kuan was a sickly man and nine years into his marriage to Lian he died. The doctor at the hospital told her that he had tuberculosis, and it was at his funeral that she learned that his mother had also died of the same illness.

Being a widow with four young children was an impossible nightmare. Min was only six moths old, and Jen the oldest was not quite eight. She remembered standing at his graveside seeing his coffin being lowered into the hole in the ground; she lost all sense of reasoning and she tried to jump in with him, but was held firmly away by the strong arms of Mrs Ong.

The memories of it all brought great big shuddering sobs. Years of sadness and frustration hit her like a sledgehammer and suddenly the room was reverberating with her distressed howling. She howled and cried and howled and cried until the tears had dried up and her throat was sore. Suddenly she remembered the lump in her throat, she felt nervously for it with her hands, there was nothing there. She took a few hard swallows but the lump seemed to have disappeared. Anxiously she took a few sips of the water, whatever that was blocking her throat had definitely gone away. Reassured, Lian dried her eyes, flopped down on her pillow and fell into an exhausted sleep.

Jen, on hearing her mother's sobbing had crept up the stairs and stood outside the bedroom listening and agonising. She was terrified but felt as if her feet were nailed to the floorboards, unable to move away. In the end she just stayed there until the room went quiet and then she panicked about what to do next. She pressed her ears to the thin wall when she heard her mother's hoarse breathing. Very quietly she got down on all fours and crawled into the room, she stayed there for a couple of minutes just to make sure that her mother was still breathing, then she backed out of the room, ran down the stairs, out the back door and straight up the lane to Mrs Ong's home.

Chapter Eighteen

Jen arrived at Mrs Ong's front door breathless and in a cold sweat. She stood on tip-toe at the half-opened door yelling, 'Mrsss… Ong, it's… it's Jen, Mrs Ong!'

Min on hearing Jen's voice came running down the corridor, 'Big Sister, Big Sister, you've come. I open the door for you.'

Min struggled with the bolt and Jen leant over the half door to give her encouragement, but all she managed to say was, 'Hurry up, Min, just… just pull it back the other way,' she said waving her hand about.

'J… een! Is that you? Oh! It is you.' Mrs Ong sauntered towards the door. 'Let me do that, Min, your little hands aren't strong enough.' She stepped aside to let Jen in and nudged the bolt back into the hasp with a snap. 'How's your mother?'

Jen eyed her sister and debated if she should tell the old lady her concerns in front of her younger sister. 'Min, can you go and play in the garden, I want to talk to Mrs Ong on my own.'

'Why? I won't tell,' Min protested.

'You help yourself to a piece of that bun and go and play in the garden while I speak to Jen, go on, that's a good girl,' Mrs Ong said and put a firm hand on Min's shoulder to propel her in the direction of the kitchen. Her maxim in life has always been that bribery goes a long way, followed swiftly by a threat that it would be taken away if not accepted at once. She now turned her attention to Jen, 'You look starved, have you eaten anything?'

'Err… I can't remember… I'm very worried about my mother.'

'We are all worried about your mother, Jen, but she's going to be all right,' she emphasised.

'She… she was crying! I heard her, very loud… and…' Jen shivered and hugged herself.

Mrs Ong patted a chair, 'You sit down here and have something to eat, then you can tell me all about it. There's some buns under there,' she pointed to a dome-shaped mesh, 'eat as much as you want. What do you want to drink, Chinese tea, or I have some coffee left over from this morning?'

Jen, while she was delighted to be offered food was impatient to express her fears and was more than a little agitated that Mrs Ong was not taking her seriously about her mother's health. She sat down, her legs were shaky, but she refused to eat. 'Can I have water instead please? Mrs Ong… do… do you think my mother will die… soon?'

Mrs Ong swung round. A trail of water followed her in an arc splattering her trousers and the concrete floor, the kettle and mug were still firmly gripped in her hands. 'Jen? What made you say that? Your mother is just sick because she is not eating the right food. She doesn't get enough sleep, but she will get better,' Mrs Ong said soothingly once she had recovered from the shock. She hadn't realised that Jen was carrying the burden of her mother's mortality on her tender shoulders. She stood behind Jen and put her arms gently on her shoulders, 'Listen to me, Jen. I won't let it happen, not as long as I am living. Now, have something to eat and I am coming back with you to see to your mother.'

A solitary tear slipped down her pale cheek. 'Thank you, Mrs Ong,' Jen whispered. She helped herself to the water and took a few bites out of the bun. The kitchen was as she remembered it, large, airy and stocked full of utensils that Jen had only ever seen in one of those large shops in town. She wondered if Mr Ong earns lots of money in the market stall and why they have no children. Jen had a good mathematical mind but was inclined to let ideas run away with her; she was still musing about how much she could earn if she learned how to make cakes and buns like Mrs Ong when she felt a slap in her back.

'Big Sister, Mrs Ong is talking to you!' Min said reproachfully and delivered another slap to Jen's back.

'Oh! Oh! Sorry, Mrs Ong, what did you say?'

The old lady was holding a squat earthenware jug aloft. It had a spout like a kettle and a large handle like an ear stuck to the side of a face as an afterthought. The lid sat snugly on the top like a baby sucking on a dummy. It was a dirty brown colour with black soot stains on its lower half.

'You must remember to take this home,' Mrs Ong said as she placed the implement on the table.

'We don't need it…'

'What is that?' Min asked as she clambered on the chair and leant across to have a closer look.

'A clay pot!' Mrs Ong said as she took a chair next to Min.

'What's a clay pot?' Min asked as she attempted to take the lid off but Jen parried her hands off.

'Don't touch it, it's not a toy,' Jen admonished her.

'It's a medicine pot,' Mrs Ong said. 'The medicine doctor in the village gave your mama some medicine. You have to boil it in a clay pot.'

'Why?'

'All those herbs make stains in a metal pot. Clay pots let the herbs breathe. It's better for the medicine,' Mrs Ong explained.

'And Mama will get better when she eats all the medicine,' Min said looking at Mrs Ong wide-eyed and innocent.

'Yes, that's it. I think it's time we go and see your mama.'

The boys were already home when Jen came in with Mrs Ong. Min, who had run on ahead was now poking on a bag of flour that they had brought home. There were several chicken eggs being carefully unwrapped by Tam and stored in a wicker basket.

'Mrs Choy gave me the eggs for Ah Ma. She said it will help her get better if she has one egg a day,' Tam said to Jen. 'The vegetables are over there, she also gave me a fish, a fresh one.'

Jen eyed all the food that the farmer's wife had given them and felt like crying. 'Did you apologise that I couldn't go today?'

'Yes, she said it's more important to look after Ah Ma. She said you don't have to go again, don't worry, she said she will come to see you here tomorrow.'

Jen was worried. Very worried. She was promised a sum of money after her month's work at the farm, as it was she had absented herself twice that week. Any deductions meant less money for essentials like pen, paper, ink, a pair of proper shoes, and a pair of shorts – shorts! Jen suddenly realised she had qualified for a pair of shorts, those horrible bloomers that she had to wear at primary school made her look like a turkey, she need never wear them again. A beginning of a smile played on her lips when the thought occurred to her but it was short-lived as Lee shot out of nowhere and ran smack into her. 'LEE!' she screamed at him.

'WHAT!' he retorted, very red in the face.

'All right, boys! Go and have a wash, Min, you help me cook, and Jen, you go and take the laundry back to the hotel.' Mrs Ong decided a bit of grown-up discipline was in order.

Jen was reluctant to hand over her house duties to Mrs Ong much as she liked the old lady. She stood in the kitchen looking lost while Min was being educated on the practicalities of de-scaling and gutting a fish.

'Eh! Jen, haven't you gone yet? Dinner will be ready for you when you come back, go now, there's a bus due soon,' Mrs Ong said with a smile.

Jen had to admit that it was really nice to come home to a meal cooked and ready for her to eat. Her mother was up and sitting in the kitchen with Mrs Ong. They were deep in conversation when she walked in on them. The boys and Min were upstairs; Lee could be heard teasing Min with a dead insect.

Jen wrinkled her nose; there was a bitter cloying odour wafting around in the kitchen. 'What's that smell?' she asked no one in particular and then noticed the clay pot on the stove glugging and puffing clouds of vapour.

'It's the herb potion for your mother,' Mrs Ong answered. 'Now you're home, you can see to it. I must go home to cook some rice for my Old Man.' As she got off the stool she winced, 'I must get some more herbs for those knees. Remind me, Lian, when we go to the herbalist next week, remind me to get some more herbs...'

'Thank you, Mrs Ong, thank you for all you've done,' Lian said, her voice hoarse yet weak.

Jen walked her to the door. The old lady looked Jen up and down, a shadow crossed her eyes and she said, 'Watch the clay pot. Don't let it boil dry. When it's ready, pour it into a rice bowl and make sure your mother drinks all of it,' she told Jen.

'How do I know when it's ready?' Jen asked.

Mrs Ong thought for a moment, 'Use a pair of chopsticks and push the herbs down to see how much water is left. When you think there is a bowl of water left, it's ready. Don't add too much charcoal either; if the heat is too high it will cook too quickly. It needs slow simmering to bring out the goodness of the herbs.'

Jen nodded. She returned to the kitchen and noticed her mother staring at the pile of sewing. 'Ah Ma, do you want rice, I am going to have some?'

Lian, lost in thoughts, took a few moments to respond. 'I've eaten. I think I will go to rest. Could you bring me the herb medicine when it's ready.'

'I will, Ah Ma. Shall I help you, go up the stairs?'

Lian waved her away.

Alone again Jen sat down to her evening meal facing the stove. She watched and listened to the glug, glug, glug, as the liquid boiled and bubbled in the pot. The rising herbal vapour became more pungent the longer the boiling went on. When the tension of waiting got the better of her she got up and took the lid off to have a look inside. Peering into the depths of a bubbling clay pot of black foaming herbal brew did not give Jen any indication of how much liquid was in the pot. She decide to take further action, one that she felt was more accurate that Mrs Ong's 'prod with a chopstick and see'.

She got a rice bowl, a cloth to wrap around the handle of the pot and a pair of chopsticks. Jen squatted by the stove and removed the pot with one hand, in her other hand she held the pair of chopsticks to keep the lid in place. As she tilted the pot, thick black liquid plopped into the bowl. When the bowl was full Jen righted the pot and gave it a gentle shake, she heard gentle swishing of more liquid, satisfied that she had more than the required amount of medicine, she tipped the bowl of liquid back into the pot and returned it to the stove.

Jen got on with her other house duties while she waited for the herbs to infuse further. It was another half hour before she was confident that it was ready. When the bowl of infusion was cooling on the table Jen put her nose to it and took a few sniffs, it made her eyes water and gave her face a good steaming. It looked more like a bowl of tar than herbal remedy as it sat in the middle of the table with a fine plume of rising vapour hovering over it.

As she nursed the bowl gently between her hands, Jen offered a silent prayer to the kitchen God before she took it upstairs. She sat opposite her mother while Lian drank the liquid in one long gulp. Lian pulled a face and shook her head as the bitterness hit the back of her throat.

'Erghhh…' more shaking of her head, 'Erghhh… that's really bitter,' she said.

'Shall I bring you some water?'

'No, the taste will go away soon. It's getting rather late, why don't you go to sleep.'

'I haven't finish—'

Lian cut her off gently, 'Leave the work for another day; you look tired, go to bed. You worked very hard… Thank you. You've been a good daughter, you've worked hard,' Lian said and watched Jen as she got up and dropped the curtains that separated their sleeping space. The conversation she had with Mrs Ong earlier in the evening made her look at life from another perspective, Jen's perspective.

Chapter Nineteen

Jen got up reluctantly from the warm spot on the floorboards that was her bed when she failed to block out the defiant and triumphant cockerels crowing from the neighbouring houses. She had been awake for some time listening for the signs of life. Min had a gentle purring snore while her mother's was more of a grunt, followed by a whoop, that finished off with a snort and a wheeze.

She padded quietly downstairs and slipped on her clogs at the bottom of the stairs. A quick check in the water urn, the charcoal bucket, sugar jar and the empty biscuit tin told her that she had to do some fetching and shopping to replenish supplies. She sat on the stool to collect her thoughts and scratched her head with one hand and her knee with the other.

A gentle knocking on the back door made her jump. It was so unexpected; she stood very still and waited. Another knock. This time she was sure it was coming from the back door. She slipped off her clogs and tiptoed towards it, and as she put one eye to a hole in the door another knock resounded and she jumped back.

'Who's that?'

'Jen, it's me, open the door.'

Jen shot the bolt back and opened the door. Mrs Ong stood there looking as fresh as the new day.

'Here, I've brought you these buns for breakfast. Steam them in the wok to keep them warm.'

Jen took the plate, too surprised to speak. There were half a dozen soft fluffy buns on the plate and they were still warm.

'Is you mother alright? Did she sleep well?'

'Yes, Mrs Ong… and thank you for the buns,' Jen said, regarding the buns with mixed emotions.

'I've got to go now I will come over later,' she said as she walked off.

Jen stood watching her receding back for some time.

Tam, Lee, and Min were extremely pleased with their breakfast. The buns were filled with soft sweet mashed red beans. Lee licked his fingers and asked for more, so Jen tore one of the buns into three pieces and gave a portion to each of her younger siblings.

'There's two left, can I have another?' Lee asked.

Tam intervened before Jen could reply. 'No, you can't have anymore!'

'I didn't ask you?' Lee protested.

'The answer is still no!' said Jen.

'Why not, Mama won't want hers. Anyway, she's got eggs, you brought them home yesterday,' Lee reasoned with Tam.

Tam looked at Jen and then at Lee. 'Ah Ma is sick, she needs more food to get better.'

'I'm hungry, and I need more food to grow bigger,' he argued.

Min feeling left out piped up, 'I'm going to Mrs Ong's house later, and she has lots and lots of food. I'll get you some, Brother Lee,' she said.

The noise from the kitchen woke Lian up. She opened and shut her eyes several times to adjust to her surroundings. She had slept very heavily. Taking a deep breath made her cough, but the pain in her chest seemed to have eased slightly. Sitting up made her a little light-headed; and she steadied herself by backing up against the wall. After some minutes she stood up; feeling more confident she went down the stairs holding on to the rickety banister.

The children looked up in surprise at her appearance. Her hair was hanging loose around her shoulders and sleep had marked a long ridge from the corner one eye and down her cheek. A trail of white saliva stain blotched the corner of her mouth. She was still wearing her nightclothes. They were used to a neat and well-scrubbed mother who never allowed a hair to stray past her ears, and here she was looking like a tramp.

Lian flicked a few strands of stray hair off her face with her hand and sat down. Jen got up quickly and poured her mother a mug of coffee. Lian looked around at her children and put a hand on Min's head and brushed her hair away from her pink cheeks. 'Your hair is getting long, must get it, cut soon.' Then she turned her attention to Tam and Lee, 'You boys have grown up so much lately, it must be the food Mrs Choy gives you,' and she smiled benevolently at them. 'Are you going to the farm again today?'

'Yes, Ah Ma,' Tam confirmed quietly.

'I don't want to go today!' Lee said.

'You promised to help me dig over the vegetable garden,' Tam said.

Lian got hold of Lee's pointing finger and said, 'You go with Tam today, and then you can stay at home tomorrow. If you make a promise you must keep it,' Lian said still holding on to Lee.

'Yes, and I will bring you lots of food,' Min reiterated.

That seemed to pacify Lee and he went off with Tam to the farm feeling really pleased with himself. He salivated as he conjured up the images of cakes and buns that Min was going to bring home that evening.

'Ah Ma, would you like me to make you a soft boiled egg?' Jen asked as soon as they were on their own.

Lian thought for a bit, having a whole egg to herself, was, in her books, too extravagant. Jen knew what she was thinking too.

'Tam brought them home yesterday especially for you. Mrs Choy gave them to you, she said they would help you to get better,' Jen added, she felt that she needed to back up her argument to convince her mother to accept what she considered luxury food.

'That sounds good. Yes, I think I will have an egg. Could you cook me one? I'll have a wash and change; maybe I'll do a bit of sewing later.'

Jen felt buoyant. Her mother hadn't coughed once since she got up and she appeared less tired and even her voice was livelier. She removed the wok from the stove and put the kettle back on the boil. Very gently she unhooked the basket secured by a string to a large nail on a wall. She gazed longingly at the half dozen brown eggs nestling on layers of newspapers. Jen ran her fingers over them; the smooth ovals seemed so perfect and so right next to each other that she was reluctant to take one away.

The abrupt coughing and huffing from Lian in the bathroom brought Jen back to what she was doing. She quickly took out an egg from the basket and put it in a tin canister that was sometimes used as a lunch box. When the water boiled she poured it over the egg until it was completely submerged and then she fitted the lid over the canister. When she judged that five minutes had passed she emptied the hot water away and left the egg in the canister to keep warm.

Lian came out of the bathroom with wet hair wrapped up in a towel and her face pink as a cooked prawn where she had scrubbed the sleep off her face. Jen thought her mother looked quite comical but didn't dare laugh or make any flippant remarks for she would think her rude and disrespectful.

'The egg's ready, Ah Ma,' Jen said pointing to the canister.

'Thank you, I'll have that now.'

'Let me do it for you,' Jen said. She picked up the egg

and smacked it into the sharp edge of a bowl, a perfect crack appeared on the smooth shell. As she dug both thumbs in to hinge it apart, some of the egg white splattered onto the table. Lian looked on but didn't comment. Jen hurriedly scraped the rest of the egg with a spoon into the bowl and gave it to her mother. Lian added a drop of soy sauce, stirred the runny egg yolk into what was left of the white and tipped the lot down her throat in one go. Jen watched her mother intently as she licked her lips.

'That was very good, Jen. Why don't you make one for yourself, you deserve one too. You worked hard,' Lian said without a hint of irony.

Jen was pleased, and shocked – she was not used to her mother being so reasonable. She wondered if all herbal remedies have the same effect on everyone. Jen looked forward to brewing the second herbal medicine for her mother that evening, but meanwhile she had to finish the washing and then do some shopping in the village.

Jen was energetically rinsing and spinning the sheets clock-wise when she heard her name being called. Thinking it was her mother, she ran indoors and up the stairs. But Lian was fast asleep and she had forgotten to draw the curtains. Min had gone to Mrs Ong's house so she knew it wasn't either of them. As she got to the bottom of the stairs she saw a familiar silhouette at the front door.

'Hello, Mrs Choy, sorry I didn't see you there,' Jen said with a mixture of surprise and trepidation.

'Hello, Jen, how's your mother? Tam told me that she wasn't well.'

'Please come in.' Jen led the way into the kitchen.

Mrs Choy noticed that the little front room was bare except for the altar. Three Chinese prints presided over the three colourful urns where joss sticks were still burning. Two of the prints depicted deities of the Buddhist faith and the third was a framed print of Chinese characters conveying the names of the ancestors of the household.

'Please take a seat, can I get you a drink? I can make you some tea or a cup of coffee,' Jen said clasping and unclasping her hands.

'No thank you, I've just had my breakfast. I've come to speak to you about… you've been a good little worker. I will miss having you…'

Jen blushed. 'Where are the children, is Mr Choy looking after them?'

Mrs Choy laughed out loud, 'Mr Choy only understands things that grow in the ground or if they have four legs, are pink and snort,' she giggled at her own observation. 'No… my husband is not any good as a childminder. My mother has come to stay for a few weeks. I have to take Siu Min to school on Monday, and my mother will look after the others. I'll probably take him myself for the first two weeks, after that I'll try to arrange for a rickshaw to pick him up and bring him back every day. Let's not talk about me, I came here to talk about you, how's your mother?'

'She's better. Thank you for the eggs, I boiled one for her this morning,' Jen answered.

'Good… I'm glad your mother's feeling better.' She felt in her trouser pockets for her purse, as she pulled it out she said, 'I've brought you this, I hope you think this is a fair payment for the work you've done.' She pushed a few dollar bills across the table.

Jen sat staring at the notes on the table. She was surprised, she was delighted, and she was speechless.

'Do you think that's a fair pay?' Mrs Choy asked stretching her neck towards Jen.

'Oh yes! Yes it's very fair; it's more than fair. I… I don't think I deserve that much,' Jen answered.

'Of course you do. You work hard, Jen. Tam is the same as you, my husband said that he is very good with his hands,' Mrs Choy smiled and crinkled her eyes.

'I must go now; I've got some shopping to do. Remember, if you have any free time, do visit us.'

'I will, Mrs Choy,' Jen replied with a slight bow of her head.

'Do call me Auntie Lin, Mrs Choy is so formal.'

'Thank you,' Jen hesitated, 'Auntie Lin, I will come to see the children some time.' Jen walked her to the front door. As she watched her walk down the lane Jen couldn't help feeling sad, she had enjoyed the company of the farmer's wife who is about the same age as her mother but much jollier and softer in her manner.

Back in the kitchen Jen studied the money sat teasingly on the table. There were three five-dollar bills and several single-dollar bills. She thought that Tam and Lee should have a share of the money too; but the reality was she would have to hand the money over to her mother to decide what should be done with it. Surely her mother wouldn't deny her a new uniform, she thought. After all she did earn the money!

Chapter Twenty

Saturday morning turned out to be an optimistic and equally hectic day for Jen, but for very different reasons. After her last evening discussion with her mother, presided over by the indomitable Mrs Ong, Jen found herself wandering in a bazaar in town looking for materials. Her mother was well enough to do so some sewing and had promised Jen a new uniform if she could buy the fabric for her school colours, Lian would help her cut and sew them together.

The bazaar was like a warren of secret passages pitched with rows and rows of tiny stalls where a lot of bartering went on. Buckets and brooms stood shoulder to shoulder with ready-made shirts vying for space with lurid coloured sarongs and bales of cloths. Ladies underwear was more discreetly displayed on shelves under glass counters. The place was buzzing with customers haggling and hectoring to bring the prices of goods down. The owners of the stalls were just as vociferous in their clamour for business and keeping their margin of profits high. Jen walked along the narrow passages listening and looking for the materials she came for. She spied several stalls selling them but was unsure which was the cheapest. After she went round the same stalls three times, one young man called out to her.

'Miss! You'll go dizzy if you keep going in circles,' he laughed. 'Come and have a closer look,' he said rubbing his hands over bales of brightly coloured cotton materials. 'This one suits your skin tone,' he continued as he pulled out a tightly folded bale of fine cotton in apple green with tiny pink blossoms splashed haphazardly all over it.

Jen smiled coyly and shook her head.

'Tell me what you're looking for and I'll see if I can find it,' he persuaded Jen.

'Thank you, I'm just looking,' she said and walked on. She went round the next corner and stopped in front of another stall where an old lady was sitting with her head bowed, sewing noisily on her treadle machine. Jen gazed at the columns of colourful cloth packed tightly together at the front, but at the back of the stall she saw the white and the blue materials she needed for her school blouse and pinafore. She stood and waited until there was a pause in the clacking of the old machine before she spoke. 'Auntie! How much is a yard of those cloths there?' Jen asked pointing to them.

The old lady looked up and gave Jen a smile showing her gold front teeth. She stood up and pulled down the bales of materials that Jen had pointed to and brought them to the narrow counter. 'This one is one dollar ten cents for a yard and this one is one dollar twenty,' she said.

Jen, unsure if that was a fair price, asked softly, 'Auntie, can you take some money off, I haven't got a lot of money with me.' She kept her eyes steadily on the old lady's face.

The stall owner, used to haggling customers, knew the quietly spoken ones were just as sharp. 'Little Miss, my price is already cheap, I have to earn a living…' she left her words hanging in the air.

Jen watched how her lips moved over those gold teeth and wondered how much profit she must have made to afford them. 'Can you take a little off the price please?'

'And how much do you need?'

'I need two and a quarter yards of the white and three of the blue,' Jen confirmed. She was pleased that she had managed to convince her mother it would not cost much more to have two sets of uniforms. Having Mrs Ong on her side in the argument was a great help Jen thought. 'So how much would that cost?'

'Six dollars and ten cents in total and I'll take thirty-cents off the price,' she said firmly.

'No, that's too much, how about you charge me one dollar a yard for both of them?' Jen was getting into the swing of it and quite enjoyed herself.

'Ai… yah! Little Miss! I have to make a living, my profit margin is already very narrow,' she said.

Jen was unmoved now that she noticed that even her back teeth had gold fillings. 'I only have five dollars and some change on me,' she un-knotted her handkerchief and showed the old lady the money and waited for the sympathy vote to win her over. 'I've got to leave some change to take the bus home,' Jen gave her best pleading look.

The old lady made to shake her head and then noticed Jen turning and walking away. 'Come back, come back, Little Miss, you are a hard barterer! You win! Just this time I will let you have it at this low price,' she said good-naturedly. She unrolled the material and stretched out a tape measure, 'So how much do you want of this one?' she asked pulling the tape taut over the edge of the white cloth.

'Two and a quarter,' Jen replied.

'You sure that's enough? What's it for?'

'My school blouse,' Jen answered. She wished the old lady wasn't so nosey.

She looked Jen up and down, 'Mmm. I think you need more than two and a quarter yards, don't forget you have sleeves and collars as well.'

'Okay, I'll have two and a half yards if you charge me the same price as two and a quarter.'

'Ai… yah, you're not only thrifty but smart too ha!' she smiled broadly at Jen. 'I'm feeling generous today, I'll let the tape slacken a bit so that will be nearly two and a half,' she said as she picked up a pair of scissors and ran it cleanly along the width of the cloth. After she had cut out a three-yard length of the blue cloth she folded them both into a neat rectangle and dropped them into a brown paper bag.

Jen handed over the money and walked out of the hot and stuffy building into the mid-morning sunshine, feeling like a bird being let out of her cage.

Back home that afternoon Jen was seated by her mother's hand-sewing machine watching Lian measuring and cutting the materials into curves and slants that even Jen's mathematical mind couldn't fathom. She was rather surprised when her mother explained how the curved edge of a pattern became a sleeve when sewn and fitted into the right hole. The pinafore was much easier to handle as it only had straight edges, and when it was pinned together it looked like a long box with openings on either end.

Her mother left her to sew all the pieces together while she went for a nap. Jen, sitting in front of the quaint sewing machine, moved the wheel around with her hand and watched the metal teeth in the opposite end glide up and down before tangling up into a knot. She cut away the knot and put a scrap of material between them to test her sewing skills. With her right hand she gripped the handle of the wheel and turned it several times. The material slipped effortlessly between the metal teeth and came out the other side with a fairly straight line. Pleased with her first attempt she placed the pinafore material into position. Gingerly she started the machine up. It went fine for a few seconds before she noticed that she was not sewing in a straight line.

Jen decided that sewing wasn't as easy as her mother said it was. She unpicked the stitches and tried again, much more slowly. The wheel went round clack, clack, clack, clacking like a mouth full of loose teeth. It took her nearly five minutes before she came to the end of the first side seam. She smiled and ran her tongue over her top lips delighted with her efforts. It took her nearly two hours to join up the sides of both pinafores. She held them up to admire her handiwork and noticed that one was an inch longer than the other. She sighed, annoyed with her carelessness. She got up from the stool and stretched herself. Her shoulders were aching and her eyes felt peculiar through watching the needle going up and down, up and down.

She took a walk to look out the back door; apart from the chicken rooting around in the dirt there was no one about. The chicken, a gift from Mrs Choy, was certainly getting fatter on scraps brought home from the farm and the stale leftovers from Mrs Ong's kitchen. Jen wondered if the chicken knew it was being fattened up for the Chinese New Year, she felt sorry for the poor animal.

Lee had refused to go to the farm with Tam that morning. Instead he opted to join Min to visit Mrs Ong, ostensibly to help in her kitchen. Jen smiled when she thought of Lee helping in the kitchen, he was about as useful as a pair of paper chopsticks.

After a long drink of water Jen sat back down to continue her sewing. She picked up one of the front panels for the blouse and pinned it to one of the back panels and then stood back to admire her needlework. Satisfied that she was on the right track she sewed them together. She felt the sleeves were too complicated and left them for her mother to finish off. Before she could start on the second blouse Lian had woken up and came downstairs to see how she was doing.

'The pinafores look good, you've done well,' Lian said, and then she saw the blouse. 'Waaah! What have you done?' she exclaimed.

Jen looked baffled. She looked at the blouse that her mother had picked up and held out like a piece of evidence in court.

'You forgot to change the thread, you can't sew white cotton with blue thread,' she said with almost a smile.

'Oh! I... I didn't know,' she answered feeling quite silly.

Lian seeing Jen's expression, her hand over her mouth, eyes wide, suddenly felt chastened. Her face softened and she said consolingly, 'It's only a small mistake. If you unpick it I will do it for you, it won't take long.'

'I can't do the sleeves either. Sorry!'

'It's fine, I will do it, you made a good job of the pinafores. You will look really smart on Monday.'

Jen felt a tingle all the way down her spine.

A few rays of the setting sun found their way through the kitchen window and glinted off the enamel plate, casting a glow to the dish of braised pork.

'The pork tastes wonderful. It's very kind of Mrs Ong to cook us a beautiful dish,' Lian said. It was the first time in weeks since she joined her children at the dinner table.

'Yes! And I helped to carry it home from the market,' Lee said tucking into another large piece of meat. His chopsticks were going from bowl to mouth at quite a frantic pace.

'I helped too!' Min raised her voice.

'Lee, slow down, you'll choke eating so fast,' Lian was looking at Lee with disapproval. 'No one is fighting you for food!' Lian added.

'Ah Ma,' Tam addressed his mother with his chopsticks poised halfway to his mouth, 'I asked Farmer Choy today if he wants a permanent helper in the farm. He said that he would employ me if I was not going back to school,' Tam finished quietly and looked across at Jen for support.

'But you are going back to school!' Lian smiled fondly at him. 'I could see you like going to the farm, but more important for you to go to school. You need an education if you want to earn a good living.'

On the other side of the table Jen was thinking that

wasn't what her mother said when she told her that she wanted to stay in school. 'Perhaps,' Jen paused, 'Tam wants to be a farmer,' she said.

Tam, catching on, said, 'Yes, Ah Ma, I think farming is a good way of earning a living. People need to eat, someone has to grow the vegetables and rear the animals… and I enjoy working on the farm much more than reading in class.'

'Tam, you are too young to leave school… you need to read and write well to get a good job. Before your father died he said if he were educated we would have a better life. If your father was alive today he would insist you stay in school.'

'But he isn't alive…' Tam stopped when he saw the colour drained from his mother's face, but he still felt very aggrieved.

'That's no way to talk to your mother!' Lian said sharply.

'Sorry! Sorry, Ah Ma, I don't mean to upset you, I don't really like school,' Tam said as he put his chopsticks down and kept his head bowed.

Lee and Min continued eating as if nothing had happened. Jen felt her heartbeat quicken. She didn't know whom she felt for most – her mother for keeping to tradition and doing what she thought was best for her children, or Tam for having to make a choice and then denied that choice.

By now everyone had stopped eating, Lee because the pork had all gone, Min was full, and the others had lost their appetite. Jen stood up and started to clear the dishes.

'Lee, go and fetch some water from the well for Min to have a wash,' Lian said.

'Why can't she wash in here? There's water in that urn,' Lee complained.

'Please do as I ask, Lee, I don't want anymore of your backchat!'

187

Jen got hold of Lee and Min and walked them through the back door and out of earshot.

Chapter Twenty-One

Unusually for Tam he slept badly. It was still dark outside when he untangled himself from Lee's arms and legs and crept downstairs. He sat on the bottom step rubbing the sleep from his eyes and looked about him. The house was quiet and all around him was still and familiar. He rested his elbows on his knees and cupped his chin in his hands; his eyes followed a cockroach as it wound its way across the mud floor and disappeared behind a piece of timber. The upright wooden stake, a support for the main wall of the house was crumbling, a pile of wood dust had gathered at the bottom. Tam stuck his foot out and wedged his big toe into the hole in the timber, he waited for the cockroach to re-appear. His mind wandered, and he debated if cockroaches had to make difficult decisions, or do mother cockroaches make all the decisions like his own mother.

He had failed to convince his mother that leaving school would be to his advantage, and when he said that she was wasting money by sending him back to school she got really angry. After much talking he did persuade her that if he failed his entrance exams to secondary school in a year's time she would not insist that he tried again but allow him the dignity of leaving. He hated the thought of being put back a year and re-do the exams the following year with the younger pupils. A knot of anger twisted in his stomach, humble he may be, but even he had some pride in his lean muscular body. But respect for his mother had to come before his own choice for the time being. His

189

twelfth birthday was coming up soon, not a boy anymore but a long way from being a man.

He seldom thought of his father, but at that moment he wished he was alive and that he could have a man-to-man talk with him about his future. Of late he had been having those conversations with Farmer Choy and found the latter easy to confide in and much more in tune with his own wishes for the future. He let out a long sigh that echoed around the stillness in the room. Standing up he stretched himself and yawned until his jaws clicked. He muttered to himself and went out to the backyard for a wash.

Lian was already awake when Tam made his way down the stairs. She had spent part of the night lying awake going through all the options she could have given him. She felt the one she decided was the best way out. She was aware and equally irked that it was Jen and not Tam who was the more academic of the two. She so wanted her sons to do well, having sons was an insurance to cushion her own life in later years. That was the order of things in life and order gave Lian security.

She reflected on her own childhood – the elusive father, her poor humiliated mother, the untimely death of her birth mother, her own husband's short life; and what became of her own brother? Questions, questions and more questions. Nothing was constant, nothing was certain, Lian rolled over on to her side and stifled a sob. Her children were growing up, one day they might all leave home and travel far away and she might not see them again! The more she thought about her destiny the more dispirited she felt. The tears swam out of her eyes in a continuous flow until her pillow was sodden. She turned the pillow over and before long that side was wet with tears too.

The night before she found her troubled mind had kept her awake until the early hours of the morning when her dreams took over. It was all a jumble, one moment she was talking to her mother and then suddenly her husband would appear and then disappear. She called out to him each time he appeared but he seemed unable or reluctant to speak. Her children's faces showed up when her back was turned, she knew they were her children because she heard them talking to each other. When she tried to turn around to speak with them she found that her feet were too heavy for her to move and her neck was too stiff for her to swivel her head round. It was all so frustrating and depressing. It was a relief when she woke and realised that it was all a bad dream.

Jen was having a dream of a different kind. She was late for school. All her classmates were lined up in their smart uniforms standing in a perfectly straight line watching her. They tittered and jeered when she entered the hall. Patricia was nowhere to be seen. She heard someone whisper that Patricia had left the country and was at that precise moment in an aeroplane flying off with her father to England. She decided that it was malicious gossip; she was probably in the toilet. Having decided that, she straightened up, brought her shoulders back and then strode proudly to the front of the queue only to be told that she was in the wrong class. Oh! The shame of it all! Jen woke fighting with her blanket and calling out for Patricia. She lay there for some minutes trying to separate her dream from reality before falling back to sleep and dreaming some more.

As Lian got up, Jen followed. A bucket of freshly drawn water from the well splashed onto her face was as invigorating as an hour's running on the spot Jen thought as she dried her face off with the threadbare towel that the whole family shared. The kettle was boiling merrily when she came back into the kitchen and she saw her mother scooping a spoonful of ground coffee grains into the dented coffee pot. Her spirit lifted a little, life might get back to normal, she hoped. They had hardly spoken, each mulling over the events of the past few days and pondering over the uncertainty of the future. They went about their morning ritual like two cogs in a wheel of living – Jen to do the washing, Lian back to her sewing.

The herbal remedy had done Lian a power of good, her chest had felt less painful and her coughing was more intermittent. She had also slept much more and eaten at least two meals a day. But Lian thought she was poorer, she hadn't done any sewing for three days and some of her money had gone to pay for her medicine. As she was feeling so much better she felt the need to convince Mrs Ong that it would not be necessary for her to see the herbalist again. Sometimes she found the older lady too outspoken and opinionated, but she couldn't deny that she had been very kind and considerate towards her and her children. She let out a long sigh and started up her old machine, her mother's old machine. She stopped and looked at it again, she remembered watching Mrs Tang sitting at the table just like her then, head bowed, lips pursed, one hand on the wheel and the other guiding the cloth along. She took in a deep breath, she wondered if spirits do survive the body after death, she hoped so.

Sunday was such a strange day as far as Jen was concerned. She knew that Patricia and her family considered it an important day for the family. But then Patricia had a different kind of family, they were Catholics, they went to church and had family gatherings unlike Jen's family where one day merged into another in a cycle of work and more work. There was no school on Sunday, but no fun either, just much quieter as most of the shops were shut. Jen sat on the edge of the well, the washing lay at her feet and she stared hard at the ground; what, she wondered, was the meaning of life? She felt so empty sometimes; when she didn't feel empty she was filled with dread and fear. She was fearful of the future and what it held for her and her family.

Her eyes wandered over to the house, it was falling down she mused. The roof leaked, there were more nails in the wooden walls than timber, the mud floor in the kitchen flooded whenever there was a heavy downpour. She looked at her own hands, there were calluses on her palm where the flesh should have been soft, the skin on the back of her hand was criss-crossed with fine lines, and her knuckles were red raw through constant immersion in soapy water.

Jen's quiet contemplation was soon shattered by the shape of Lee running a jagged path to the lavatory. He was followed swiftly by Min, and they were both giggling into their hands. Lee slammed the lavatory door shut with a bang and left Min standing outside pleading with him to hurry up.

'What's so funny?' Jen asked her sister.

Min looking flushed and still giggling said, 'Brother Lee, he's making naughty noises.' She giggled some more and pinched her nose at the memory of Lee's 'naughty noises'.

Mrs Ong popped round after lunch to remind Lian she would be going to the village between nine and ten the next morning and asked if that was a good time for Lian.

'Are you looking forward to going back to school?' she asked Jen.

'Yes, I am, Mrs Ong,' Jen answered with a half smile.

'I'm not,' Lee shouted from across the room. Smack! And smack again – Lee had one of his flip-flops in his hand and he was swiping a fly that had landed on a stain on the floor.

'So what do you like doing instead?' Mrs Ong asked.

'I want to join a ship and go to sea.'

'Can you swim then?'

'No, you don't have to swim, you'll be in a boat,' he replied contemptuously.

'Lee! You are very rude,' Lian admonished her son. 'Now apologise to Mrs Ong!' she commanded. Secretly she wished that Tam had more of Lee's brashness.

'Boys will be boys, Lian, don't worry about it,' she said. Mrs Ong liked Lee's spirited nature, she reckoned he would go far in a world where 'One who shouts the loudest will be heard the clearest,' she thought.

Before she went to bed that evening Jen ironed her new school uniforms. She admired them from every angle and sniffed the newness of the material before she hung them up on hangers made out of a length of bamboo and a piece of string. Her plimsolls were washed and whitened and lined up alongside those of her brothers. She had dug out her brother's old school shirts and shorts and pressed them ready for the morning. As she ironed, she let her thoughts roam and whenever she came upon any unhappy thoughts she skipped over them. In her young life she had encountered too many unhappy events to give them space, instead she concentrated on the happier events to come.

She felt a shiver of excitement at the prospect of going back to school though she worried whether Patricia would be in the same class as her. But what worried her most was whether her former bullies were in also the same class too, she hoped not. She wasn't afraid of them but their constant taunting and gossiping got on her nerves and made her really, really cross.

Just before she went to bed Jen lit a bunch of joss sticks, knelt before the altar and kowtowed a hundred times. She asked the Gods and the spirits of her ancestors to make it possible for her to stay in the same class as Patricia and keep those bullies away from her. She prayed with her eyes shut for her mother's health, for Tam that he may do better in school, for Lee that he may grow up soon and behave better, and to keep Min safe. After she had embedded the joss sticks into the urns she returned to kneeling in front of the altar and kowtowed another hundred times. She reasoned that if she wanted something that much she must show humility and sincerity.

She blew out the candle, her only source of light, and fumbled in the dark to the bedroom. A gentle wind was blowing and the rhythmic patter of raindrops on the corrugated-iron roof sent her into a dreamless sleep.

Chapter Twety-Two

'If you wait long enough for the clouds to clear you will see daylight!' another one of Mrs Ong's sayings. It didn't make sense then but suddenly it speared Jen's mind with its clarity and woke her up. She padded downstairs, fumbled on the windowsill for the box of matches and lit one to check the time on the small wind-up clock. Five-thirty, too early to get ready for school she lamented, but as she was up she might as well start the fire and boil the kettle to make the coffee. Out of the corner of her eyes she spied two rats drinking from a depression in the floor at the base of the water urn. She watched them idly and waited for them to leave before she took the lid off the urn and topped the kettle up with fresh water.

She washed, and brushed her teeth carefully; pulling a comb through her wet hair she winced as the knots and tangles got caught between the fine teeth of the comb. She checked her face in the mirror and then pinned her hair back one way and then another. She looked into the mirror again, she raised her eyebrow and then tilted her face and decided she preferred her right side better. Her lips were full; her nose though straight was pressed too close to her face. She gave her nose a pinch and narrowed her eyes, that was not an improvement either she thought. She smiled at the thought of Patricia's protruding teeth and she decided that she preferred her own face after all.

She smiled to herself as she did the buttons up on her school blouse. When she pulled the pinafore over her head she shivered with joy and ran downstairs and picked up the mirror. She held it at arm's length to check how she looked; she brought the mirror to her right side and then her left and then her front. She liked what she saw and with a flourish she did a curtsey to the water urn.

She woke Tam and Lee up and gave them breakfast. Tam walked around as if in a daze and Jen had to remind him to get dressed for school. He looked decidedly unhappy but he kept his feelings to himself. Lee grumbled because it was too early to be up and he complained some more because Tam was holding him up brushing his teeth, there was only one toothbrush between them. Jen had bought a new one for herself on Saturday, but she wasn't going to share it with Lee.

The school bell rang at seven-thirty sharp. Patricia was still looking for Jen. She hoped that her friend was not late; in her school bag were several books that she had acquired from her cousin Mary, and she was keeping them for Jen. It was her mum Suzie who suggested keeping Mary's textbooks for Jen and Patricia could have new ones as her dad was paying for all her schools books.

Jen had arrived in school five minutes before the bell which left her little time to look for Patricia, but she did however spot the trio of adversaries – Bee Bee, Meena, and Wei Wei. The gang of three were talking among themselves and eyeing up the opposition. Jen looked around her new surroundings, this part of the school was alien territory to her and she felt nervous.

In her last year at primary school, which was right next-door, this side of the fence felt like another country to her, even though she had often stood at the dividing fence looking in awe at the older pupils. She had often told herself that they must be very clever to get into secondary school and here she was standing on the same side of the fence as they were. For a very brief moment she felt light-headed that she was now in Form 1, and next year she would be automatically moved up to Form 2 and then 3.

She would have to sit for another exam to gain entry to Form 4 then 5. She suppressed a smile as she surveyed all the first year girls; she recognised their smart new uniforms, and how they huddled in groups talking in subdued tones.

A nun was standing on a podium, addressing the school through a microphone. 'Good Morning!'

'Good morning, Sister Pious' echoed around the fields, bounced off the concrete floors and walls and rippled along the long corridors.

'Could all the pupils in Forms 2, 3, 4, and 5 please line up over here, here and here,' she waved her arms about like a conductor in a musical arena. 'Those who are starting Form 1, please wait over there until I call for you.' There was a lot of shuffling and talking until the nun boomed, 'Please be quiet, girls! Now! Pupils! Could you all line up according to your class please? Thank you. When I ring my bell,' she lifted up a hand bell to demonstrate, 'you move off to your class in an orderly fashion,' she finished on a high note. Sister Pious gave her hand bell two hefty swings and the peel of the bell sent the girls smartly to their classes.

Patricia caught a glimpse of Jen and waved, she was about to wave back when the microphone crackled into life again, 'Good Morning, Form 1! Welcome! Please listen carefully, when I call your name, you walk up here quickly and form an orderly line. There are five classes, A to E, and I will call those in class A first and so on.'

In the silence of the assembly hall Jen heard her heart beat violently against her chest. She would soon find out if Patricia was in her class. Suddenly the silence was broken by the entry of five teachers who smiled and spoke to each other and Sister Pious in turn. All the girls craned their necks trying to see if they could identify the teachers – they were all female; one was in a sari, one in a grey suit and the others were wearing dark skirts and complimentary tops.

Sister Pious was introducing the teachers; Jen had missed what she was saying. She saw the teachers move around until they were standing next to each other; she assumed the one standing nearest to the nun was the form teacher for Class A, but she wasn't sure. She wished she had paid more attention and prayed that she wasn't the first to be called to assemble in front of two hundred pupils.

There were more whisperings between the nun and the teachers and then one of them stepped forward and the nun faced her microphone, 'When I call your name you line up in front of Miss Perez, your teacher for Class A. I will call you in alphabetical order,' Sister Pious announced.

Jen sighed with relief. Her knees were a bit shaky and her arms felt weak too as she transferred her school bag to her other hand. There wasn't much in her bag, as she still had to get all her textbooks for that year. The wickerwork bag held her pencil case, her dictionary, several new exercise books, a one-foot ruler and an old exercise book for scrap. She hoped that she would receive her textbooks soon as she was impatient to read them, and then felt a stab of fear, what if she didn't get the scholarship after all, how was she going to get the money to buy all the books she needed for that year?

It was the second time that Sister Pious was calling out over the microphone, 'Lau Li Jen,' before Jen realised she was being called to line-up with her classmates. As she pushed her way through she looked up and caught the eyes of Bee Bee and her friends. She felt a delicious sense of mischief rising in her, she looked Bee Bee in the eye and winked, in reply she received a hard stare. She was in such a euphoric state that she didn't care how much she was being stared at. Once she was standing in-line she remembered that Patricia was still standing with the masses, and she immediately scanned the sea of faces for her friend.

It took half an hour before all the pupils in Form 1

were finally allocated their places. To Jen's elation the 'three musketeers' were not in her class but neither was Patricia. She felt sad that Patricia was in Class C even though she would see her every day in their break-time. Jen looked across the second row of pupils on her right and saw Patricia smiling and waving at her, she smiled back and mouthed 'see you at morning break,' as Miss Perez introduced herself and welcomed her pupils before taking them to the class.

The room was at the end of a long and airy corridor. On one side was the bicycle shed where dozens upon dozens of gleaming chrome handlebars reflected the sunlight back into the room. Stretched across the other side of the classroom were the playing fields. There were three doors on each side of the classroom but no windows. Jen took a seat behind one of the sloping desks at the back of the class by the end door. There were forty pupils in her class – a mixture of colour, culture, and languages but only English was to be spoken within the school grounds they were told.

Miss Perez introduced herself, she spoke with an accent, her voice was high-pitched and she rolled her 'r' and emphasised her 'eth' and 'ed' in a most forceful manner, Jen thought. She had jet-black wavy hair that had been cut very short to tame the curls and they looked like they had been stuck down with grease, every hair in its rightful place. Her black skirt clung to her slim hips and her white top had tiny motifs on the collar and across her chest. The brightness of the shirt seemed to show off her dark brown skin. Her eyes were like pools of dark liquid that darted in all directions at once. Jen was sure that she could see all the way round the room all at the same time too.

The desks were arranged in rows of twos; Jen had taken the one in the furthest corner by the door, overlooking the bicycle shed. On her left sat a rather sad-faced girl with thick-rimmed glasses. Jen had never seen her before;

she knew most of the girls who came from the same primary school as she did. She wondered if she was a boarder, she knew that the Convent took in boarders from outlying areas.

'Now, class,' Miss Perez was addressing the class from the platform in front of the blackboard, 'I want you to copy down your Timetable.' She drew lines on the blackboard and filled in the squares with words like, Maths, English Lit, Domestic Science, Religious Knowledge, Geography – and then one that Jen had never encountered before, 'Moral'. It was the first lesson of every day and it was only a half hour long, unlike all the others which ran for forty-five minutes. She puzzled over it but decided not to ask silly questions on her first day.

Snivelling from her neighbour made Jen turn her head ever so slightly, she didn't want to appear nosey, and saw the girl dabbing her eyes with her handkerchief. She was used to sitting next to Patricia, who was always laughing and joking, that she was at a loss how to react. She wasn't sure if she was to alert her teacher about her snivelling classmate or say something to the girl herself. In the end she decided to ignore the periodic sobbing and eye dabbing but wished the teacher would pay more attention to her pupils under her charge.

Miss Perez was saying something again. 'When you have all finished with the blackboard, please come up to my desk, one at a time to register, this way I may get to remember your name and face sooner. Class!' she smacked her table with the ruler, a hush fell and everyone looked up, 'when you get up please lift the chair away and not let it scrape the floor,' she said. Then she sat down and put her knees together.

It was Jen's turn to register, she remembered to tilt her chair and lift it away before she slipped out from behind her desk. She held her head up and walked down the aisle towards Miss Perez's table and dutifully gave her name.

The teacher looked her up and down and wrote her name down on the register without making any comments. The brief eye contact between them gave Jen an impression that made her heart sink to the floor. When she finished writing she nodded and Jen was dismissed.

When the bell rang for morning break all the girls stood up at once and scraped their chairs on the concrete floor. Miss Perez's eyes disappeared into the top of her head and her lip pulled together like a string bag. She announced that the class may go for their break but most of the girls were already out of the door. The girl next to her, Grace, was still sitting down blowing her nose; Jen waited, she was desperate to speak to Patricia but she was worried about Grace who had been crying off and on for two hours.

'Are you sick?' Jen asked.

She shook her head, 'I'm fine, just homesick,' she answered and stood up slowly.

Jen hesitated, 'Are you coming for your break?'

'You go ahead, I'm going back to my room for a minute.'

'Okay.' Jen walked off to look for Patricia, so Grace was a boarder she thought.

Patricia was waiting for her behind one of the columns along the corridor. She jumped out at Jen as she walked past.

'Oh! You scared me,' Jen slapped Patricia in the arm. She beamed at Patricia and they both spoke at once.

'So what do you think?' Patricia asked.

'Think of what?'

'The school, the teacher, being here…?' Patricia was clucking her tongue at Jen.

'Okay I suppose.'

'Okay! Stop being funny, you are not funny at all!'

'I'm serious. Who's your teacher, what's she like?'

'A cross between a dragon and a chitchat,' Patricia guffawed.

Jen laughed in spite of herself, 'How can someone be

202

between a dragon and a chitchat, one's big and one's so titchy,' Jen said waving her arms and curling her fingers to demonstrate her point. 'What's her name? Is she the one in the suit?'

Patricia nodded and rolled her eyes, 'that's her, Miss Tan! All she said was, "stop talking, stop playing with your pencils and pay attention if you want to get off on time," she got on my nerves!' Patricia said and chuckled.

'Miss Perez is not much better, she's so stiff, and the way she speaks makes me want to laugh all the time,' Jen said.

'Let's forget the teachers, come on,' Patricia got hold of Jen's arm, 'let's see what we can have at the tuck shop.'

Jen only had ten cents to buy herself something for lunch; morning break was exactly that, a break from the classroom, but for Patricia any break was an eating break.

'I'll wait here for you, I don't want anything,' Jen said.

'I buying you a treat, my dad's given me lots of pocket money,' Patricia answered and dragged Jen off to the tuck shop.

Sitting under the shade of a large magnolia tree the two friends discussed their various views on life in general. They seemed united in their different home lives rather than divided by it, they were particularly united in avoiding Jen's bullies. Patricia had seen them at the tuck shop and had given them a cursory glance but with no acknowledgement of warmth or humour towards them. She disliked them for calling her names because she was half Chinese and half English and the fact that her parents were divorced and her father lived in another country. But what she hated them most for was taunting Jen about her ill-fitting clothes, the holes in her shoes, and Jen's lack of money for all the things they needed in school. Meena and Bee Bee were in her class, and she had made a point of sitting as far away from them as it was possible. Wei

Wei, was in Class B so there was one problem less to face every day.

'Hey Patricia! What is Moral class? What do you study in Moral? I've got to go to that class from seventy-thirty to eight o'clock every morning,' Jen pulled a face. 'Will you be there?'

'I don't have to attend moral class, I go to Catholicism class instead.'

'Why is that then?'

'Because I am a Catholic, and you are not, so you attend moral class.'

'What do you learn in moral class?'

'Morals!'

'What are Morals?'

'Well you know!'

'No!… I don't know, so I'm asking you,' Jen was getting impatient.

'Well, you learn how to behave yourself, like not commit a sin and things like that,' Patricia wasn't entirely sure.

'I don't commit sins anyway! You've already said that I am not a Catholic, so how can I commit a sin?'

'Everybody commits sins, just because you're not a Catholic doesn't mean you don't.'

Jen eyed her friend and smiled faintly, 'I'll find out tomorrow morning and I'll tell you what they teach in Moral class,' Jen said with a nod.

'Oh, I nearly forgot, I've got some books for you, they are in my bag in class.'

'What books are they?'

'You know, text books for this year.'

'Don't you need them then?' Jen knew that Patricia usually had the books that her cousin Mary had the year before to save money.

'Nope! This year my dad's paying for all my books,' Patricia confirmed.

'Aren't you lucky,' Jen said feeling just a tinge of jealousy, but Patricia was frowning at her. 'What? What's wrong? Was it something I said?'

'No! You didn't say anything wrong.'

As ever the sensitive friend, Jen noticed the subtle change in her friend's mood. She moved closer and said quietly to Patricia, 'It's your dad isn't?'

Patricia was silent, she had a faraway look in her eyes.

The peel of the bell cut across their conversation. And as they walked off together to their respective classes Patricia said, 'My dad's flying back to England on Saturday.'

Jen was silent. She couldn't find the right words to console her friend, and wondered if it was far worse to lose someone forever, like her own father, or like Patricia, who was unable to see her father often because he lived half a world away.

Chapter twenty-Three

Miss Perez had taken up position behind her desk on the raised platform. She held up a textbook, her eyes scanned the room and waited until she was satisfied that she had the attention of forty pairs of eyes. Jen thought those liquid dark eyes spoke volumes. And when she spoke her voice was like a sharp stone striking an empty can.

'I expect some of you may already have the required textbooks for this year, if you haven't please try to get them by next week. Did all of you get the book list for this year?' Heads nodded, a few braver ones answered and some ignored her question. 'That reminds me, Lau! Lau Li Jen!' Jen blinked and jerked her head up on hearing her name. 'Stand up when I'm talking to you,' she commanded.

Jen stood up but forgot to lift her chair out of the way, the scraping of wood on concrete sounded like a violin being played badly. Jen winced. Miss Perez looked disapproving. 'Sorry,' she whispered.

'Thank you, Lau.' It was customary to be addressed by a person's surname in school, but Jen was so used to be addressed by her last name that she was inclined to ignore anyone calling her by her surname. 'Before you go for your lunch break could you please go to see Sister Pious in her Office.' All thirty-nine pairs of inquisitive eyes turned in her direction, any pupil called before Sister Pious was either in trouble or in merit. As it was the first day of secondary school for the class they were even more curious. Even Grace stopped snivelling and looked at Jen with curiosity.

Whisperings went round the room. 'Sit down, Lau, and the rest of you settle down.' After a short pause the whisperings didn't show signs of stopping. Miss Perez with one hand on her hip raised her voice another octave, 'I am waiting for all of you to finish talking!'

By this time Jen was in a world of her own, a quiver of delight zigzagged through her, she knew for sure that the scholarship was indeed hers. She wanted to run out of the class and tell Patricia the news, but one look at the teacher told her that it was out of the question. The rest of the morning's lessons went too slowly for Jen. She fidgeted and played catch with her pen and slid her bottom back and forth on the hard wooden chair.

When the bell rang she shot out of the room before Miss Perez had given the class permission to leave. She looked for Patricia among the throng of white and blue. She was being swept along the corridor by the surging bodies going for their lunch break. Standing on tiptoe she looked up and down the corridors, and then she waited for a couple of minutes standing on the second step of the stairs for a better view, but Patricia didn't appear. She checked the clock on the wall of one of the classes and decided she had better go to the Office, it wasn't wise to keep Sister Pious waiting she told herself, especially on her first day.

Jen followed the instructions that Miss Perez had given her – down the corridor, turn left, up the stairs, turn left again, down another corridor and the office was on her left. The place was quiet as a grave, even the typewriter looked bored. Jen stood at the opened doorway looking in, there were three large windows on the far wall and the bright sunlight slanting through made her look very small and insignificant. Someone coming out of a side room made her jump, 'Can I help you?' the stranger asked.

'Ah... m, I am Jen, Lau Li Jen,' she stammered, 'I... I am here to see Sister Pious.'

'I see,' she smiled, 'Sister Pious's office is that way, second door on your right.'

'Thank you,' Jen dipped her head and walked further down the corridor.

On the door was a big bold plaque that said 'Sister Pious' on it. Jen stood and examined the heavy door and the gleaming doorknob. She adjusted her uniform and straightened the pleats and checked that her plimsolls were clean; she inhaled deeply and knocked very lightly on the door.

'Come in,' a heavy-accented voice called from the other side.

Jen turned the doorknob very cautiously and slipped in noiselessly. Sister Pious was sitting behind her desk. Several piles of books were neatly stacked on the table and there was one opened in front of her. She looked up, not a flicker of a smile passed her face. Jen stood very still with her hands by her sides and her eyes were fixed on the nun's spectacles. She was wearing a white habit with a wimple and apart from her nose and lips her spectacles were the only visible part of her. Her arms were folded across her chest and her hands were hidden in the long loose sleeves.

'And who are you?' the nun asked.

Jen moistened her lips with the tip of her tongue before answering, 'I am Lau, Lau Li Jen, Sister Pious. My teacher, Miss Perez told me you wanted to see me,' Jen said pronouncing each word slowly and carefully.

'Ah yes, Lau, yes, now where is my piece of paper,' she shuffled the books and papers around on her table. 'Yes, I've got it here… Mm! So! You are Lau Li Jen.'

Jen nodded and suddenly remembered where she was, 'Yes, Sister Pious, I am Lau Li Jen.'

The nun gave Jen a once-over with her blue eyes and then stood up and extended her hand, 'Congratulations for getting the scholarship. This is the confirmation letter, and this is the voucher for the books. You take the voucher to the bookshop downstairs and they will supply you with all the necessary books. The school will pay your monthly fees, and all you have to do is work hard and show your appreciation.' She paused and gave Jen a few moments to digest the information. 'Now, have you got any questions?' She sat back down, rubbing her chin with a forefinger and thumb, studying Jen with her keen eyes for the first time.

Jen's hands shook as she looked down at the two pieces of paper in her hand. She wanted to know what would happen if she didn't do as well in the next year, would they take the scholarship away from her, but she was too nervous to ask; the room, Sister Pious, the books, the chair, the whole world was making her nervous. Instead she said, 'Thank you, Sister Pious, I will work very hard, Thank you.' She stood for a few moments longer wondering what to do next.

'You may go now,' Sister Pious said with a nod.

Jen slipped out of the room, closed the door quietly, looked around and then ran down the corridor and took the stairs two at a time. When she got to the bottom of the stairs Patricia was waiting for her.

'Hello! How did it go?' Patricia asked.

'How did you know where I was?' Jen was pleased and surprised.

'I asked one of your nosey classmates,' Patricia said wrinkling her nose, 'they thought you were in trouble – were you? And what's that you've got there?'

'I did look for you. Here, you have a read of this and tell me what it says,' she handed the letter to Patricia.

Patricia read and re-read the letter before she looked up and smiled broadly showing all her teeth. 'Congratulations! You've got the scholarship! I am so happy for you, I want to hug and kiss you,' she said teasingly knowing Jen did not hug or kiss.

Jen smiled and cocked her head, 'Thank you, I am really pleased too. What time is it?' she hadn't eaten any lunch and her tummy was making loud gurgling noises.

'I've saved you a sandwich, you won't have time to buy anything from the canteen now,' Patricia said looking at her watch.

They both walked out towards the playing fields, on the way Jen stopped by a tap and drank copiously from it. The bell went before they reached their spot of shade under the magnolia tree.

Jen looked at the clock on the wall above the blackboard, it said twenty-five minutes past one. Another five minutes to go. She started putting her pen and pencils away. Grace was still busy scribbling in her notebook. Jen looked out over the bicycle shed, she wished she had a bicycle. It would make life easier for her in the morning, to cycle to school. Catching the bus every morning was so tiresome, a long walk to the bus stop, and another long walk from the station to her school and besides it must be cheaper cycling to school she thought.

Grace nudged her in the arm, 'The teacher's talking to you,' she said.

Jen turned round to see Miss Perez standing on her podium looking straight at her. 'Is something interesting going on outside?' she asked raising her eyebrows.

'Sorry, no, I mean no Miss Perez, there isn't anything interesting outside.'

'Then could you please pay attention while you're in my class, keep your daydreaming for after school. Have you been to see Sister Pious?'

'Yes I have, Miss Perez, thank you.'

'Class dismissed,' she said, her voice tight and shrill.

Some of the older pupils were already scrambling for their bicycles; many more were running across the field to the opened gate. Jen picked up her bag, took out the book list and read the titles as she made her way to the bookshop.

The bookshop stayed open until four o'clock in the first two weeks of a new term and thereafter was only opened for a couple of hours in the morning. The local bookshop ran the business; the school took a cut of the profit and also charged a rent for allowing them to use the premises. It worked well for both these parties, but for those pupils whose parents were unable to purchase all the required textbooks the system was very unforgiving. No money, no books, no negotiation.

Many of the pupils from poorer families bought their books from the pupils of the previous year at half the price; in that way many more children were able to have an education. The school did not keep a supply of textbooks for their pupils as education was not then compulsory nor was it necessary for any family to send their children to school. Those children given the opportunity to attend school did so with the knowledge that they were privileged and if they were not able to buy or borrow the necessary books from friends, none complained. Half an education was better than none was their motto.

Jen was waiting in the queue for the books when she remembered that she had promised to see Patricia after school by the gate, the queue was long and it moved slowly. There were only two people serving behind the counter and at least half the pupils from Form 1 were waiting to be served. Jen was getting restless, she hated letting Patricia down, but if she didn't try to get her books on that day the supply may run out and she might have to wait days and sometimes weeks for more books to arrive from abroad.

'Hello, Jen! I see you're on your own. Where's your joker, the one with the strange colour hair and sticky-out teeth?' Titters and sniggering erupted behind her.

Jen looked round and gave her meanest stare at Bee Bee, Wei Wei and Meena.

Bee Bee gave Jen a poke in the arm when she continued to ignore her, 'I am talking to you,' she said.

'Yeah, we are being friendly and you are so rude,' Meena said.

'Perhaps she's lost her tongue,' Wei Wei said, 'let's help her find it.'

The trio pretended to search the ground and look around each other. 'You're not standing on it are you?' Bee Bee addressed Meena in mocked anger.

'Of course I'm not standing on it, it's her that's standing on it,' Meena replied pointing to Jen, her finger almost touching Jen's cheek.

'I think she keeps it in her school bag, that's why she's holding it across her chest,' Wei Wei said.

The three girls decided it wasn't much fun when Jen continued to ignore them, so they took their game to Jen. Wei Wei tugged at Jen's school bag while Meena tried to prise her fingers from the handle. Bee Bee got hold of Jen from the back to stop her wriggling free. None of the other girls took much interest, as they were more concerned with getting to the front of the queue.

Wei Wei noticed the piece of paper in Jen's hand and snatched it off her. It was the book voucher.

'Give it back!' Jen snapped.

'Come and get it back!' Wei Wei laughed.

Jen saw her future in that voucher and Wei Wei's grubby fingers were all over it. She lost her temper. She grabbed Wei Wei by the ear and pulled as hard as she could. Wei Wei let out a piercing scream, Jen refused to let go. Instead she whispered menacingly, 'Give me that piece of paper back or I will tear your ear off.'

Meena and Bee Bee had stepped back from Jen on hearing Wei Wei's scream. They were surprised and shocked at Jen's reaction. From previous years Jen had behaved more like a mouse and it was Patricia who generally came to her rescue. A few of the other girls in the queue had gathered what was going on and had chosen to ignore Wei Wei's scream. Most of them knew the trio of reprobates from primary school and at one time or another had been on the receiving end of their bullying.

Jen casually removed the voucher from Wei Wei's fingers with one hand while her other hand was still around the latter's ear. 'You do that again I will bite your ears off and don't think I am bluffing,' Jen whispered in Wei Wei's ear as she loosened her hold on the ear.

Wei Wei rubbed her ear as tears welled up in her eyes from the pain. 'I am going to get you for this,' she hissed.

The three of them then regrouped and pushed past Jen to get to the front of the queue. Jen suddenly felt very tired and weary. She walked off to look for Patricia.

Patricia had waited for almost twenty minutes, seated in the back of her mum's car. Suzie had waited even longer; she was always the first at the school gate to ensure that she could park her little car near the main exit of the school. She knew that Patricia, due to her mixed parentage, came in for a lot of teasing from the other children and that generally happened outside the school compound. She had often stood watching from the school fence praying that her only child did not suffer too much at the hands of the bullies. So when Patricia asked her to wait for a little longer for Jen she agreed, her daughter's happiness was the most important thing in her life. She herself would never marry again and she would never have another child.

Apart from a few stragglers, the lane by the entrance of the school was almost deserted. Patricia got out of the car as soon as she saw Jen running across the field.

'There she is, Mum, I told you she would come,' Patricia said.

Jen was panting more with anger than exhaustion, 'I'm

213

sorry! Oh, hello, Auntie Suzie. I was trying to get my books… but there were too many people. I'll have to go back and wait. I've just come to tell you…'

'You are all red in the face, did you fall over?' Patricia asked.

'No, it's them!' Jen said furiously and turning her face and pointing a finger in the direction she had come from.

Suzie had got out of her car and came round to speak with Jen. 'Are those girls being nasty again? Would you like me to come with you to speak to them?'

'No! No thank you Auntie Suzie, I have already…' Jen stopped, realising that it was against school rules to fight and according to her mother nothing was achieved by fighting, not to mention the shame it would bring to the family.

'What did you do?' Patricia asked, her eyes wide with curiosity.

'I got hold of Wei Wei's ear and twisted it. I was so angry I wanted to pull it off!' Jen replied with anger and passion.

Patricia laughed, 'You should have called me; I wanted to see her face when you did that. Did she cry?'

'Patricia! That's not… it's not ladylike to fight, and it's wrong to hit,' Suzie tried to admonish Patricia.

'But, Mum, they are always getting on to Jen, you should see them. They are like cats. Sometimes I want to smack them myself, but I'll only hurt my hand,' said Patricia, justifying her case for Jen's retaliation.

'Just because they behave badly doesn't mean you have to—'

'It's all right, Auntie Suzie, I won't let Patricia get into trouble,' Jen said.

'Me! I never get into trouble,' Patricia said and rolled her eyes towards the heavens.

Jen laughed at her antics. Suzie looked away so that they couldn't see her having a sly smile.

'Oh, Jen, the books,' Patricia said as she crawled into the back seat of the car and hauled her bag out. 'These are the books... I don't know if you want them, if you don't it's okay. I know you've got the voucher for all the books...'

Thanks, thank you... could you keep them today, I've got to go back to the bookshop, there's too many for me to carry home...'

'Mum will take you home, won't you, Mum?'

'Of course I will, we'll wait here, you go and get your books.'

'I'll come with you,' Patricia said and ran off across the field before Suzie could protest. Watching her daughter holding on to Jen's hand in a show of friendship more than compensated for the long wait, besides, there was nobody at home waiting for her.

Chapter Twenty-Four

When Jen struggled through the back door laden with all her textbooks, she was feeling jubilant. The bookshop had all the books she needed and she even managed to make arrangements to sell the rest of her old books through Suzie. There were many school children like Jen and her family where books were a hard-to-come-by commodity.

'Big Sister! You're home,' Min greeted her.

'Hello, Min Min, have you been good?'

Min nodded, 'I've been very good, and, I've been helping... washing the dishes, sweeping the floor, and I saw the old man in the shop,' Min added excitedly.

'What old man in the shop? Where did you go?'

'In the village, that old man!'

'She saw the herbalist,' Lian interrupted. 'You're late, what time does school finish now?'

'I finished a long time ago, but I had to wait for the books,' Jen said and took her bag over to show her mother. She picked them out one at a time and read the titles out loud and explained what each subject meant. Lian couldn't read a word of English, but she was pleased that she had made the decision to send all her children to English schools; her reasoning was that since the English helped to banish the enemies from Malaya during the Second World War, they must be clever. And cleverness was respected the world over.

'Are they all free?' Lian asked. She hadn't quite grasped the concept of a scholarship.

216

'Yes, they are free to me because I've won their sponsorship. And they will also pay my school fees each month too.'

Lian took a few moments to digest all the new ideas that Jen was telling her. 'What about next year?'

'It's the same next year; the school will pay for my books and fees.'

'That's kind of them. What do you have to do in return?'

'Nothing.'

'Nothing?' Lian looked doubtful.

'I have to pass all my exams to show them that I was worth it.'

'What do the school get out of it?'

'Well, it's good for the school's reputation, so more students would want to go to that school,' Jen explained.

'I'm hungry,' Min said. She was bored with Jen and their mother's talk about school.

'Where's Tam and Lee, aren't they home yet?'

'They've gone to see a neighbour about Tam's books. Lee's got Tam's old books but Tam is still short…'

'Ah Ma,' Jen hesitated, 'what did the herbalist give you today, the same medicine?'

'No, my chest is better. Don't need strong herbs today. He gave me smaller packets, less bitter he said.'

'Shall I start the cooking or the ironing?'

'I iron, you cook. Later you must read your books, if your school pays your fees you must show them you deserve it,' Lian said.

Jen was rather taken aback. In the past reading and homework were something Jen did when she could fit them in between her housework. But Jen was pleased with the new arrangement; she rather enjoyed grappling with her homework than hauling buckets of water from the well. Her sense of joy was only marred by her worries about money for food for her family.

217

'What about taking the linen back to the hotel, what time will it be ready for me?'

'I've been thinking, maybe I should speak to Mrs Lim.' Lian paused and then added, 'Yes, I will go tonight, I must speak to the manager. We must change things. You look after Min and the boys...'

'Ah Ma, it's all right, I can take the laundry back and I will still have time to read my books,' Jen protested. Her mother's health was constantly on her mind.

'No, tonight I must see Mrs Lim. I want to talk to her about changing things. I want to put the price up and only take the laundry three times a week, every day is too much for you.'

Jen was astonished at the change of her mother's attitude. The mother Jen knew was always subservient, compliant, and lived her life by other people's philosophies. Her maxim in life was to live within the confines of her ancestral moral code. Jen had often wondered why her mother had allowed others to dictate how she should conduct her life, and as she got older she was at times irritated by her mother's lack of fighting spirit.

What Jen didn't know was that Lian had had plenty of time to think over the past years about how stale life had become. The hours she had spent bent over the sewing, washing and ironing, she had often berated herself for her inability to speak out. But the events over the past week and the many talks she had with Mrs Ong had made her realise that she must change things herself. She must leave the past where it belonged, in the past. The future, her future and her children's future, that's what she must build on. As Mrs Ong said, she has talent. Lian had never looked upon her beautiful sewing as a talent, merely a way of earning a living. She looked at the back of her hands, her fingers were bony and slender, the knuckles stood out like knots, not pretty but versatile.

She took a deep breath and exhaled deeply, she decided

that it wasn't going to be easy having to tell all her patrons that she was putting her prices up but it had to be done. Some of her patrons went back a long way, some of them had known her since she was nine years old when she threaded a needle for the very first time. She had her mother to thank for her expertise in turning a plain cloth into a garment to fit any size and shape. Lian smiled to herself as she recalled some of her fussy customers with oversized bodies making impossible requests. Her life was not without humour after all she thought as she thrust the hot iron onto the white cotton sheet spread out on the table.

Jen and her mother shared the golden glow from the kerosene lamp at the table, both absorbed in their own pursuits. The smell of new books, the sharpness of each new page, the way they rustled when the pages were turned and the neatness of the printing thrilled and grabbed her attention all evening. Her appetite for all knowledge new was voracious and she was impatient to read every page of every textbook.

Lian was also feeling pleased with herself. Mrs Lim, the hotel owner and manager was easy enough to persuade that a price increase was in order, but Lian had to use all her diplomacy to convince her that while her service was being reduced to three times weekly she was still getting the same service. Lian pointed out that daily delivery meant more money wasted on bus fares, and that meant she would have to put the price up further. Mrs Lim reluctantly agreed that Lian made a valid point and even invited her to have a bowl of noodles to celebrate their new agreement.

Jen sniffed as the herby brew filled the stagnant air; she gave the bubbling clay pot a cursory glance. 'Ma, should I take a look,' she nodded in the direction of the pot.

'Mm… the medicine? Yes, take a look.'

By now Jen had mastered the art of guessing the murky depths of a clay pot, she took the lid off and tilted the pot to the light, she blew on it to clear the rising vapour as she checked where the inky liquid came up to in the pot. 'I think it's nearly done, maybe another ten minutes and I'll pour it out for you.'

'Thank you. What are the books like, what kind of things do they teach you?' Lian asked. She had never been inside a school as a pupil because she was a girl; if she had been born a boy she would have been sent to school, she thought sadly.

Taken by surprise Jen looked at her mother open-mouthed. 'What, this book?' she asked, lifting the book in her hand higher towards her mother.

'Well, all the books,' Lian said feeling suddenly embarrassed. She had never asked nor been curious what her children actually learn in school.

'This one is about other countries, what kind of food they grow and what they export, that kind of thing.'

'Oh, I see. What countries are they then?'

'All the countries in South East Asia.'

'Why do they teach you that?'

'I suppose that what's they call education,' Jen answered cheekily.

Lian frowned and asked, 'What else do you learn in school?'

Jen picked up another book and said, 'This one tells you how plants grow and what kind of nutrients they need to produce better crops.'

'Do you think then, if someone wants to be a farmer, they have to study about such things?'

Jen knew where the conversation was going and decided to help it along. 'Of course some knowledge about plants will be important, but you don't have to read all about them in books. If you have someone who knows about farming to work with I think that would be better. You see, Ah Ma, you didn't learn to sew from a book…'

Lian was surprised how astute her daughter was. 'When you finish school what do you want to do?'

'I've got another five years before I finish school, I've plenty of time to think about it,' Jen replied. She wasn't ready to commit herself, neither did she feel confident enough to confide in her mother that her wish was to attend Sixth Form if money could be found to fund her.

'It's late, are you going to bed? Here, take this, I will forget in the morning, you need a little more food at school.'

Jen took the coins her mother gave her. 'Thank you, Ah Ma.' An extra ten cents for school lunch! Jen immediately made plans on what she could spend the money on; food was not on her agenda.

Lian went to bed with the herb potion sloshing inside her as she mounted the stairs. She felt good; she wasn't going to die after all. The herbalist had assured her that it would take a few weeks for her to regain all her strength. He advised her on the food she must eat to balance the heat and damp in her body.

Sleeping on the hard wooden floor had never been a problem for Lian; it just re-affirmed the hard life she had led. But on that night she thought a bed might be more comfortable. When her husband died she sold their bed to buy food for the family and she had been sharing the same floorboards with her children since. Where she had lost so much weight her shoulder blades were like knives on the wooden boards nipping and pinching her skin.

The following morning when the three older children had gone to school Lian got up and searched in the bottom of her wardrobe for the key to the locked drawer. She lifted the faded white paper lining and stuck her hands inside feeling for the small key. Her heart was pounding in her ears; she was about to do something she promised herself a long time ago that she would never do; to pawn the pieces of jewellery her mother and husband had given her. They were locked up in that drawer, without purpose or meaning. Life must have a purpose and meaning she decided.

She got Min out of bed and told her to wash and change as she was going for a bus ride into town. Min needed no further encouragement. As the youngest, she had missed out on most of the adventures of her older siblings.

'Where are we going, Mama?' she asked excitedly.

'Into town,' Lian answered distractedly. She was looking in the drawer; a glittering array of bracelets, necklaces and rings shimmered nostalgically at her. Memories of her mother and her husband Chee Kuan bounced around her head. She felt sad and sentimental in waves. She couldn't decide if she should pawn them all at once or one piece at a time. She picked up a jade bracelet that had once graced her mother's wrist. The smooth cold circular burnished brown gleamed in the half-light. A tear slid down her face and landed on the bracelet. The cold hard metals were not simply objects that she could exchange for money but they were memories that charted her life. Her fingers lingered over them as she recalled how each piece of jewellery marked the passage of time.

Min was standing on tiptoe with both hands on the side of the drawer trying to look inside. Her mother's motionless stance had aroused her curiosity. 'What's that?' she asked touching the bracelet with a finger.

'Let go!' she said as she prised Min's hands off the drawer.

'What are they?' Min asked again.

'Just something I want to take to the shop,' she answered as she slammed the drawer shut and locked it again.

They were about to leave when Mrs Ong turned up with a plate of cakes.

'You looking nice, Min,' she said.

Min was more interested in the plate of cakes.

'You going out, Lian?' Mrs Ong had a habit of stating the obvious.

Lian had put on her best blouse with matching trousers. Her scrubbed face was given a hint of powder made from ground rice. 'Yes, I'm going into town,' she said looking away.

'It would do you good to go out for a walk in town. You're looking better. I won't keep you… if you want to send Min over later when you need a rest…'

Lian was feeling irritated and embarrassed. Mrs Ong's impromptu appearance only served to increase her conflicting feelings about pawning the jewellery, but good manners prevailed and she said, 'Sorry, I forgot my manners, thank you for the cakes. Yes, I think Min would like to come over to see you later. Yes, Min?'

Min, her mouth full of sticky rice cake nodded in answer.

There were three pawnshops in town. Lian felt nervous and guilty as she held her purse firmly in her hand. After much deliberation she had picked up a gold bracelet that had belonged to her mother, it was the smallest item and probably the least expensive. She had no idea how much gold was worth and felt that her plan to pawn one piece of jewellery at a time was the best way to use her only asset left to her.

Lian visited all three pawnshops. She spoke quietly but bargained doggedly to get what she thought was the best price. In each shop she used the same tactic, when a price was given for the bracelet by the shopkeeper she upped it another twenty per cent. By the time she came out of the third shop she was worn out but felt pleased with herself.

In fact she was so pleased she bought a bowl of noodles and shared it with Min.

On the bus home she squeezed her purse to make sure that the bracelet was still in there. Now that she had worked out how much she could sell the bracelet for she was in no hurry to sell it, it was enough just to know how much it was worth. She had worked out that if she finished sewing all the garments that were sitting at home, the money she would get for them should cover the food, fuel, and bus fares for the next month. The money from the hotel laundry should provide for some extras for the Chinese New Year.

She got off the bus two stops early, she had a plan and she must carry it out before she lost her nerve. Min was tired, she didn't enjoy being dragged around town and they hadn't even bought anything, but Lian chose to ignore her complaints about her sore feet and empty stomach.

All in all it was a productive day. She visited most of her existing patrons in their homes. She thanked them all for their long patronage and she hoped that they would continue to do business with her, but she said that it was time to put her price up. She pointed out to them that she was still the cheapest, quoting the price of each garment as compared to the prices charged in the village shop. They were a bit put out but in truth they knew that they had had good services from Lian. Her price, in spite of the increase was still the most reasonable, and another ten per cent extra because of the coming Chinese New Year was not extortionate by comparison.

All her plans put into action, Lian walked into the village butcher's and bought a fresh piece of pork to cook for their evening meal. Min grumbled all the way home, but Lian, exhilarated by her day's accomplishments took no notice.

Chapter Twenty-Five

Jen's second day at school had not gone as smoothly as she would have wanted. She arrived at the gate just as the pupils were making their way to their respective classes. Hiding behind a column she waited until the last of the girls were passing and she slipped into line. When she walked past her class she slipped in through the last door to her chair, only to find someone sitting on it. She looked around quickly for a vacant seat but they were all occupied. She glanced across the room to where the teacher's table was, only to find a stranger staring at her. Miss Perez was not in the room.

'What's your name?' the teacher asked.

'Lau, Lau Li Jen,' came the nervous reply.

'What class are you in?'

'This class, Miss,' Jen thought, what a strange question.

'No, I mean what lesson should you be at,' the teacher had a melodious voice, and a lovely smile too, Jen thought she looked more like a film star than a teacher. She was wearing a pink cheongsam and her lipstick matched her dress.

For a brief moment Jen lost track of what was going on, she turned up in her class to find a lot of strangers in it and the teacher had transformed into a friendly smiley person. And then it hit her. She was supposed to attend Moral class from half seven to eight o'clock every morning. 'I'm sorry, I should be at my Moral class,' Jen said as she retreated from the classroom and into the corridor. As she walked along the long corridor past all the opened doors, distracting all the other students, she felt her face get hotter and her pace quickened. She tried to look into each class discreetly as she walked by to see if she recognised her classmates. By the time she reached the end of the corridor she had run out of ideas about what to do, she couldn't decide if she should go upstairs or go back the way she had come when along came Sister Pious. There was no hiding place and she had been spotted.

'Good morning! It's Lau isn't it?' Sister Pious asked.

'Good Morning, Sister Pious, yes, I'm… I am Lau Li Jen,' Jen replied with a quiver in her voice.

'And what are you doing in the corridor? Shouldn't you be in class?'

'I'm sorry; I was late. The bus was late,' Jen answered looking at her feet.

'That's no excuse! You just have to catch the earlier bus. Now go to your class.' Sister was just about to walk off when Jen decided that as she was already in trouble she might as well throw herself in deeper.

'I am trying to find my class, Sister Pious. I have Moral class this morning but I don't know where it is,' Jen said and looked Sister Pious in the eye.

The nun cast a critical eye over Jen and checked the papers in her hand. She shuffled them about and ran a finger across the page and then said, 'You should be in class Form 2B for your Moral class.'

'Thank you, Sister Pious, I will make sure that I'm not late again,' with that she ran up the stairs to find Form 2B.

All the pupils in Form 2B had their faces turned towards the front of the class. They were listening intently to the teacher, their eyes glazed over with awe and conviction. Jen felt awkward standing outside the door waiting to catch her attention. As the teacher swivelled her head round, a finger poised in mid air, a question on her lips, she noticed Jen standing erect and conspicuous.

'Are you attending this class?' Miss Ng asked.

'Yes, I am. I am sorry I'm late,' Jen hung her head in shame.

'Do come in and join us. There's a chair over there,' she waved her hand to her right.

Jen walked across the classroom to the vacant chair in the corner at the front of the class, aware that all eyes were trained on her. She sat down feeling flushed and embarrassed. She crossed and uncrossed her arms several times and finally rested them primly on her lap. She tried to look interested at Miss Ng when she stole a look at the clock on the wall. She was fifteen minutes late. It appeared that the teacher had been telling the class a story and Jen was annoyed with herself for missing it.

When the bell sounded for morning-break Patricia was waiting by her classroom door for Jen. She grabbed Jen's arm as she walked by. 'Didn't you see me? I've been waving like mad, look, my hand is about to fall off,' Patricia laughed.

Jen looked sombre. 'I'm sorry.'

'What's wrong? You look like you've seen a ghost.'

'No, but I've seen my teacher,' Jen said.

Patricia giggled and linked her arm with Jen's. 'Tuck shop here we come!'

'I was late this morning, and guess who caught me? Sister Pious! She must have told Miss Perez, so I got into more trouble. That's not the worst of it, those three were in the same Moral class as well!'

Patricia stopped walking and turned to face Jen, 'What! You mean Bee Bee and…'

Jen nodded, she couldn't believe her luck either.

'Poor you! Can you change class? It's only Moral class,' Patricia tried to console Jen.

'Never mind change class, after what Miss Perez said to me I will have to change to someone else. I don't think she likes me.'

'Teachers are not supposed to like their pupils, if they do…' Patricia was waggling a finger at Jen, 'if they do… I don't know what happens if they do,' Patricia chortled.

Jen burst into hysterical laughter. Patricia always knew how to make her feel better.

Bee Bee and her two friends had waited until lunch break to tease and provoke Jen. They had looked at each other meaningfully when Jen turned up late, and Wei Wei's ear was still sore where Jen had grabbed her the day before. They hatched a plan at their morning break and as soon as they had finished their lunch they went in search of Jen.

Patricia and Jen were sitting under the magnolia tree. Jen was telling her about how worried she had been about her mother's health; deep in conversation they didn't see the approach of the three girls.

Wei Wei came up behind Jen and grabbed both her ears while her two friends grabbed an arm each. 'See how you like having your ears detached from your head,' Wei Wei whispered through clenched teeth as she kneed Jen in the back. Patricia was too shocked to move or say anything for a moment.

Jen struggled to free herself but Bee Bee and Meena held on firmly to her arms. She kicked out with her feet but the girls moved out of the way and Meena gave her leg a shove for good measure. Patricia stood up and looked around her for help but a few girls who had seen them walked away, they were too afraid of the trio to intervene.

Suddenly the air was filled with Patricia's scream and moments later she slapped Wei Wei round the face. And then everything went quiet; Patricia was breathing hard, Wei Wei let go of Jen's ears, Bee Bee and Meena stood back and glared at Patricia. Jen was still sitting on the ground rubbing her sore ears. She was about to lunge for Wei Wei's legs when she saw a teacher running across the field.

'Stop that at once!' the teacher commanded. She arrived at the scene breathless and irritated, having had her lunch interrupted was not a welcome intrusion.

One of the girls who had witnessed the trio approaching Jen was sitting on the steps next to the teacher's rest room. As Wei Wei went on the attack she knocked on the window and informed the teachers about the impending fight. The teachers then took up positions by the windows and saw what happened.

All the girls tried to speak at once but the teacher held up a hand, 'You can all explain yourself in Sister Pious's Office,' she said. 'Now, all of you, go and wait outside the office upstairs,' she said and stalked off without a backward glance.

Standing shoulder to shoulder outside Sister Pious's office the five girls were silent. For once even Patricia couldn't think of something to say to Jen. Jen's mixed emotions of shame and anger was like a tornado gathering momentum and threatened to engulf her.

Muffled voices could be heard from inside the office; the teacher was giving her account of events and when she left the girls were called into the office one at a time.

After Sister Pious had heard all the different versions of the event she sent the girls back to their classes when she contemplated the punishment to fit the crime. From the description the teacher had given it appeared that Jen and Patricia were telling the truth, but according to Wei Wei and her two friends Jen had brought about the chain of events when she gave Wei Wei's ear a bashing the day before. Jen hadn't mentioned what happened the day before and Patricia was not involved in that incident, in fairness she had acted in defence of Jen.

Was she to judge what was witnessed that afternoon or was it fairer to give all the evidence the same consideration? If both events were to be considered then

Patricia would be unfairly judged, as she had no part in the incident of the day before. Whatever the decision she must deal with it for the good of the school, at that moment she wished she were in her convent tucked up in the hillside in Ireland. She shut her eyes and rested her face in her clasped hands as if in prayer.

Decisions made, she wrote them down and went to speak to the form teachers to inform them to keep a closer eye on those girls. All five girls were to remain in their classrooms for their breaks for the rest of the week. Wei Wei and her two friends must each write a letter of apology to Jen. Patricia had to write a letter of apology to Wei Wei for slapping her. All five girls had to write one hundred lines, 'I must not fight in school' to be handed in the following day. A letter would be sent out to all their parents informing them about what happened.

Jolting uncomfortably on the bus home from school that afternoon Jen had time to think about what to say to her mother when the letter arrived at the house. She was hanging on to the railing on the back of a seat to steady herself as she stood swaying with every turn and twist of the road. The bus was packed full of school children and the constant chattering and laughter brought home to her the seriousness of what she had done, but a tiny part of her rebelled against the unfairness of it all.

Sister Pious had told her that she knew about Jen attacking Wei Wei the day before. The nun said that her actions had provoked the three girls into retaliation, and she was warned that her scholarship was in jeopardy if she was called into her office again for unacceptable behaviour.

When she returned to the class from the office all eyes bore into her, they knew where she had been. Jen felt really ashamed, and to make up for her poor behaviour she paid rapt attention to both lessons, and even Miss Perez looked pleased with her performance. Maths and English were her favourite subjects after all.

There was nothing as boring as having to repeatedly write, 'I must not fight in school'. Jen broke her pencil twice when she pressed the lead too hard into the paper and pierced it. The lines of writing started off straight and neat but as line number thirty-two ended almost half an inch to the right of line twenty-six Jen sat up and sighed loudly.

'What is wrong?' Lian asked as she stitched another button into position. She was pleased to see that Jen had taken to her schoolwork so well and she even felt a tinge of guilt when she saw Jen leaving the house that evening with the bundle of clean linen for the hotel.

'Homework! I made some mistakes in school today, so I have to practise to get it right,' Jen said, and immediately felt ashamed at how easily the lie tripped off her tongue. 'Ah Ma, from now on I have to catch the early bus, I was nearly late this morning...'

'Do the boys have to go early too?' Lian asked.

'No, they get off the bus outside the school; I have to get off at the station and walk, that's why I was nearly late. I... If I go early I won't be able to see them to school...' Jen had promised her mother years ago that she would see both her brothers to school safely and she had kept that promise to date, but circumstances had changed. She decided against telling her mother the whole truth about the problem she had encountered after only two days in school because she didn't wish to worry Lian. To ensure she got to school on time every day meant she must catch the earlier bus at half past six in the morning. There was no way she could persuade Lee to get up before six each morning, Tam was much more amenable but that still wouldn't solve her problem.

'Tam is old enough now; he can see Lee to school. You

wake Tam before you leave the house. I have to get up early too, all these have to be finished soon,' she said gesturing to the various garments draped over the stool waiting for the buttons to be sewn on.

Jen woke up very early the next morning to finish off her homework. What with her maths and English essay she didn't get to bed until well after midnight and at five o'clock that morning sleep was still thick in her eyes. She lit a candle stub and stuck it on a shallow dish and in the flickering light she completed her penance. The lines weren't very straight but legible; she counted them one last time to make sure she had written one hundred lines before she put them away. She stared at the rows of writing for a few moments pondering if the teacher would actually count them to catch her out, for a brief second she considered adding an extra line just for sheer devilment, but the moment passed.

It was still dark when she left the house to catch her bus. There were few people about and the air was still cool and dewy. She looked about her as she walked through the back of the houses; the worst of the rainy season had passed and the ditch that was once swollen with rainwater and supported families of frogs was only half filled with muddy stagnant pools. The world looked a different place seen through the dawn light and she pondered on the distant beacon at the top of the hill where the rising sun, casting its long shadows, would soon obscure the leafy backdrop.

Jen had a spring in her step as she bounced across the makeshift bridge that took her across to the bus stop. Getting a seat on the bus was a bonus that she hadn't envisaged, after having always stood in the aisle to and from school all these years. Jen felt different that morning, she felt somewhat light and free. She went through the events of the past two days and wished she could go back and do it all over again, but differently.

She arrived at the school gate just as Patricia was getting out of her mother's car.

'Morning!' Jen called out before Patricia could enter the school gate. 'Good morning, Auntie Suzie.'

'Morning! Did you get into trouble with your mum?' Patricia asked.

'Did you?' Jen asked.

Patricia nodded and turned to wave her mum goodbye. 'I had a good telling off, Mum was not happy with me,' Patricia said but the smile on her face reassured Jen. 'Did you finish the lines?'

'I did, but I don't want to do that again!'

'Me neither! I didn't get to bed until ten o'clock, I'm still tired now.'

'You're not the only one, I could fall asleep right here,' Jen said pointing to the grassy verge.

'What did your mum say when you told her?' Patricia asked again.

'I didn't tell my mother,' Jen replied looking away.

'What are you going to say when the letter arrives?'

'I'll say that it was to confirm that I've got the scholarship. My mother wouldn't know, she can't read English,' she answered.

Patricia gave her a curious look. It wasn't in Jen's nature to fib. 'You sure that's… that's… I hope you don't get found out or you'll get into more trouble.'

'I am in so much trouble already, what's one more?' Jen replied shrugging her shoulders.

During their morning break Jen and Patricia saw Bee Bee and Meena at the tuck shop but Wei Wei was missing.

'I wonder where she is?' Patricia wondered aloud.

A smile played on Jen's lips and she said, 'Maybe she is still writing her lines.'

'Maybe she only wrote ninety-nine lines and the teacher

made her do it all over again,' Patricia replied.

Jen's face was serious, 'Do you think so?'

'NO! I'm only joking,' Patricia laughed.

'I don't think she is in school today, I didn't see her at Moral class,' Jen said.

'Let's go and ask them,' Patricia got off the ground and made to go after the two girls who were now sat hunched together on a bench.

Jen grabbed Patricia and pulled her back down beside her, 'Don't!'

'Why not? I am not going to do anything!'

'What? Like slapping one of them?'

'Well, she deserved it.' Patricia said stubbornly.

Back in the classroom Miss Perez told the class that as they were now in secondary school it was customary to elect a Prefect for the class. The person elected must represent the class in weekly meetings and take turns at the gate to book late arrivals. Her duties included reporting any misdemeanour committed by any pupil outside the classroom. The Prefect was also responsible for supervising the pupils in the absence of the teacher. She advised the pupils to think it through and put a few names forward the following day, and the class would vote on the final decision in a week's time.

Jen listened intently and had a chuckle to herself; she thought if she was a Prefect she would have to book herself first, being late was something she was familiar with. She had found out that late arrivals had to pay a penalty meted out by the Prefects on duty. That morning there were five pupils who arrived after the bell and they were told to spend their lunch break patrolling the school grounds and pick up any rubbish left behind by other pupils. She heard a rumour that the next day if anyone was late she would have to pay a fine. Jen thought that was unfair but by now she had learned to keep her opinions to herself.

There were too many rules and regulations to remember and she found some of them unnecessarily harsh. Gone were the days when she was able to run around the fields chasing Patricia just for the fun of it, it was now not considered ladylike to run. If any student was caught yawning during a lesson a fine was levied against her for being rude and inattentive. Jen wondered if the teachers who made these rules up ever yawned or passed wind.

Jen looked around the class, though she recognised nearly all the faces she didn't know any of them well enough to put a name forward for election. She turned to Grace who had stopped crying and was feeling less homesick, and whispered, 'Whom are you picking, Prefect I mean?'

'Pardon? Oh! I don't know yet. Do you?'

Jen shook her head and was about to continue when Miss Perez's voice cut across the room. 'Stop whispering down there! You are interrupting the lesson.'

'Sorry, Miss Perez,' Jen apologised disguising her annoyance with her teacher in her soft modulated voice. She sighed inwardly, she hopped that her next year's form teacher was less strict and smiled a bit more.

Chapter Twenty-Six

Much to Jen's surprise, her name was one of four put forward to be voted as Prefect for the class. All week she had been walking on air alternating with hot coals. The pleasure and terror kept her awake at night and stopped her food going down her gullet. Patricia was full of praise and admiration. When she told Lian about her unexpected honour her mother was less than enthusiastic, instead she worried about where the money for the new uniform would come from.

Jen was too overjoyed to join in with her mother's pessimism. She was pragmatic about the whole saga, she might not be elected at all but the fact that her name was put forward for election gave her such pleasure that she decided to enjoy the week of anticipated glory. She hadn't noticed that Wei Wei was still missing from Moral class until Patricia pointed it out to her one lunchtime.

'I wonder what happened?' Jen asked no one in particular.

'Maybe she is sick,' Patricia answered in between mouthfuls of sandwiches.

'It's been a week, she must be very sick,' Jen observed. 'Her two friends look miserable,' Jen nudged Patricia as she clapped eyes on Meena and Bee Bee across the field. 'They look like a pair of shoes with no feet, don't know where to go or what to do.'

Patricia laughed out loud. 'You are wicked! They do look miserable though.'

'Do you think we should go and talk to them?' Jen asked teasingly.

'Why? I don't even talk to them in class. They might think we are scared of them if we talk to them,' Patricia was thoughtful.

'Sometimes people change,' Jen said. She looked pensive. Her mother had changed lately she thought.

'They haven't changed! Remember, they used to taunt you in primary school. Everyday they called you a new name,' Patricia said, anger in her voice.

'They weren't very nice to you either,' Jen said and noticed that Patricia's cheeks were red and she was staring at the two girls sitting some fifty yards away.

Patricia was deep in thoughts, her father had flown back to England and she didn't know when she would see him again. He had told Patricia that she was most welcome to visit him in England and he would pay for her airfares. Her mum had said that she was too young to be flying half way round the world on her own and she had to wait for a few more years. When he suggested that she accompany Patricia, Suzie said that she was afraid of getting into a plane. She further qualified her statement by saying that she didn't feel safe when her feet were not on the ground, on her home ground she meant. Patricia felt sad and angry.

Jen nudged Patricia, 'Do they still call you name?'

'Hmm? Oh! No, I just ignore them and they ignore me.'

Just then the bell went and they both got up and walked towards the assembly hall. Their daily school routine was predictable, as soon as the bell rang, be it in the morning, after mid-morning break or lunch break, all the pupils had to line up in the assembly hall before snaking off to their classes in silence and more or less in straight lines. Jen, feeling daring and defiant on this particular day, gave Patricia a surreptitious wave as she went past. Patricia winked and waved back with both hands but her smile turned into a grimace as she came face to face with one of the teachers.

When Jen got home from school that afternoon her mother was acting most peculiarly. She dashed about between her sewing and ironing like an agitated child. She muttered to herself constantly, and when Jen asked if she was talking to her she told her to stop eavesdropping and cook the dinner instead. It wasn't time to cook the dinner but Jen decided to cook it anyway.

As Jen squatted by the water urn, washing the fine grains of rice and picking out the bits of husks, she stole a glance at her mother. Lian didn't look any different, but she wasn't coughing, her cheeks had more flesh on them than the week before and she was eating and sleeping well as far as Jen knew. It must be money, Jen thought, her mother must be worrying about the extra expenses with the Chinese New Year less than four weeks away. She wished she hadn't told her mother about the possibility of being elected as a class Prefect; a new Prefect uniform was out of the question. And if by a miracle she was elected she must refused it. Jen heard her mother mutter something over and over again and as she repeated the words she nodded to herself as if to confirm that she was saying it correctly.

The family sat around the wobbly table to eat their evening meal and as usual Lee and Min were chatting and entertaining the family with their daring-do when Lian snapped at them to stop talking. They all looked at their mother but none spoke, and after a few moments eating resumed, the silence in the kitchen was all consuming and oppressive. As soon as the words were out Lian reproached herself for being so harsh on her children. In her heart she promised her dead mother's spirit that she would try harder to be a better mother and that evening she would kowtow an extra hundred times and ask for forgiveness.

Late that night when all her children had gone to bed Lian lit a bunch of joss sticks and knelt in her front porch and prayed to the God of heaven for enlightenment. Then she went indoors and knelt before the altar and prayed to her ancestors' spirits, the God of All Wisdom and the merciful Goddess of Mercy to help her do the right thing by her ancestors and her children. She shut her eyes and begged for forgiveness for all the sins that she knowingly or unknowingly committed. She asked for answers to her latest dilemma – should she or shouldn't she meet with the stranger who claimed to be her longed-lost brother. She kowtowed many times on the concrete floor to ask the Gods to show her the right path to follow.

Lian lay awake going over every detail of the conversation she had with Mrs Ong that afternoon. Old Mr Ong had come back from the market that day and told his wife excitedly that a well-dressed gentleman had been walking round the shops and market stalls asking for a family by the name of Lau. He said that he was a businessman from the capital and he was looking for his sister's family whom he believed lived in that village. Old Mr Ong had said that his wife knew a family by that name. The businessman had given his name and the telephone number of the hotel he was staying to Old Mr Ong and said that he would like to meet the family if only to eliminate them from his list.

Mrs Ong was insistent that Lian was not to meet the man without an escort. She didn't volunteer herself but neither did she exclude herself. Lian was unsure; why would her brother, whom she had never met, want to find her? Her mother had never told her his name. Tang Kwai Chai, the Chinese characters said on the piece of paper Mrs Ong had given her. How could she be sure that he was her brother? She worried and puzzled over her problem, and her tossing and turning had kept Jen awake until the early hours of the morning.

Jen woke the next morning after having had four hours of sleep. She had temporarily forgotten about her mother's strange behaviour from the day before. There were other things on her mind. It was the day her class was to elect their Prefect. She scrubbed her face with extra care and combed her hair until the parting in the middle was in line with her nose and then she plaited it into two tight ropes, fastened into place with two rubber bands.

For breakfast she had a mug of cold water, they had run out of sugar, and the strong bitter black coffee made her screw her eyes up and she had to spit it out. When she tried to eat the cream cracker dunked in the unsweetened coffee it just made her gag. She left the house much earlier than the day before. Her tummy was making gurgling noises as she threaded her way through the narrow path between the back of the houses that led to the waterlogged ditch. As she bounced across the narrow plank bridge she smiled a secret smile, the croaking of the frogs sounded like good luck wishes. Stopping for a moment she watched the many circles of ripples made by flying insects on the surface of the stagnant pools, she marvelled at the workings of nature and walked on.

Jen had little memory of the bus journey; her mind was like a many-headed arrow, darting here there and everywhere. Patricia had to restrain her by the arm to get her attention when she arrived in school. 'Have you gone deaf?' Patricia asked.

'Oh! It's you! What did you say?'

'What's the matter with you? I called you twice, you just ignored me.'

'Sorry! I was thinking.'

'Are you going to tell me then?'

'It's nothing. I... I was just thinking who... well, it's election day...'

Patricia looked at Jen not comprehending. 'What election?'

'Prefect! Don't you listen when I tell you things?'

'Oh… that! Are you excited? I hope you get it,' Patricia said as she squeezed her friend's arm. 'But I have something really important to tell you,' Patricia whispered and looked around her to check if anyone else might be listening.

Jen, seeing the expression on Patricia's face, also looked around her. 'What are we looking for?'

'No one! I am just checking. I was reading the newspaper yesterday and guess what?'

'Yes? What did you read about? Go on then, tell me.' Jen moved her head a fraction closer to Patricia.

'Wei Wei has run away from home!' Patricia whispered into Jen's ears.

'What? Where did she go? Is she back?'

'No, she is still missing.'

'What! Stop joking!'

'It's the truth, cross my heart and hope to die,' Patricia said as she crossed herself.

'How did you find out?'

'It's in the papers, my mum read it and asked me if I knew her,' Patricia said just as the bell rang for assembly.

Miss Perez was addressing the class, standing erect on her podium. They were a few minutes away from their morning break and most of the girls had already put their textbooks away. 'Class, I want all of you to write the name of the person you have chosen as your prefect and put it on my desk before you go for your break,' she said as she placed a small bundle of paper squares on the desks of the front pupils to be distributed down the line of desks. Silence descended on the class as heads bent to their tasks. The sound of pens scribbling on single sheets of paper on wooden surfaces echoed mutely across the room.

Jen's palms were slippery with nervous sweat. She shut her eyes and repeated the four names in her head and decided that she shouldn't include her own. The other three candidates were equally deserving of the position she thought. She recited the alphabet to keep her concentration from straying; what Patricia told her that morning kept invading her thoughts.

'You may go for your break, girls,' Miss Perez was saying, Jen had missed the bell.

The scraping of chairs and hurried footsteps spurned Jen into action and she scribbled the first name that came to her head. Quickly she went up to the teacher's desk and placed her scrap of paper on top of the pile under the watchful eyes of Miss Perez.

'Come back here, Lau,' Miss Perez's piercing voice rang out after her.

Jen shuffled back and stood in front of the desk. Miss Perez looked about seven foot tall standing on the podium.

'Are you trying to be clever, Lau Li Jen?'

'No, Miss Perez?'

The teacher picked up the piece of paper and held it under Jen's eyes. Jen recognised her own handwriting. 'What is the meaning of this?' Miss Perez asked. Jen had printed in bold capitals 'Chang Wei Wei'.

'Sorry, Miss Perez, I didn't... mean to do that.'

The school had been aware of the missing pupil for a week. Mrs Chang had been to the school to speak to her daughter's form teacher. Subsequently Sister Pious had a meeting with all the teachers and had asked them to squash any gossip or speculation about the disappearance of one of their pupils. Publicity of that nature was detrimental to the good name of the school. After a week with no news of her daughter, Mrs Chang had made an appeal in the newspaper for her safe return with no questions asked.

It was not a practice in Jen's family to buy a daily paper as it was considered frivolous and a waste of good money. Lian had often said that most of the news was made up by people with nothing better to do. Most of the pupils in the school, with the exception of Jen, had seen the appeal in the papers and the gossip being bandied about was too shocking for any of them to freely articulate in the playground.

Jen went for her morning break not knowing that she had committed a most heinous crime. In Miss Perez's eyes Jen was questioning their authority by boldly writing Wei Wei's name. It was like a slap to her face delivered with venom and spite. She stared at the piece of paper wondering what to do. Before she went to see Sister Pious she sat down and went through all the pieces of paper on her desk; she made four piles, one for each candidate. When all the papers were accounted for she went through each pile again to check the number of votes for each candidate. After going through the four piles of votes for the third time she sighed deeply in frustration. There was no mistake. Jen had the most votes. She picked up all the pieces of paper and went to see Sister Pious.

Walking along the long corridor she had time to ruminate; was there a conspiracy among the pupils? Did they plan the whole thing? Why? If there was a conspiracy she thought, then the votes become null and void. If that was the case the solution was staring in her face – a re-vote, without Jen. She had disqualified herself by her impertinence Miss Perez decided. Having decided that, she knocked on the nun's office door.

Jen, unaware that Miss Perez had taken her momentary confusion as a sign of dissent, was happily munching on a biscuit. 'They are really nice,' Jen said to Patricia. 'Did your mum make these too?'

Patricia wasn't listening. Her eyes were staring into the middle distance. Jen followed her line of vision and saw Meena and Bee Bee deep in conversation.

'Oh, you were telling me about Wei Wei, she's missing?' Jen asked. She didn't believe that the girl was really missing.

Like her mother said, most of the news was made up to boost the sale of the papers.

'It's my fault,' Patricia said.

'What is your fault?'

Patricia turned sharply to Jen, her eyes were welling up, 'If I hadn't slapped her and she didn't have to write the lines then she wouldn't have run away!'

Jen was silent. She hadn't thought of it that way. In her way of thinking if you misbehave you take the punishment, besides, writing a hundred lines wasn't exactly hard work. 'No it's not, don't say that, She ran away because... because she was unhappy,' Jen said with sudden insight.

'She didn't look unhappy, she was always laughing with her friends...'

'Just because she laughed a lot... it... she didn't run away because of you,' Jen said stoutly and gave Patricia's arm a squeeze.

Miss Perez wasn't in class when Jen returned after her break. Obediently all the girls sat down quietly and looked about them as if that would make their teacher suddenly materialise. Minutes passed, a buzz went round the room, muted at first, but got louder as the gossiping gathered momentum. The braver ones spoke in normal tones, and soon the buzzing could be heard in the next classroom. Jen, deep in thoughts was roused to attention when she heard Wei Wei's name mentioned. She strained her ears when a group of girls in the far left corner were discussing what they had read in the papers. One of the girls who sat by one of the doors was posted as a lookout for Miss Perez's return. Jen could see her darting her head out the door every few seconds. Soon the whole class was animated, each girl giving her own opinion about what happened.

It slowly became clear to Jen that it was no idle gossip;

Wei Wei had indeed run away from home. A tiny doubt implanted itself in her brain – perhaps Patricia was right, Wei Wei's disappearance was connected to that incident which in turn was connected to her. Jen felt a sudden stab of guilt in her chest, she realised that everything that had happened was her own fault, and she should never have pulled Wei Wei's ears in the first place. Just then the lookout girl gestured with her fingers to her lips and the class fell silent. Miss Perez appeared a few moments later looking severe.

The teacher tidied the books on her desk. She opened and shut a couple of drawers. The girls waited in silence, the tension in the room was taut, and Jen's breathing became uneven as she watched Miss Perez playing for time.

'Class!' The girls jumped, so sudden and shrill was her voice, 'you have all voted for your Prefect before you went for your break. It's a democratic decision, and I have counted all the votes and the decision has been made.' She cleared her throat, 'I have written how many votes each candidate received and you can all read it later, I will leave the paper on my desk, but I will tell you now whom you've voted for to represent the class.' She paused and eyes panned the room, 'Jen,' Jen jumped and immediately her heart rate went up, 'Yes, Jen has the most votes, so she will be your class Prefect for the year. Congratulations, Jen!' she said and sat down.

A buzz went round the room. Jen felt all eyes on her; most of them were warm and smiling. Grace congratulated her and other girls followed. A shiver went up Jen's spine, she was embarrassed and proud, a part of her wanted to run and shout to the world and a small part of her wanted to hide in a dark cupboard. She had completely forgotten that only the day before she had told herself she must refuse the honour. She tingled from head to foot and held her smile inside. All manner of thoughts swam around in her dizzy head. She gripped her desk with both hands, hypnotised by her own white knuckles and unable to release her fingers she stared at them cross-eyed until she was startled by her teacher's voice.

'Is there anything you wish to say, Jen?' Miss Perez asked after watching the reactions of the girls. Among the smiling faces she couldn't detect any foul play. At first she didn't agree with Sister Pious that Jen should be given the position but when the nun explained that if Jen was given the responsibilities of a Prefect she might toe the line and change her attitude. She pointed out that the best way to discourage Jen's disruptive behaviour was to make her responsible for the demeanour of any unruly pupils in the class. Miss Perez grudgingly agreed that the nun might be right.

Jen looked around her and stood up, with a shaky voice she said, 'Thank you,' and sat down again.

When the bell rang for lunch break, all the girls who had voted for Jen went up to congratulate her with a friendly tap on the arm, a few even shook her hands. Those who didn't vote for her went up to their chosen candidate to commiserate. Much to Jen's delight the three losers came up to offer their congratulations too. She went to look for Patricia; her footfalls were light and seemingly weightless. She remembered not to run, especially now that she was a Prefect.

Miss Perez had called her aside before she left the class to inform her that she had to attend a Prefect meeting the following day after school to be formally told about the ins and outs of being a Prefect. As she scanned the girls gathered around the tuck shop for Patricia she was overcome with anxiety – what if she couldn't fulfil the responsibilities of a Prefect, would the honour be striped away from her she asked herself. No, she mustn't allow that to happen, she decided that she must fulfil her duties;

she owed it to the girls who voted for her. She would not let herself or the spirits of her ancestors down by bringing dishonour to her name.

Patricia felt two arms around her waist; she turned her head and nearly gave Jen a kiss on the cheek. Jen released her hold. Her lips were pulled back to a wide smile revealing her evenly-shaped white teeth. 'What are you so happy about?' Patricia asked.

'I've got something to tell you, come on,' Jen tugged at Patricia's arm.

'Stop, stop! You are hurting my arm,' Patricia yelled. 'Where are we going?'

'Nowhere,' Jen was shifting her weight from one foot to the other. She fidgeted with her hair and then her uniform. All of a sudden she squealed, 'I've got it!'

Patricia narrowed her eyes and asked, 'Got what?'

'I am a Prefect! Aren't you going to congratulate me?'

A slow smile spread across Patricia's face and she lunged for Jen and picked her off the ground yelling, 'Congratulations!'

'Put me down! You mustn't do that, we are supposed to be little ladies remember,' Jen said in mock disdain and then gave her friend a big smile.

'That's great! I am really happy for you. How do you feel?'

'Nervous, sick, happy, hungry...' and she burst into fits of giggles when Patricia pinched her arm to stop her babbling.

Walking home from the bus stop Jen had calmed down sufficiently to worry about how she should tell her mother the good news of her new status. All her school life had been routine and predictable in spite of all the little mishaps that came her way. In the main the other girls had accepted her as one of them, but only like a chair or a desk in a classroom, to make up the numbers. But since receiving her scholarship things had changed – why would the girls elect her as Prefect otherwise, Jen mused.

Chapter Twenty-Seven

When Jen entered the house by the back door, unusually for that time of day it was pulled to – normally it was left wide open. As she stepped into the kitchen she found the place deserted. She called out to her mother and then to Min but no one came. There were a couple of half-finished garments carelessly thrown over the sewing machine. She went up to the stove and lifted the lid off the rice pot. It was cold and there were several gouged marks left by the scoop on the stodgy clump of rice. She went across to the food larder and peered in through the wire-mesh. There was a plate of vegetables and two small fried fish lying white-eyed on another dish. She decided to wait for her brothers before eating her meal, they were usually home before her but sometimes if they missed their bus they could be an hour late.

She was upstairs changing out of her uniform when she heard a commotion at the front of the house. She looked through the bedroom window just as her mother entered the house followed closely by Mrs Ong. As she ran down the stairs she heard Tam and Lee arguing about the goodness of one type of noodles over another. Min was holding on to a parcel of food wrapped in leaves and tied up in strings like a pyramid-shaped handbag.

'Ah! Jen! You're home,' Lian said.

'Big Sister, this is for you,' Min said excitedly as she handed over the food parcel.

'Thank you, Min. Good afternoon, Mrs Ong.' Jen studied their faces for clues as to where they had been.

Her mother looked rather flushed and she had her best clothes on. Min looked scrubbed, and she was wearing her going-out dress and sandals. The boys were still in their uniform. Mrs Ong looked positively resplendent with a pair of gold studs in her ears and a jade bracelet on her left wrist, the colour contrasted well with her grey blouse and loose black trousers.

'That's noodles for you,' Min said pointing to the parcel in Jen's hand.

'Eat it while it's still warm,' her mother said.

'Did you have a good day in school?' Mrs Ong asked.

'We caught the early bus and met Ah Ma in the village,' said Tam.

'I had a big bowl of noodles,' Lee said, exaggerating the size of the bowl with his hands.

She was momentarily dazzled by all the attention. Looking from one animated face to another, Jen was about to speak when she became distracted. Droplets of cooking fat were leaking into her hands. She hurriedly fetched a plate, untied the strings, and allowed the warm stodgy noodles to slither on to it. A small mound of finely-cut red and green chillies lay in one corner daring Jen to eat it. She suddenly felt very hungry, and with everyone watching she picked up a pair of chopsticks and pinched a few strands of noodles and started eating ravenously. After the third mouthful she looked up, suddenly remembering her manners she stopped eating, 'Sorry, Mrs Ong, please have some noodles?'

Mrs Ong gave her a warm smile and said, 'Don't worry about me. I've eaten. You just carry on.'

Jen tried to catch Tam's attention but he was busy play-fighting with Lee who had challenged him to an arm-wrestling contest. Min was laughing and encouraging them on the sideline. Meanwhile her mother and Mrs Ong had gone into the front room to continue their conversation.

All afternoon she had been hearing snippets of news

about her family's outing but nothing to suggest anything out of the ordinary took place According to Min, Mrs Ong took her mother into a shop to use a telephone and then they went into the market where Mrs Ong treated them to noodles. Later they saw a friend and then they waited at the bus stop for Tam and Lee and had more noodles and then they came home. Tam and Lee said that they didn't see any friend of their mother's apart from Mrs Ong and her husband.

Thursday was one of the days when Jen had to deliver the laundry to the hotel, so she waited until late that evening to speak to her mother.

Jen had just walked through the door when her mother called to her, 'Jen, what is this letter about? It arrived three days ago. I left it in the drawer and forgot it. Is it important?'

'Ah! Oh! Letter? Let me see.' Jen took the letter with shaky hands. The brown envelope with the neatly typed lettering looked frighteningly formal and made Jen quite sick. Very slowly she slipped a finger under the flap of the envelope to ease it open, she tried hard to still her hands. Her heart went boom, boom, boom, in her chest and the hot flush crept up from her neck to her cheeks. She pulled out a typewritten letter and studied it with infinite care. Her mind was racing, to tell or not to tell the truth she agonised. She remembered she hadn't told her mother about being elected as a prefect for her class and now might be a good time she thought.

Lian was bent over her sewing. The image of her brother Kwai Chai whirled around her head and made her quite dizzy. He told her that he was in the restaurant business in Kuala Lumpur where he lived with his wife and four children. His father, their father, had died three years previously and left him some money. On his deathbed he told his son that he had a sister. Kwai Chai had grown up thinking that his baby sister had died with his mother, and therefore the news came as a terrible shock. He felt cheated and was very angry for a long time after their father's death. With his wife's encouragement he decided to look for Lian to make amends for past misdeeds. He told her that it had taken him nearly two years to track her down and Lian found his honesty very moving.

He brought with him a photograph of their father as proof of his identity. Seeing the image of her father gave Lian a terrible shock, those hooded eyes seemed to penetrate into her soul. It brought back to her many of the unhappy memories of her childhood.

Her brother had said that his restaurant business was thriving and when he was growing up he had benefited from his father's money, but Lian hadn't. He said that it was only fair that the money he left should go to Lian instead. He didn't say how much it was but he had asked if he could come to see Lian and all her children the following day. Lian told him that she wanted to have a day to think about it and said that she would ring him back the next day.

'Ah Ma,' Jen addressed her mother again.

Lian looked up, roused from her introspection. She had forgotten about the letter.

'You know I told you last week about… being a prefect? I was picked to be my class Prefect today,' Jen said and waited with bated-breath.

Lian took a few seconds to register what Jen had said. 'You! Prefect! That is very good.'

Jen wanted to laugh and cry all at once, but she kept her expression serious and grave. She cleared her throat, 'I… um… need a new uniform to be a Prefect. I will work very hard to help… to make up the extra money,' Jen said.

'You just pay more attention to your school work, I will get the money for your uniform,' Lian said matter-of-factly. 'What did the letter say?'

Jen swallowed twice, 'This letter?'

'Are there two letters? I only see one,' Lian said.

'Well… last week… I was waiting at the bookshop, these girls came to bother me. They called me names, so I pulled… this girl's ear,' Jen stopped and watched her mother's reactions.

Lian's face was a mask. She stopped her sewing and gave Jen her full attention. 'Why did they call you names?'

'I don't know. They used to do it in primary school too,' Jen was groping for the right words.

'What's their names? I go and see the teacher,' Lian's voice was firm.

'No, Ah Ma! No, it's all right now. The teachers have spoken to them. This is what the letter says,' Jen said and swallowed hard.

Lian pressed her lips together and looked intently at Jen. 'Tell me the names, next time I go and see their mothers.'

'Well, there's three of them. They call Patricia names too.' Jen shifted uncomfortably on her stool.

'What's their names? I speak to Patricia's mother too. What's their names?' Lian asked again.

Jen licked her lips, 'The Indian girl is called Meena, she is in the same class as Bee Bee, and they are both in the same class as Patricia.'

'You say there are three,' Lian said and waited.

'Yes, the girl whose ear I pulled, Wei Wei…' Jen said as her voice became softer and quieter. She looked down and studied the grains on the table.

'Is her surname Chang?'

Jen's head bobbed up in a flash and stared at her mother. 'I think that's her surname.'

'Is it her surname or not?'

'Yes, that is her surname.'

Lian inhaled loudly and sat very upright. Jen waited but her mother was silent. The wick in the kerosene lamp had burnt to a black dot and Jen stretched out a hand and gave the knob a turn, the flame immediately expanded casting a bigger glow and longer shadows on the uneven mud floor. The only sound in the room came from their breathing.

'She is not at home.' Lian made the statement after a long pause, and carried on stitching an obstinate button into position.

'Patricia told me she is missing. She read it in the papers,' Jen said softly.

'Oh! It is in the English papers too? Mrs Ong read it in the Chinese paper.'

'Where's she gone?' Jen asked. 'She hasn't been in school for a week.'

'Bad news, sad news, all the same, family suffers, everybody talk. Her father is a big boss in business in town. He is shamed. She runs away. Now all the town people know he gets drunk, visits cheap woman and beats his wife,' Lian said and pressed her lips together as if she had already said too much.

Jen listened but didn't offer her opinion. She wasn't expected to. In the school playground she had seen evidence of family violence, children turning up in school with empty tummies but their arms and legs full of weal marks. These unfortunate children often became victims of school bullies too. The teachers turned a blind eye to the plight of these children and that of their broken-down families. They didn't consider it their business to ask questions. In a society where hardship was the backbone of daily grind, families were left to deal with their own broken dreams and broken hearts, outsiders were not welcomed. There was no shame attached to being thrashed by one's parents, only acceptance of one's fate. But running away from home to expose one's family to public humiliation was unforgivable. Jen knew better than to give voice to what she thought of people like Wei Wei's father, rich, influential, brutal and immoral.

Some minutes later Lian spoke to break the silence, 'This morning I went to see a relative. He is my brother. He lives in the capital and he wants to meet all of you.

Jen, taken by surprise, opened and shut her mouth like a fish. 'W…who? I didn't know you have a brother!'

Lian smiled. 'Yes, I have a brother. We were separated when we were little. I was adopted by your grandma and he was brought up by your grandpa's other family.' Lian had decided that she would tell her children her family history, the cleaned-up version, after they have met her brother.

'When are we seeing him, Ah Ma?' Jen asked, sudden excitement gripped her insides.

'I will telephone him tomorrow. He will come here… on Saturday, but now you better go to bed.' As Jen gathered her books together Lian spoke again, 'Tomorrow… after school, you go and get some clothes in the bazaar, for yourself.'

'What clothes, Ah Ma? I don't need any new clothes,' Jen said, surprised at the request.

'You are growing up now… a girl needs to wear extra clothes, under clothes,' Lian said with some difficulty.

Jen blushed and said shyly, 'I… don't know what size to buy.'

'You go to see a woman clothes seller and she will advise you. Take this money and buy two… remember to ask for discount if you buy two,' Lian advised. 'Another time I will talk to you about other things,' she hinted mysteriously.

Jen was thankful for the poor lighting. She felt her blush deepen. Patricia had told her about girls' things, how their bodies change shape and the inconvenience of monthly menstruation, and how she may find hairs growing in the most unlikely places. Jen had grimaced when she heard all the gory details about being a woman and wished she were a boy. Patricia had reassured her that it was normal for all the girls to go through the same changes because her mother had told her so. Patricia was already wearing a bra in school and Jen wondered what it would feel like wearing one as she went off to bed.

Chapter Twenty-Eight

Standing in the dark corner of the unlit bathroom Jen gave the two gentle mounds on her chest a furtive glance. She was too embarrassed to give her changing body more than an occasional peep. A deep-seated voice told her that it was immodest to draw attention to the female shape and now that her mother had mentioned that she should be wearing under garments she suddenly became very aware of her expanding chest. As she got ready for school Jen tried to clear out the clutter in her head, the conversation she had with her mother the night before was still very present.

She imagined her mother's brother to be tall, dark, and rich with a hint of cruelty to his character. All the images of rich men she had ever seen in her yearly visit to the pictures were rich and cruel, villains really. A shudder of excitement went round her shoulders and chest and she hugged her arms close. Her father was gentle and kind Jen remembered, but then he died young. Jen concluded that life itself could be so cruel and unkind, she realised she had so much to learn. She noticed lately that her thoughts returned rather too frequently to her father, perhaps she was getting older, and learning and curiosity was part of becoming older. She picked up the cracked mirror and peered at her reflection, her dark hair that fell below her shoulders with a jagged edge could do with a cut. Her brown eyes were round not almond shaped like her mother's. She didn't like the way the bridge of her nose sort of sunk into her face, her mouth was too full and took up too much space, but she liked her skin that was smooth and clear. She smiled at her own reflection, a crease appeared at the corner of each eye, she puckered up her lips and held the mirror at an angle, that was when she caught sight of the clock.

She would miss the bus if she didn't hurry. She dashed up the narrow staircase and ran into Tam who was yawning, his arms outstretched at the top of the stairs. His skinny body was poking through the holes of his sleep shirt.

'Don't forget to get Lee up,' she said to Tam as she dodged past him.

Tam stood for a few moments not moving as if deep in thought, and then reluctantly returned to his bedroom where Jen could hear him calling Lee in a gruff voice. Jen noticed lately that Tam's voice was changing, some days his voice was deep and hoarse like a grown man and sometimes his tone was boyish and a bit shrill. Jen wondered if boys go through the same changes as a girl, she must remember to ask Patricia.

'What's it like being the Prefect?' Patricia asked. It was their lunch break and they were sitting in their favourite place under the magnolia tree.

'Mm, just like every day really,' Jen answered screwing her eyes up to think.

'Did you have to do any of the Prefect things… duties?'

'Not yet, I have to go to a meeting after school today, maybe they will tell me what I have to do.'

'Are you excited?'

'I'm scared! What if I can't or don't know what to do?'

'You'll be alright, you are clever, you'll learn very quickly.'

'Thanks. I am glad you're my friend. Oh, I have something exciting to tell you,' Jen teased.

'What? Tell me,' Patricia said shaking Jen by the arm.

'It's my mum really. She found her brother, no, her brother found us.'

Patricia frowned and looked at Jen quizzically. 'You mean your uncle came to see your mum?'

'No! My mum didn't know, no, it was her brother who didn't know that he had a sister, that is my mum.'

Patricia looked confused and Jen looked just as puzzled. 'Anyhow he is coming to see us tomorrow,' Jen said.

'What, at your house?'

'I think so… there's something I want to ask you,' Jen said, feeling herself blushing.

Patricia waited. Jen stared at her feet. Patricia waited some more. Finally she turned to face Patricia, but at that moment the school bell sounded, announcing the end of their lunch break.

Patricia whispered as they walked back towards the assembly hall, 'What were you going to ask me?'

'I'll tell you later,' and with that Jen went and joined her classmates.

All day Jen had been surreptitiously looking around her class to see who was wearing a bra and who wasn't. The blue pinafore and white blouse that they all wore was proving to be a good camouflage. A few of the girls had telltale bumps on their chests and Jen deduced that they must have been wearing bras. She didn't know any of them well enough to ask where they bought their garments from and she felt a bit queasy at the thought of having to get some on the way home from school. Her mother wore bras but Jen had never accompanied her to the shops before and she wasn't even sure if they had special names or were they just called under garments.

It was just as well she had to attend the Prefect's meeting after school; it bought her a little more time. It was her first meeting and she felt shy and awkward but the other Prefects made her welcome and were patient in explaining to her the duties and responsibility conferred on her. It wasn't as bad as she had envisaged and as she left the meeting she suddenly felt very proud. She was accepted for whom she was, no one called her names, and they listened when she spoke. Being a Prefect Jen decided was a blessing, it gave her a certain authority over her schoolmates; it pleased and frightened her at the same time.

The dreaded moments had arrived; she walked hurriedly through the narrow corridors of the bazaar, head bowed, eyes darting left and right Jen scoured the shelves of jumbled goods for likely looking undergarments. She felt hot and uncomfortable and the heat of the afternoon hadn't helped. It was noisy in the bazaar; the shopkeepers and customers were bartering and bantering outrageously which only served to embarrass Jen further. She walked past several stalls that sold women's underwear, but she didn't stop to look at them. She walked through the maze of narrow corridors and right out of the bazaar and then stood in one of the many entrances wondering what to do. As she turned around to go back in she saw Meena and Bee Bee walking towards her.

Her first instinct was to turn and run in the opposite direction, but at that moment something inside held her fast to the spot. A little voice in her head urged her to face up to her school bullies, besides she was tired of running away. So she squared her shoulders, brought her chin up and looked them in the eye as they walked past. To Jen's surprise they both nodded and smiled shyly in return. She followed their progress down the road feeling a little light-headed and confused. She must have been standing there for some time when she felt someone touch her arm.

'Are you alright, Sister?' one of the stallholders asked.

'Oh! Sorry I'm in your way,' Jen apologised.

'You were standing so still like you've just seen a ghost,' she replied.

'I was just thinking…' Jen said as she swivelled herself round and looked at her stall. Nestling in the glass-topped cabinet were rows upon rows of bras, all in white. Jen edged forward, she was fascinated, and she didn't know that there was so much to choose from. Some had lace over the cups to make them look feminine and delicate, some had circular stitching to make them stiff and pointed, there were padded ones that stood up proud, and there were plain cotton ones that looked flat and forlorn.

'Do you want to buy some?' the stallholder asked.

Jen blushed and stammered, 'I… yes, I want two please.'

'What size?'

'I don't know,' Jen blushed and stammered some more.

'Let me look at you,' the lady smiled kindly at Jen. She cast her critical eye over Jen and said, 'You want this size,' and pointed to a row of bras in the cabinet. 'Is this your first time?' she asked.

Jen nodded. Her cheeks were burning hot and she was acutely aware that the man in the next stall was watching and listening to their conversation. She handed all her money over and almost snatched the brown paper bag off the woman's hand and made a hurried exit. Stuffing her purchase in her school bag Jen ran all the way to the bus station.

Once indoors she was caught in her family's excitement and preparation for their uncle's impending visit the following day. Her mother was in earnest conversation with Mrs Ong about what would constitute the better ingredients for the soup she was going to make for her brother's visit. Tam, Lee and Min were busy poking around in the various paper bags of dried food and sniffing the different herbs strewn on the table.

'Big Sister, we've been shopping,' Min said with a beaming smile.

'Big Uncle is coming to visit us tomorrow,' Lee added excitedly.

'Is he? Do you know his name?'

'Big Uncle of course!' Lee said.

'Yes, his name is Big Uncle,' Min said and nodded several times to affirm her statement.

Jen was about to question Tam when he looked up abruptly and said that he was going to the farm. Without another word he slipped out the back door and was gone before Jen could speak to him. All the talk about the long-lost uncle didn't sit well with Tam. He felt that his position as the head of the household, being the eldest son, had been usurped. He was worried for his mother too, she was not usually so trusting of strangers but for some reason Lian appeared positively happy about her so-called brother's forthcoming visit.

'What do you think about your uncle's visit?' Mrs Ong asked Jen.

'Err... I am looking forward to meeting him,' she replied politely. But was she looking forward to meeting her uncle she wondered. She grew up with only vague memories of cousins on her father's side of the family and but her mother had never mentioned any relatives on her side of the family. Jen had never met any of her cousins before; she wasn't even sure how many cousins she had. Her mother had said that they lived in another part of the country when asked about their whereabouts. Jen suspected that distance was not the only reason she had not visited or been visited by their relatives. For the first time in her life it came to her that her family had led a very insular life. Perhaps a visiting uncle may give her some answers. She reasoned that if her father had been alive she could have asked him why his family never visited but she couldn't ask her mother the same questions, she didn't know why but just sensed that was the way it was.

Meanwhile Tam was walking down the dusty lane towards the farm, kicking up dust and stones and dirtying his school plimsolls. He was angry and frustrated; his fists were bunched up in his pockets as he recalled the conversation he had with his mother that afternoon. Lian had told him that he could not go to the farm the following day as his uncle was visiting, and in defiance he said he was going that afternoon. Tam looked forward to his weekend spent at the farm, working in the vegetable gardens, feeding the pigs, talking and learning about farming from Farmer Choy, but a stranger had come along and disrupted his orderly life.

Chapter Twenty-Nine

Kwai Chai's eyes traced the ceiling fan as it circled on its axis. His concentration wavered as he watched the bevelled blades slicing through the stagnant air. He had been awake before daybreak, listening to the familiar sound of bicycle bells tinkling away in the dawn traffic below his open window. The occasional raised voices of greetings and good-natured bantering jolted him from his reverie as the hawkers went past.

His first floor room in the Tai Wah hotel-cum-restaurant was sparse but clean. He had opted for the more expensive room for its prime position; situated in the corner of the building it gave him a wonderful view of the life beyond. One window faced east and the other north, each depicting an ever-changing portrait of life in the little market town that nestled at the foot of the mountain range. The morning air, crisp, fresh, and invigorating, brushed past the whitewashed brickwork and escaped through the louver windows beckoning Kwai Chai to the world beyond.

He peeled back the pristine white sheet and swung his legs off the bed. As he stood up he yawned and stretched his arms up towards the ceiling, almost touching the blades of the fan. Kwai Chai was rather taller than most of his countryman at six-foot two. He had retained the lean and muscular body of his youth that he was justly proud of – but he wasn't a proud man. Unlike his father before him, he was sensitive, generous in currency and spirit, and he believed in honour and justice. It was with this resolution that he had come back to his birthplace to put right the wrongs perpetrated in the name of tradition.

When his father's health was failing he had spent more time with the taciturn old man. During their nightly conversations by his father's sickbed Kwai Chai learned about his family history and the way the old man had behaved throughout his life. Kwai Chai was not proud of his father's view of life but he also realised that he was a product of his times and his own history, and in time he came to accept what happened was his father's burden, not his. But the money left to him by the old man became a constant reminder of that burden. And it was for this reason he came looking for his sister, Lian.

As he stood leaning on the sill by the east-facing window Kwai Chai's attention was drawn to a hawker's stooped frame silhouetted against the charcoal stove directly below. He was energetically waving a straw fan to coax the coal into life. Sparks of burnt orange flew and danced every which way as the embers became a roaring fire. He looked away and smiled. The hawker had invoked a memory locked away inside his mind, a memory tinged with pleasure and pain. As he cast his bleary eyes further ahead he saw the familiar sight of the cinema directly opposite the hotel, the Majestic. The paint on the lettering was now faded, blistered by the sun and washed away by the rain. He only wished that his memories had been erased in the same manner. He sighed and turned away from the window.

Out of curiosity he stepped to his left and looked out the north-facing window. The streetlights threw a dull white glow on the tarmac and picked off shadows where the potholes were big and wide enough to swallow half a bicycle wheel. There were several three-wheelers being ridden recklessly by their owners to market. The fresh produce packed into the side-platform jumped and slid around in their restraints. One rider even had several baskets strapped to the platform of his three-wheeler containing live ducks and chickens. Their quacking and clucking emitted at various pitches could be heard from a long way off as they were transported to their fate.

There were no cars about, taxis were expensive to hire and beyond the reach of the poor. Those who owned their own vehicles were still asleep in their beds, only those who scraped a living had to get up before dawn to fill their rice bowls and keep faith with their gods. Kwai Chai had a comfortable upbringing, educated in the best school that his father chose and paid for. But he upset his father's plans when he turned eighteen and decided he wanted to travel and make his own plans for his future. In truth, he had no idea what he wanted to do with his life, but he found his father's iron-fist hold over his future and his step-mother's inability to speak up for herself too painful to watch. So one night while they were asleep he took the night train and left for the city lights, some three hundred miles down south.

It took him five years to learn his craft and save enough money to finance and set up his own business. Another two years had passed before he was reconciled with his parents. Like his father before him he learned the trade scrubbing grease-encrusted pots and pans in some dimly-lit kitchens. He shared a room with two other co-workers in a basement flat where rats and cockroaches came out regularly to raid the food larder at night. He spent many nights debating the wisdom of leaving his comfortable home to live in that hovel, but a certain stubbornness sustained him in his darkest days and he came through the seven years of exile to become a man of integrity and a formidable businessman. He winced as he remembered the journey of his early years. He reluctantly withdrew from the window scene to take a shower before breakfast.

Sitting at one of the restaurant's tables on the ground floor he took a sip from his coffee cup and pulled a face in dismay. He had told the young lad who came to take his order to put less condensed milk in his coffee but he found it just as sweet as the day before. When the same youth came back with his breakfast, a steaming bowl of noodles, he asked for another coffee, black and strong. He looked at his bowl of noodles critically; the few strands of anaemic-looking chicken criss-crossed over the pale golden egg noodles. Mechanically he dug his chopsticks into the tangled strands and turned them over, exposing the limp bean shoots glistening in the hot soup.

After a couple of mouthfuls he put his chopsticks down, he had lost his appetite as his thoughts ran over the events of the past few days. His second coffee arrived, he got up and picked up the newspaper from the next table and sat down to read it. He glanced at the headline on the front page. He was not in the right frame of mind to read the invective of a young politician and with a flick of his wrist he turned the page over. A photograph on the third page caught his attention. It was that of a young girl in school uniform. He read the column of news below the headlines and a chill went up his spine when he realised the girl in question lived in the same town. Chang Wei Wei was found dead. Her body was discovered at the bottom of a ravine by a group of ramblers who were staying in one of the holiday bungalows on the side of the mountain.

As he continued reading he felt a shadow over his back, he turned his head round and came face to face with another man reading the paper over his shoulders. 'Sorry. Have I taken your paper?' Kwai Chai asked, embarrassed at his own mistake. He had assumed that the paper was free for the patrons of the hotel.

'No, no, I was just reading about that girl. Family problem!' he said unabashed and pointed to the picture of Wei Wei. 'Sad business,' he continued and bobbed his head up and down. A few moments later when he finished reading the column of news he walked away still shaking his head.

Kwai Chai returned to his papers but by now he had lost interest. He picked up his coffee, drank the last dregs and left the hotel. He had three hours to do some shopping, he pondered over what his nieces and nephews might want for a present. He had only met the youngest, Min, and his sister Lian of course.

He walked down the main road that led him through the markets taking in the old familiar sights and sounds of his own childhood. Nothing much had changed, the metal bars that separated and enclosed the different meat markets still looked like cages to him, but the faces that sat behind each stall were unfamiliar. Walking through the narrow wet concrete path his feelings alternated between nostalgia and cynicism.

The sun was high in the sky and the heat brought out beads of perspiration across his temples, and as he pulled out a white neatly-pressed handkerchief to mop his brow a piece of paper fell out of his pocket. He turned the paper over and saw his wife's neat handwriting and he smiled. She had given him a list of things to bring back, mainly local delicatessen goods that she craved but couldn't get in the big city. A warm feeling of joy and contentment surged through his body, he was a lucky man he thought, and he had a pretty, loyal and hardworking wife. He was equally proud of their four children who took after their mother in looks and temperament. They were also about the same age as his nieces and nephews and he anticipated the fun they were all going to have when they all meet.

Kwai Chai visited several departmental stores that sold a bewildering array of clothes, toys and household utensils. After three hours of fruitless search for presents he had decided that he wasn't very good at buying presents. He made up his mind to take his nieces and nephew out the following day so that they could choose their own presents instead. Carrying a brown paper bag containing a selection of dried herbs, a catty of the best-dried mushrooms imported from China, and a variety of cakes and sweets for the children, he hailed a taxi to the village where Lian lived.

He was in a buoyant mood. As the taxi wound its way along the twisting road he looked out the windows like an excited child. The soya factory was less imposing than he remembered it from his boyhood, the few temples dotted along the way were dustier and less colourful, the reds bleached by the sun to a shy pink, but the scent from the incense was the same. The cemetery, reclining on the side of a mountain, was studded with hundreds of white tombstones like soldiers on guard duty. Patches of scrubland, parched and shrivelled, reached for the shade offered by some gnarled old trees. Further down the valley were acres of red soil, left bare of plant life. The trees and scrubs had been turned over by heavy machinery and flattened into the earth. In its place were mounds of sand and ballasts jostled among rows of bricks and steel rods on the levelled ground. Men in shorts and singlets scurried around the site emptying buckets of concrete into marked trenches where the new houses were waiting to be built.

Kwai Chai was lost in thoughts, and a germ of an idea was growing in his head. He almost jumped out of his skin when the taxi stopped and the driver spoke to him.

'I think this is the place, Old Friend,' the driver addressed him.

Kwai Chai looked out through the passenger window and was confronted with a cluster of coconut trees on one side of the dirt track, dense woodland on the other and some houses beyond where the lane rises steeply. A dog barked and a face appeared at one of the windows in the nearest house. Turning to the driver Kwai Chai handed over his fare and stepped out of the car. Mesmerised by the peace and tranquillity he was only vaguely aware as the taxi took its leave. He stood for moments looking at the fronds of the coconuts trees waving gently in the breeze with clusters of coconuts hanging enticingly below them. He put a hand up to shield his eyes from the midday sun and looked towards the houses. As he walked up the lane he saw the familiar sight of washing fluttering in the wind and muted voices coming from the dark interior of the first house. The faint aroma of spices wafted past his nostrils as he hesitated in front of the first open doorway.

He rapped on the wooden frame of the heavy door and waited. Nobody came. He knocked again, this time louder and for longer. A shuffling sound came towards him from the gloom. A middle-aged woman with a weather-beaten face looked up at him with curious eyes.

'Sorry to disturb you, Auntie, I am looking for my relatives,' Kwai Chai hesitated, 'my sister, Lian, and her children…'

The woman broke into a smile and pointed to a house three doors down, 'Lian lives over there. You are her brother are you?' she asked, curiosity written over her features.

'Thank you. Yes, yes, I'm her brother. Thank you again.' Kwai Chai walked across the lane towards a wooden house sandwiched between two large trees. He stood several paces from the front door and studied the lopsided house. He marvelled at how it managed to stay upright, the roots of the trees had burrowed into the foundation of the house. It looked as if the tree on the left was trying to push the house over while the other tree was pushing against it. He smiled and shook his head.

Kwai Chai was faintly aware that he was being watched. He turned around just in time to see the woman across the road duck back into the dark gloom of her house. He cleared his throat and called quietly through the open doorway, but the excited and spirited argument coming from the kitchen swallowed his tentative, 'Hello, hello.' He raised his voice and called out again and this time rapid footsteps charged towards him.

Lee was rapidly followed by Min; they rushed to the door and then stopped dead in front of the tall figure. Lee recovered first, and in his usual bravado put a protective arm over Min's shoulder and spoke to Kwai Chai, 'Are you my uncle? We've been waiting for you.'

Kwai Chai smiled, Lian had briefly told him about her children and he recognised Lee in her description. 'You are correct, I am your uncle, let me guess – you're Lee,'

Lee eyed the carriers bags in his uncle's hands and asked, 'Are those for us?'

Min meanwhile, untangled herself from Lee's arm and ran back into the kitchen to inform the rest of the family of their very important visitor.

The introduction over, Kwai Chai observed his relatives and their home from his vantage position by the kitchen table. He noted the uneven mud floor, the flimsy walls, the absence of running water and the rickety furniture. The stool he was sitting on threatened to tip him over every time he moved. Lian was standing over the wood burning stove quietly stirring and haranguing the vegetables to cook. Jen, squatted by the water urn was rinsing some lettuces. Tam, after a quick handshake with his uncle went out into the backyard to chop some firewood. Min and Lee sat opposite their uncle asking questions that only uninhibited children knew how, much to the embarrassment of Lian and Jen.

The simple meal was eaten amid lively conversations. Jen learned about her uncle's life in the big city and wondered if she could one day meet her cousins and spend some time in the big city too. Tam's initial reticence had thawed and found his uncle's warmth and genuine interest in him comforting. Lian felt a warm glow in seeing how her children had taken to her brother. Min and Lee's unrestrained questioning supplied the whole family with answers that would have taken Lian months of polite exchanges to find out. Outwardly Lian showed disapproval of her two younger children's bold cross-examination of Kwai Chai but secretly she was pleased to have found some of the missing pieces in her life.

The photographs of Kwai Chai's family were duly passed round the table, they were admired and commented on favourably. Jen promised to write to her cousins, she was delighted to find that her oldest cousin was the same age as herself and had also recently passed her exam to enter secondary school. Tam was no less pleased that his second cousin was only a few months younger than himself but he didn't promise to write. Lee said he would write when he learned to do joined-up writing. Min only asked if she could visit and play with all her new cousins and Kwai Chai promised that he would bring his family to see them soon.

Late that night when the family had gone to bed Lian remained seated at the table with only the flickering light of a candle stump to keep her company. She went over the conversation she had with Kwai Chai, he had informed her the sum of money her father had left her and Lian was shocked to find herself the owner of a substantial sum of money. Her brother had advised her to invest in a brick-built house as the one she was living in was slowly falling down. She looked around her simple wooden house that her husband had built with his own hands and a heavy sadness fell upon her. She had been too busy trying to scrape a living and looking after her children to mourn his passing.

A steady stream of tears ran down her cheeks. It was ironic that it was her father who came to her rescue this time yet it was her husband who had rescued her from her father's tyranny all those years ago. She asked herself time and again if she was betraying him if she accepted the money. Her brother had assured her that it was her moral right to take the money to provide a better living for herself and her children. Kwai Chai said that he would help her to find the right property in a location where it would be more convenient for the children to get to school. Lian thought about her kind neighbours, particularly the robust Mrs Ong, she decided to consult her the following day before she made any decision.

Chapter Thirty

Jen sniffed her pillow, the newness of it made her shiver with delight. She moved her head off the pillow and sniffed the mattress. It was firm and yet it yielded gently to her body. It too was brand new. She ran a hand along the wooden frame of the bed and let out a deep sigh and she smiled happily to herself. Money wasn't the root of all evil like her mother had often said but it also bought comfort and luxuries too, thought Jen dreamily.

Ever since her uncle's visit, her family's lives had been transformed. He had bought her and Tam a bicycle each, admittedly it wasn't her choice of a present but her uncle had said that it would get her to school much quicker. Jen had to agree that she would no longer have to get up at the crack of dawn to get ready for school and then spend precious minutes waiting for the bus that was always crammed to the open door with school children. She much preferred her own transport even though she was nervous of the traffic at first. Dodging other cyclists became a kind of mind game; she often found the little old ladies pedalling their three-wheelers to the market were the most dangerous. They used their vehicles like weapons, and anyone who got in their way were easy targets. Jen, having had a few near misses gave them a wide berth, being young and agile she often out-pedalled them.

Lee wasn't happy that he didn't get a bicycle. He argued his right to a bicycle for days until Lian promised him one for his next birthday. He now went to school in a rickshaw instead which made up for his disappointment. Lian had to be persuaded by her brother that the saving made by Jen and Tam on bus fares more than paid for Lee's rickshaw fares. The memories of the past few weeks gave Jen a funny feeling in her tummy and she rolled over in her bed and faced Min.

Min was sleeping with her mouth opened. Jen stretched her arm across to her sister and drew the cover off the end of the bed and over her. They no longer had to share the room with their mother. Lian now had a room to herself, a bed, a chest of drawers and a wardrobe. The boys shared a room at the back of the house leading off from the kitchen. Their beds weren't nearly as new; they came with the house that they moved into two weeks ago.

Lian, after much agonising, had agreed to spend some of her inheritance on bricks and mortar. She was reluctant to leave her neighbourhood, so instead of putting her name down for a new house as Kwai Chai advised she opted to buy an older property in the same village. The previous owner of the house had already moved his family to the city and left a relative to negotiate the sale of the house and most of its contents with Lian.

Four rattan armchairs and a low table took up most of the sitting room space. Lian had extravagantly bought a new altar table to take pride of place in the sitting room and then performed a welcome ceremony with prayers and burning of joss sticks and incense. Wads of gold and silver embossed paper money were also burnt to welcome the spirits of her ancestors to her new home.

Running water, clean and fresh that gushed effortlessly from the tap was still a novelty for the whole family. As for the electric lighting Jen thought it was a minor miracle, and what pleased her even more was that she never had to read or do her homework at the mercy of the kerosene lamp or the stub of a candle again. She shivered and pulled the cover up to her chin as she remembered the chill of the water when she had her bath the evening before. What particularly thrilled her was that she didn't have to fetch the water from the well, she only had to turn on the tap. She was just about to fall back to sleep when she heard her mother outside her bedroom door.

'Jen, time to get up, I need your help in the kitchen.'

'Mm, I'm coming Ma,' Jen replied reluctantly. She heard her mother's retreating footsteps towards the kitchen and she went back to sleep again. The smiling face of Patricia beckoned her, she was talking excitedly but no sound came from her mouth and Jen woke up with a jolt.

'Jen, J-en', she felt her mother's hand on her shoulder. 'Could you please get out of bed. You know your uncle and his family are coming today and I need your help in the kitchen,' Lian said impatiently.

Suddenly Jen was wide-awake. 'I'm coming Ma,' she replied and sat up so quickly that she nearly knocked her mother over. 'Uncle and his family are coming for the Reunion Dinner?' Jen asked.

'You know they are! How many times have I told you?' Lian said impatiently and went out of the room.

She was going to meet her aunt and cousins at last. Excited and a little nervous she jumped out of bed and ran around the room looking for clean clothes to wear, she flung open her wardrobe door and stared at the four new dresses hanging stiffly to attention. Two of the dresses were much shorter; they were Min's. She admired her mother's fine needlework, she ran her fingers over them lovingly and sniffed at the new scratchy material and hugged it to her chest. Min stirred in her sleep; quickly Jen shut the wardrobe door and pulled open a drawer instead. She scanned the neatly pressed clothes arranged in two rows according to size, Min's and her own. With great deliberation she lifted out an old blouse and a skirt. She then hid in a dark corner of her room to change.

Jen stood at the front door watching her mother. Lian was kneeling on the front porch praying with a bunch of lighted joss sticks between her clasped hands. Beside her was a table laden with food, offerings to the God and the spirits of her ancestors. The cooked chicken sat on a shallow dish looking proud, its neck in an S shape with its head resting on its back looking up to the heavens, with its feet neatly tucked in under its body. A few sprigs of scallions lay alongside it. The rather large lump of roast pork took up another plate; the cracking, brown and blistered by the charcoal, was covered in a reddish glaze. There were also several cooked dishes jostling for space, Jen recognised one of them as sweet and sour cucumber with giblets. At the front of the table nearest the joss stick urn were five little porcelain cups of Chinese tea with slivers of black leaves floating in them. Behind those were bowls of rice with chopsticks balanced precariously to one side of each of bowl.

As Lian bent down to kowtow on the concrete floor Jen picked up a bunch of joss sticks and lit them from the burning candle. A gentle breeze was blowing and Jen had to cup one hand to catch the flame, and when her joss sticks were glowing and smoking heavily she joined her mother and knelt on the floor. She shut her eyes and raised her glowing joss sticks to the heavens and thanked all the gods and the spirits of her ancestors for the good fortune that had come their way. She too kowtowed on the concrete floor. Jen whispered thanks for her family's good health, she asked for guidance for her education and her dreams to be realised and also to bless Patricia too even though she was a Christian and not a Buddhist. Jen lost count how many times she touched her forehead to the cold concrete but she didn't stop until she felt a dull throbbing pain in the middle of her forehead. When she opened her eyes she was seeing double; gingerly she stood up and pushed her burning joss sticks into the soft ash of the brass urn. She looked around and saw her mother watching her intently. She noticed she was now as tall as her mother.

Lian spoke and broke the tension. 'Where are your brothers?'

'Lee is still in the bathroom, and Tam is getting dressed. Min is still in bed. Do you want me to get her up?'

Lian shook her head, 'Let her sleep. You stay here to keep watch, I'll start cooking, your uncle will be here soon. You can bring all the food in when Tam and Lee finish with their praying,' Lian said gesticulating with her hands.

Jen stood idly waving her hand over the table to stop a couple of persistent flies trying to land on the food. She looked around her new neighbourhood; the houses had very individual characteristics. They were built according to the whim and income of each owner. Some had big gardens and verandahs that ran all the way round the house and some, like their own, only had a modest-size porch at the front of the house. There were fewer trees here than in her old neighbourhood but the people were just as friendly Jen noticed. Just then a neighbour came out of her house and smiled at her.

Embarrassed at being caught staring she looked down at her feet, now clad in new clogs with pink plastic over the top. She felt warm and happy inside standing there waving her arms over the mouth-watering food but her peace was suddenly shattered when Lee came running out of the house with Min in hot pursuit and crashed into her. Jen was knocked off-balance, as her wooden clogs were not meant for sudden movement. She put her hands out to steady herself against the table and ended up catching the chicken as it slithered across the tilted table. The chopsticks rolled off the bowls of rice and Lee caught them in mid-air but the tea was shaken out of the little cups leaving wet patches on the paper tablecloth. The roast pork was still sitting resolutely in the middle of the table although the sprigs of scallion had joined the plate with a few splashes of sweet and sour sauce over its crackling. Min, still in her pyjamas, was standing on the front step with both hands over her mouth, too frightened to speak.

'You stu-pid boy,' Jen called out in anger.

'It's New Year, you cannot call me stupid.' Lee was indignant.

'Then don't act s… well, you nearly ruined everything, and it's not New Year today, it's tomorrow,' Jen said as she placed the chicken back into its original position. 'I think you should kowtow one hundred times to apologise for spilling the tea.'

Lee, eyes wide and in a huff, retorted, 'It's you who has to kowtow a hundred times for calling me names. It was Min's fault, she chased me!'

'I-I, you hit me first, you did!' Min whimpered and tears rimmed her eyes.

Just then the crunch of car tyres on tarmac caught their attention. The black taxi rounded the corner and stopped at the front of their house. Jen and Lee watched as one very tall gentleman stepped out. Jen and Lee recognised their uncle at once, Jen stood very still as she watched the rest of his family tumble out of the taxi. Lee turned on his heels and ran indoors half calling and half shrieking for his mother. Min moved forward and hid behind Jen. She had a thumb in her mouth as she peered round Jen's side to see a little girl her size getting out of the taxi.

The two families, three adults and eight children, had a noisy and emotional introduction standing on the porch of the house witnessed by several of their neighbours. Jen dipped her head as she was introduced to her aunt and cousins, she felt dizzy and light-headed. She shivered with delight and intense pride knowing that her cousins with their impeccable manners and smart clothes were part of her family. Jen watched her cousins at the sideline trying to remember their names, Chow Wan was the oldest, then came the two boys, Yee Penh and Yee Kiang, and Chow Lin was the youngest.

A couple of hours later they were all crammed round the large round table eating a sumptuous meal that Lian cooked. The smile had hardly left her face since her brother and his family arrived. A sense of belonging coursed through her and made her voice unnaturally soft when she spoke. Kwai Chai's wife, Mei Qin, was a plump-faced woman with an infectious laugh that Lian couldn't help but join in every time she laughed.

Jen sat next to her oldest cousin, fourteen-year-old Chow Wan, a shy and quietly spoken girl who appeared to have inherited her mother's looks and her father's temperament. She felt she knew her cousin well already as they had been writing to each since her uncle's last visit. 'How long did it take on the train, to get here?' Jen asked her cousin hesitantly. Conversation at mealtimes was never encouraged in normal circumstances but this was not a normal meal.

This was a very special Reunion Dinner, a celebration of family togetherness, and a time to reflect on the events of the year that had gone before and to welcome the New Year with hope and optimism. Jen in particular, hoped that she could pursue her dreams to study in the big city like her cousins; ultimately she hoped to become a teacher. She was still chasing her dream, with chopsticks poised, when her cousin's voice brought her back to reality.

'Many hours, seven or eight I think, we left last night and got here early this morning. We went to see another relative first, and we are going back there tonight, to sleep,' Chow Wan answered and smiled shyly at Jen.

'How, how long are you staying?'

'A few days, we have many of Mum's relatives to visit.'

'Oh. We have no other relatives to visit,' Jen said thoughtfully.

'Do you want to come with us?'

'I don't know, I have to help in the house,' Jen answered as she looked across the table, watching her mother deep in conversation with her aunt and uncle. The two boys were talking excitedly with their cousins of similar age. Min didn't speak but was busy with her chopsticks; she only recently learned to use them properly.

'I'll ask my mum to ask Auntie Lian, to let you come to stay,' Chow Wan whispered into Jen's ear.

'What are you two whispering over there?' Mei Qin asked as she smiled fondly at her daughter. 'Any secrets you want to tell me?'

'Oh, Mum! Stop teasing, Cousin and I are discussing schoolwork.'

'Talking about schoolwork, how boring. Maybe you are telling your cousin how much money you'll get in your red packet tomorrow,' Kwai Chai teased his daughter.

Chow Wan blushed; her father was very fond of teasing her. She was used to his way of expressing his affection for her. 'Papa, can Cousin come to KL with us, just for a few days, please?'

'Mm, I don't know, we'll talk about it later. Perhaps you could all come, what do you think, Sister?' Kwai Chai turned to Lian for approval.

Lian, taken by surprise, replied hastily, 'Yes, I... thank you Big Brother, perhaps we could all go to the big city for a few days.'

Tam and Lee looked on in amazement at their mother. Jen felt her heartbeat rose sharply. Min saw her mother's smiling face and chuckled but was unsure what was being said, and accidentally jabbed her cousin with her chopsticks.

When the meal was over all the children were asked to help clear the table and wash up. The three adults adjourned to the sitting room to catch up on the family history and preparation for the holidays. There was a buzz in the air and Jen was so caught up in the excitement that when Lee dropped a plate and broke it she hurriedly picked up the pieces and swept up the shards of potteries without making angry eyes at him. Tam decided to take Lee and his male cousins outside to show them his bicycle with a promise to allow all of them a ride on his bike.

Min was smarting from the boys' snub and retaliated by taking Chow Lin's hand and led her to her bedroom to show off her new dresses. Chow Lin was the same age as Min but much more sophisticated and her vocabulary was much more extensive than Min's. She made appreciative noises on seeing Min's dresses which made her chuckle with pride.

Kwai Chai, after consulting his wife, changed the family's plans and decided to spend the night with Lian and welcome the New Year with her family. Lian felt a warm glow engulf her whole body and spent the rest of the day dashing back and forth making space in the bedrooms for her extended family. Laughter and hilarity filled the house as the children played hide and seek. At one stage Kwai Chai blindfolded himself and told all the children to stay in the sitting room while he tried to find them by following the sound of their laughter. Lian looked on and joined in with the fun when Min squealed for help when her uncle homed in on her under the table.

At midnight both families were out in the porch to welcome the New Year. The altar table was once again laden with food; the brass urn was overflowing with burning joss sticks and candles. All the children and adults took their turn to kneel on the cold concrete floor to kowtow and gave thanks. Lian made extra offerings to the god for finding her brother and his family. Jen reiterated her thanks she made earlier that day and asked for a few more favours to be granted.

The children watched as Kwai Chai tied the long string of firecrackers to a post and then lit it with a joss stick. Popping sounds rent the air as the firecrackers burst and released their sparks and smoke into the dark night sky. The sound was deafening as the neighbours lit their firecrackers in unison. For the first time Lian allowed her children to play with sparklers, and Lee and Tam made great efforts to outdo each other drawing big arcs and circles in the darkness. Jen was nervous of the sparklers and declined to handle any of them but instead she watched her brothers, sister and cousins enjoying themselves with great gusto.

At the dawn of the new year, a new day, and a new life, Jen's thoughts returned to the disturbing dream she had the night before. What did it mean? Why couldn't she hear Patricia? The more she thought about it the more she worried. She promised herself that she would cycle round to Patricia the next day to see her best friend. Moments later she revised her plan and decided to take Chow Wan to meet Patricia; she would borrow Tam's bicycle and her cousin could have her bicycle and they would ride over early the next morning. Her mind made up she felt much happier, and she looked forward to seeing Patricia again though it had been only three days since she last spoke to her in school.

It was one o'clock in the morning, the 8th of February 1959, the year of the boar. Jen looked up into the night sky. She craned her neck to count the stars twinkling up in the vast heavens above and whispered, 'HAPPY NEW YEAR.'